PRAISE FOR BETSEY KULAKOWSKI

"The Lost Templar is a fantastic return to the world of The Veritas Codex series. Kulakowski knocks it out of the park mixing history and the supernatural. No one does it better!"

— R.J. JOHNSON, AUTHOR OF
DREAMSLINGER

"In *The Lost Templar*, Kulakowski brilliantly weaves the past and present with historical facts in an exceptional narrative that drives the story forward with pounding intensity….This is a fast-paced suspenseful ride that keeps you gripping the edges of your tablet. Tension and family connections that tug at your heartstrings. Mind-blowing twists and turns. Lauren and Rowan are a dream team."

— JENNY SIMARD LABRANCHE, AMAZON
FIVE-STAR REVIEWER

"The Veritas Codex is an amazing series that keeps the pages turning and your mind spinning. Suspenseful like Stuart Woods, yet thought-provoking like Dan Brown, Kulakowski has the incredible ability to weave together the threads of fact and fiction and sew them into an amazing literary tapestry that leaves you wanting more."

— BRANDON MARSH, HOST AND EXECUTIVE PRODUCER, THE PARAUNITY PODCAST

"The Veritas Codex series is a hearty paranormal narrative entree seasoned with suspense. It satisfied my craving for everything paranormal! Thank goodness there are more in the series—Betsey Kulakowski has whet my appetite and I am begging for more! "

— XANDER ZWEIG, CO-HOST OF THE XANDER & STONE SCIENCE & SUPERNATURAL PODCAST

"Realistic heroes and villains. International intrigue. More plot twists than a cup of nightcrawlers. Betsey has definitely raised the bar [in *The Jaguar Queen*]."

— J. DON WRIGHT, AUTHOR OF *BEHOLD!*

"*The Jaguar Queen* keeps the momentum going in the Veritas Codex series. I am becoming very invested in the team of Lauren, Rowan, Bahati and Jean-Rene. "

— DONNA KEY

"I couldn't put [*The Veritas Codex*] down! I knew halfway through that it was going to be a late night because I couldn't quit turning the pages. I can't wait for the next book in the series."

— LISA SMALLWOOD

"Relatable characters and crisp pace…*The Veritas Codex* combines the intrigue and chemistry of *The X-Files* with the intensity of *The Da Vinci Code*."

— JAZ PRIMO, AUTHOR OF *GWEN REAPER*

"Engaging characters and remarkable plot twists jump from these pages. They pulled me into a thrilling world I did not want to leave."

— JOHN WOOLEY, AUTHOR OF *SEVENTH SENSE*

"I enjoyed [*The Veritas Codex*]. The writing is well done. I really liked the characters. It kept me engaged to the point I was speed reading (to find out what was going to happen) and I had to slow myself down!"

— TERRI FOLKS

THE LOST TEMPLAR

THE LOST TEMPLAR

THE VERITAS CODEX SERIES
BOOK FIVE

BETSEY KULAKOWSKI

For all the voices in my head.

(If you're my friend and you have a podcast, that includes you.)

"Love is the one thing we're capable of perceiving that transcends dimensions of time and space."

— BRAND, *INTERSTELLAR* 2014

PROLOGUE

Southern France – 1308

"*By the blood*, Brother Wolfgang. I bid you welcome." The French Templar stood watch at the castle gate. He had been expecting the Enclave for the past month, but the Teutonic soldier was the first to arrive. "How was your journey?"

"*Through His Blood we are saved*, Brother François. I have been too long on the road," he said, answering in French as he reined back his warhorse and slid out of the saddle. His sword caught on the saddle bag, but he freed it with minimal effort. The soldier landed on the damp pathway with a heavy thud. His tangled hair caught the pale moonlight. Even his rusty beard had a glow to it.

"*Bienvenu au Château de la Fleur.*" François caught his forearm, clasping his hand as the guest returned the gesture.

The warrior indeed appeared as if he had just come from the field of battle. The back of his leather coat was damp from the mist. The garment was torn along the shoulder. The fur lining around the neck was matted with blood — blood that was not his. His tabard beneath was equally stained and torn. Chain mail was visible beneath.

"Are you injured, Brother?"

"Not so much as the enemy I left behind on the road from the Holy Lands." Wolfgang chuckled. "Have I arrived too late?" He panted, his breath hanging in the cold night air.

"The Enclave is not yet assembled," François said. "Many of *The Order* have yet to arrive, Brother William and the Lady Elisabeth from Scotland among them. We received word when they reached the coast. There has been no message since they made it to Mount St. Michel."

"How long ago since his missive arrived?"

"Three days' time," François said. The visitor moved to unloose his saddle bag. "We are growing concerned. He traveled under a Flag of Truce signed by the King himself."

Wolfgang hesitated. "Am I to assume the English will send no envoy?"

"They will not," François said soberly. "I must hope his promise of truce was not a ruse to deceive us."

"And what of … the *holy relic*?" Wolfgang asked, glancing over his shoulder as he lowered his tone.

"Brother William and the Lady Elisabeth protect it at all costs," he said. "At this point, we must pray for their safety."

"May God offer His protection," Wolfgang said, crossing himself.

François did the same, putting a hand on his comrade's arm. "Come, Brother. You must be tired and hungry. There is food and bed prepared for you. Until all are assembled, best we tend to the needs of the body."

"God bless you, Brother," Wolfgang said, handing the horses' reins to the stable boy. He shouldered his saddlebags, reaching inside. "I have brought the gifts of my house, if you will take ale."

François accepted it. He inspected the dark glass bottle. "Ale would be most welcome."

"A gift for your House," Wolfgang said.

"I shall have a bottle of our finest wine brought from the cellar for you, in return."

"And we shall drink it together," François replied.

THE AUTUMN NIGHT HAD GONE BITTERLY COLD, AND THE LONG journey was exacerbated by the premature change of seasons. It had rained, but snow was still a few months off. Wolfgang's wool cloak provided some protection and served to hide the tabard of his order. Not everyone on the road was a friend. He was grateful to have made it to the safety of the Château and ready to accept the hospitality his host.

Shouts from the road outside the castle walls halted them at the doorway. François stopped as the guards raced from their posts to see what was wrong. Horses approached on the road in the darkness. A sorrel stallion and a white mare broke through the fog at the gate. The rider on the stallion slumped over the pommel of his saddle, limp. The white horse was riderless. Sweat from the animals' flanks turned to mist around the anxious horses as the stablemen caught the reins. Wolfgang and François both raced to meet them as the horses were led into the courtyard where the brasiers illuminated the horrific scene. The white mare's coat was matted in something dark. It appeared to be blood. It pranced in agitation and blew snot from its nose. The mare seemed to limp but calmed at the gentle hand of one of the grooms.

"Brother William?" François raced around to the rider on the stallion, lifting the man's head. His face was bruised, his eyes swollen, his upper lip cut. The broken shaft of an arrow protruded from his leg. Blood caked around the wound and stained both saddle and horse. "William?"

"*Nous avons … terminé.*" William panted. "*La rose … est tombée.*"

"Where is your traveling companion?" François asked, tears filling his eyes. "Where is your *sacred missive?*"

"My wife..." he groaned, sliding out of his saddle. He was a dead weight in his comrade's arms. "We were ... beset ... she carried the *treasure* ..."

"François!" Wolfgang shouted. The injured man's boot was caught in the stirrup. "Help me get him down."

It took several of them to free the limp form of Brother William from his horse. "Call for the physician!"

~

"THE MARE'S HOOF IS SPLIT," THE GROOM SAID AS THE knights inspected the horses. He looked for clues to what might have taken place. An arrow pierced the mare's saddle and remained lodged at the base of the pommel in the fine-tooled Scottish leather.

A rider on the path bolted through the gate and drew back his reins as he saw something was wrong. "What has happened?" Brother Alwar doffed his cloak as he landed, his boots clapping on the damp ground as he strode over. The Spaniard's white tabard was emblazoned with a cross, embroidered in gold, a red rose at the conjunction of the lateral and horizontal arms.

"Brother William was attacked on the road," François said, without the formal greetings of their order.

"And ... the *Sacred Heart of the Rose?*"

The two men had no words, but their faces spoke volumes. Alwar took the shaft of the arrow in one hand, bracing himself with the other, straining with the effort to free it. He carried it to the firelight to inspect it. The others followed. "I recognize this." He pointed to a mark on the shaft, just beneath the fletching. "I saw such marks during my time in Aleppo. It's the mark of *The Asāsiyyūn's Guild.*"

"*Asāsiyyūns?* Here? We are thousands of miles from the Holy Land. The Infidels could not have infiltrated so far into France."

"They are like maggots that penetrate our flesh while we sleep. Their numbers swell as they burrow into the darkest recesses of our realms. We must launch a counter attack," Alwar insisted. "Why do you cower in this fortress like nuns? Are we not Soldiers in the Army of God?"

"Brother William lies on his deathbed ..." François gestured toward the castle as he started to explain.

Alwar was incensed by his lack of urgency. "If you will not go after her, I will."

"Wait." François caught his sleeve, realizing he, too, wore his mail beneath. He'd come dressed for battle as well. "We must wait for the rest of our *Order*."

"Wait?" Alwar gasped. "Wait? While the Asāsiyyūns ride with *the Sacred Heart of the Rose*, what of Sister Elisabeth? It may already be too late, but I made an oath upon my life to defend and protect my brothers, and by virtue, his lady. I will not let the act of these *Asāsiyyūns* go unanswered. I will fight them all ... with or without the support of a full Army."

Wolfgang turned to François. "I will go with him," he said. "Vauquelin, fetch my horse!"

Alwar nodded, clearly pleased to have the Bohemian's support. "If we find *The Asāsiyyūn's Guild*, we will send word. When the rest of *The Order* arrives, we may need aid."

"How will your message find us here?"

"My falcon," Alwar said, pointing to the shadow at the peak of the roof above the entryway. "She is well-trained and carries letters for me in times of urgent need. She will return to her roost. I will mount it here in the courtyard." He went to his saddle and took a long post from a sheath. It might have appeared as a longsword, but the Spanish knight took the post and buried it in the compacted soil with one mighty blow. The falcon flew down and landed on it, before moving to her master's arm.

François nodded. He made the sign of the cross over each of them. "I pray, by *the Blood*, may you go with God."

Alwar bowed. *"Through His Blood we are saved."*

~

THE WARRIORS RETURNED JUST BEFORE SUNRISE, THOUGH THE day had gone gray, as was so common this time of year. François never made it to his chambers. Instead, he felt compelled to pray and kept a vigil over the fallen soldier. When he heard the beat of hooves on the bridge just outside the fortress that protected the chapel, he crossed himself then made the same sign over the patient. He rose and went to greet his brothers. He didn't get far.

The body of Lady Elisabeth had been found on the road, a dozen miles away. An arrow had pierced her heart. She wore a bloodstained overdress that appeared to be a fine silken tapestry bearing a pattern of similar red crosses and embroidered gold roses.

They had shrouded her in their tabards and brought her body to be properly entombed with her husband if he did not survive. She hadn't yet been cold when they found her, but the last warmth of life was fleeting, her flesh still pliable as they collected her from the back of the horse.

François peeled back the shroud to study her face. Despite the cold pallor of death, he could see she had been a beautiful woman. She was young, fair-haired, and bore no marks or bruises on her ghostly face.

"Take her to her husband's chambers," François instructed, moving her body to Vauquelin's arms. The man was not young, but he was robust. He had a form built by decades of labor.

"Why? What are you doing?" Alwar asked.

"The ancient wisdom says true love cannot be separated, even by death. If such things are true, and if the magic of my order holds, there may be salvation for them after all."

"But the *Sacred Heart of the Rose?*"

"Another reason to take her to her husband," François said.

WILLIAM STIRRED AS THEY CARRIED HIS LADY INTO THE chamber. His eyelids fluttered. The monks moved a second bed into the room, sliding it close to the one upon which he lay. The body of his beloved wife was lain beside him and draped in a gossamer shroud. Brother Vauquelin brought holy water and sacred oils, placing them on the table beside the lady's bed.

"Brother William?" Wolfgang knelt at his side, as François knelt beside the Laird's wife. "*By His Blood*, can you hear me, Brother?"

William rolled his head towards the man's deep voice. He muttered something that they assumed was the counter to their blessing. It was also a message *The Order* used to identify one another. *Through His Blood we are saved.*

François took the man's hand and lay it upon the shrouded hand of his wife. "She's been gone too long," Wolfgang said, keeping his voice low.

"Be of faith, Brothers. Pray with me," François said, bowing his head and lifting his hands like open cups to the heavens.

Vauquelin stood back, crossing himself, then clasped his hands beneath his chin.

"Father of the Ancients," François began, dipping his finger in the dish of sacred oil, anointing the lady's head through the shroud. "God of Abraham and Isaac, Father of Christ, First-born from the Dead. Alpha and Omega. By all Thy Names, hear our prayers. In the Name of Love, we have come beseeching that these two souls be fully restored. Open their eyes wide that they may serve at Thy command. You, O, Lord, who opens graves, who heals the sick, and raises the dead. O, Lord, we beseech that Thou restore life and health to these mortal bodies. Through the Spirit that dwells in Thee, loose the pangs of Death, and awaken Thy warrior's bride to everlasting life that we may bring glory to Thee and rescue *the Sacred Heart of the Rose*. May we see it safely delivered from the hands of our enemies, as Thou has bidden. Mend these broken bodies to full glory that their acts may magnify Thee. We ask this, our blessed Redeemer, as You raised Your Son from the grave, bring forth our Sister from the dead."

François breathed in a deep breath and let it out slowly. An unseen surge of energy seemed to pass through his body, lifting his hair and sending goosebumps across his flesh. William too, drew in a deep breath. He cried out, "Elisabeth!" His voice was weak, but the word was unmistakable.

As if the windows had been thrown open, a gust of wind swirled into the small chamber. Brasiers and candles flickered. A deep huffing echo came from the fireplace and ashes blew from the bed of coals. Sparks erupted like fireflies on the summer air. They swirled and danced, coalescing as they hovered above the shrouded body.

The luminaries stopped short of contacting the linen that draped the lady's delicate features. They seemed to throb with a heartbeat all their own. The *lub-dub* of it echoed loudly, repeatedly. François noticed William's hand wrap around the smaller one of his wife. A gossamer voice found its way into the room.

"What God has joined together, let no man put asunder …" The words, coming from nowhere and everywhere, were soft like the prayer of a small child. Just as soft was the sigh of the Lady St. Clair as her chest rose and fell, then rose again. The sparks twinkled into nothingness. The shroud pulled from her form, as if by unseen hands. It fell to the floor beneath the cot.

William rolled over, reaching for her cheek. "My beloved …" He buried his face in the tumble of golden curls that lay on her shoulder. She was a young beauty — he, not much older.

"You came back for me," she said weakly. An angelic smile curled in her cheeks as her hand went to her husband's.

Alwar stood in the door, aghast. "We could not leave you to our enemies, Lady Elisabeth." He crossed the room and fell to his knees beside François, taking her other hand. He kissed her ring in reverence.

"They road with us in the guise of friends … we were … betrayed," William said.

"Did you see who it was, Brother William?"

"I did not recognize him at first. But … it was my beloved wife who discovered it was Lord de Lacy." He lay back, his hand still entwined in his bride's. "The … Earl of Lincoln. The … seneschal of the King."

Sharp glances passed between François, Wolfgang, and Anwar.

"But … I did not detect the deception quick enough. I fear God is not pleased," Lady Elisabeth said faintly. "We have enemies to the Faith in the kingdom."

"Enemies that must be defeated," William said. "We must find and retake *The Sacred Heart of the Rose.*"

The sound of hoofbeats echoed outside the chamber. "The rest of our Enclave has arrived." François made for the door.

William rose to his elbow with great effort. "Good," he said. "Bring me … my horse. I will … lead … the charge."

Elisabeth caught his arm. "Husband," she said. "You are not yet mended."

"And I am … not yet done taking scars to secure … the *Sacred Heart of the Rose*," he said. "Scars I … will gladly bear."

Elisabeth reached for him as his hand clutched his wounded side. She moved to rise as well. "So be it, my love. Brothers, saddle our horses."

1

Lauren stood outside her mother's house as Rowan unloaded their bags from the back of their SUV. The movement of a silhouette against the light in the window told her that her mother was still up. Her eye went to the mist-shrouded moon above.

"Lauren?" Rowan nudged her, handing over her backpack. "Okay?" he asked, setting her suitcase beside her. He pulled out the collapsible handle for her.

"Yeah." She yawned. "I'm ready for a few hours' sleep in a real bed." She took her bag and turned to the house, finding her mother on the front porch in her nightgown and bathrobe.

Diana was barefooted and her gray hair hung long down her back. "Welcome home," she said as Lauren approached, leaning down to kiss her cheek.

"Hi, Mom." She sighed. "How are the boys doing?"

"It was everything I could do to get them to go to bed," she said. "They've missed you." She let Lauren pass and brightened as Rowan approached with his bags. "They've missed you both." She stood on her tiptoes to kiss Rowan's cheek. Playfully she caught a tuft of his long beard and tugged. "Welcome back. I thought you were going to shave."

Rowan turned away but laughed. "Thank you," he said. "It's almost winter. I might need it to keep my face warm."

"It's not that cold."

"Winter's not that far away," Rowan said.

"You don't hear me complaining about it," Lauren said over her shoulder, catching Rowan's eye. "Sorry we're so late."

"Eh, flights get delayed all the time." Diana let it go. "How was France? Any luck finding the lost treasures of the Knights Templar?"

"Not as much as we had hoped," Rowan said. "But we did find a few interesting things."

"Well," Diana said, following them into the house, lowering her voice. "You can tell me all about it tomorrow over breakfast. Your bed is ready, and I can see how badly you need it."

"I got a little sleep on the plane," Lauren said. "But not enough."

"I'll make sure the boys let you sleep 'til at least 9:00," Diana assured her, as they found the guest bedroom she had ready for them. The lamp by the bed was on, emitting a soft pink glow in the room. The antique wrought iron bed with a thick pillow-top mattress reminded Lauren of something from a five-star boutique hotel — not a place they were accustomed to staying — unless they were hunting for ghosts. The comforter had already been turned down. Lauren half expected to find a mint on the pillow.

"The boys aren't the ones most likely to wake me up," she said, dropping her bags, her hand going to her stomach. "This one's using my bladder for a punching bag."

Diana gave her an impish grin. "Are you trying to outdo me?" her mother asked. "I'm afraid you're getting a late start if you plan to have seven. Don't you think?"

Lauren shrugged out of her jacket, then stepped over her bags. She pushed her way past Rowan as she stopped at the door. "I didn't realize I was expected to one up you," Lauren said. "And it doesn't seem to matter how hard we try. Nothing seems to prevent it."

"Nothing?" Diana asked with a wicked grin, inuendo thick in her voice. She glanced at Rowan as he peeled out of his jacket.

"If you'll excuse me," Lauren said, pressing past her, headed to the bathroom.

~

DIANA WAS MAKING PANCAKES JUST A FEW HOURS LATER WHEN Lauren staggered wearily into the kitchen.

"Mom!" Henry popped up from his chair.

"Momma!" Jamie and John Carter chorused. The boys raced towards her, wrapping their arms around her at varying levels. She wrestled her braid out of one of the boy's grasp. "You're home!" John Carter added.

"Yes," she said, kissing each of them, mussing their hair. "I am."

"We missed you!" Jamie gazed up at her, bright-eyed and freckle-faced.

"I missed you, too, sweetie." She kissed him again.

"Coffee?" Diana already had a cup out of the pantry.

"Please." Lauren accepted it and carried it to the table. Henry held her chair out for her. He had observed his father long enough to fill in when he wasn't around. Rowan was still snoring. Lauren could hear him even down the hall.

"Where's Uncle Jean-René and Aunt Bahati?" Jamie asked.

"They'll be joining us next week," Lauren said. "They went to visit Jean-René's mother in Nice."

Diana brought a plate and put it on the table. John Carter pushed it over in front of his mother then rose and went to the refrigerator to get the butter. Henry got the syrup from the shelf in the pantry. "What'd you find at *Rennes-le-Château?*" Henry asked.

"Was it beautiful?" Jamie asked.

"Did you find *Bérenger Saunière's* treasure?" John Carter added to the barrage of questions being peppered at her as she cut into her pancakes. Lauren focused on her food, knowing her boys all too well.

"Did you see the *Tour Magdala?* Was the view as spectacular as the pictures Uncle Jean-René sent us?"

"Did you meet any Visigoths?" Jamie asked.

"Visigoths?" Lauren's brow shot up as she started to take a bite. "Where did you hear about Visigoths?"

"Uncle Jean-René," Jamie said. "He told me all about them. He said some of his favorite relatives were Visigoths."

"Maybe some of his ancestors," she said, smirking. Jamie loved his Uncle Jean-René's stories. It didn't surprise her to hear he'd been telling the boys about his more ancient forefathers. Ever since they'd discovered the ties in Rowan and Jean-René's family history, they'd talked about doing an episode on the Knights Templars and their shared history. They were getting the chance — finally — though they barely found anything in France. The Network would assign researchers to follow some of the clues they'd found and eventually, they would circle back around to finish the episode. They were on a tight schedule as they neared the end of the season's production year. They had a public appearance here in Oklahoma in just a few days, then they had another episode to film.

"Some of ours, too, by the way," Henry said to his little brother.

"*We* have Visigoths in our family?" Jamie asked his brother, as if that were scandalous.

Jamie, who'd just turned five, still had much to learn, and he often turned to his older brothers for answers. Five years his senior, Henry was bright for his age. He was a studious pupil, and whenever he had a free moment, he was reading. He patiently worked his way through his father's library and was now attached at the hip to his Kindle. Lauren had gotten him a library card and taught him how to download books. If they'd had to buy him physical copies, he could run them into the poorhouse. John Carter, two years older than Jamie, liked to read too, but he was into music. Rowan had started teaching him to play guitar.

He'd signed all of them up for Boy Scouts, and they spent most of their weekends home at scout meetings, doing community projects to earn badges, and learning camping skills. They were now going to get to put them to good use. Rowan and Lauren were starting to take them on certain investigations, choosing them with the greatest of care — and the least risk.

"Mom!" Jamie nudged her.

"Why don't we wait 'til your father wakes up, so we can tell you about it together?"

"I'm up," Rowan grunted as he came in rubbing his eyes. He had a serious case of bed head ... and bed face.

"Dad!" The boys forgot their mother and charged Rowan, mobbing him as they had her just minutes before. Lauren chortled to herself, taking up her cup. She took a long sip of her coffee before she turned her attention to the dark brown pancakes. They were just the way she liked them.

She watched her mother at the stove as she took a bite. While their relationship had been rocky, they'd found a happy accord that allowed them to forget their old hurts. Diana Boudinot was immensely helpful when they were working. The boys had spent the whole summer in Tahlequah getting to know their cousins and uncles, as well as their grandmother. Oklahoma was a better home-base when they were working anyway. Hawai'i was off the beaten path, and it was a much more expensive flight if they needed to go to San Diego to meet with their Network executives.

This season had taken them from Oklahoma to the Alaskan back-country, to the southern tip of Chile, and down to Antarctica. From there, they'd gone to Australia and New Zealand before they went to Cambodia, then Thailand. The team took a mid-season break which gave them a couple of weeks at home, before they were off to Tibet, Switzerland, and finally, southern France.

Rowan had gotten his 100th country stamp in his passport in Chile. Lauren got her 100th when they went through customs in Cambodia. It was a milestone of which she was proud.

"Sit down. Sit down," Diana commanded. "Let your poor father have some coffee before he starts his debrief." Lauren's brow shot up at her mother's comment. She *had* been paying attention and was starting to use the same verbiage as Rowan regarding their work. The boys were always excited for a *debrief* of their expeditions. Diana fetched another cup from the pantry and filled it, handing it to Rowan. She reached up and smoothed down his rusty beard. "Getting a little gray around the edges, son."

Lauren knew he loved it when she called him *son*. "I'm not twenty anymore," he said. "Unlike my wife, who hasn't aged a day."

"Excuse me," Lauren scoffed, lifting her braid off her shoulder. There were threads of silver in her raven locks, but they were rare, and Rowan said as much.

"Please." He sat down with his cup, leaning over to kiss her. "You're as lovely as our wedding day."

"You're still a sappy son-of-a--" She was cut off when her mother put a plate of pancakes in front of Rowan.

"Eat your breakfast," Diana said, patting him on the shoulder.

Lauren peered up at the three bright-eyed boys on their knees in the chairs across the table, leaning on their elbows. "So?" Henry asked. "What'd you find?"

Rowan glanced at Lauren and laid his fork down, reaching into the pocket of his pajama pants. He retrieved a tarnished old coin in a protective case. He laid it on the table in front of him. He pushed it over to Henry. "See that?"

Henry picked it up and inspected it, then turned it over.

"Let me see!" Jamie snatched it out of his hand.

John Carter did the same then inspected it closely. "How old is this?"

"Seventeenth Century," Rowan said. "What do you see?"

"Is that … a UFO?" Henry asked, gazing at it in John Carter's hand. "Like a UFO hovering over a Roman army. Is this a French coin?"

"It's an ancient *jeton*. It was used for counting. It's not the first one ever found, but the first one found in that region of France. Skeptics over the years have offered a slew of possible explanations, arguing that it appeared more like a drifting mushroom or flower, or even a shield."

"Some have linked the image in the token to the Biblical story of Ezekiel's wheel," Lauren picked up the story. "There are some alien enthusiasts that claim this story is a Biblical account of a UFO sighting."

"It's kinda like the *Madonna with Saint Giovannino* or the *Annunciation With Saint Emidius*," John Carter observed. Both were renaissance paintings which supposedly had UFOs in them.

"Do you get to keep it?" Henry asked, taking the token back as Jamie finished inspecting it.

"Unfortunately, no," Rowan said, as Jamie laid it in his palm. "I have to give it back to its owner, but he thought you guys might want to see it, and he was kind enough to let me borrow it."

"Us?" Jamie asked.

"The conservationist at *Rennes-les-Château* saw you all on the episode we did in Wyoming and was impressed at how interested you were in the hunt for Butch Cassidy's lost treasure."

"Wow!" Henry arched an eyebrow, the perfect imitation of his father.

"We're famous?" Jamie asked.

"Don't let it go to your head, dork." John Carter mussed his little brother's hair.

"I'm not a dork!" Jamie smacked him in the shoulder with the back of his hand.

"Hey," Rowan scolded. "So, who did their homework for our expedition next week?"

"I did," Henry said.

"What did you learn?" Lauren asked, not surprised at her oldest.

"The Kiamichi Mountains are a subrange of the larger Ouachita Mountains," he said. "The elevations are significantly lower than the mountains in Colorado because of the increased erosion."

"How high is the tallest mountain?" Rowan asked.

"About 2,700 feet," Henry said.

"And what kind of animals live there?" Diana asked.

"All kinds," Jamie piped in. "Black bears, cougars, bats, deer, bobcats and bald eagles, too."

"Which means there are some hazards," Rowan said.

"Jamie didn't even mention the swamps to the south." John Carter's voice was deeper than his brothers, and the dark-haired child could go from teasing to sober in seconds, much like his mother. "There are alligators there."

"And snakes, too," Henry added.

"All hazards we will need to keep in mind," Lauren said.

"And the weather?" Rowan asked. The boys had gone on two expeditions before. Their Scout training had been more than just fun and games. It gave Rowan a chance to test their mettle and make sure they were ready for any potential dangers.

"It's a humid subtropical climate, and while temperatures this time of year are in the 50's, a low of -1 degree Fahrenheit has been recorded, and thunderstorms are not uncommon." Henry had a near-eidetic memory for anything he read. As a result, he often sounded like a walking Wikipedia.

"What did you learn about the geography?" Rowan asked, sipping his coffee.

"Well, the Ouachitas are part of the Ouachita Fold and Thrust Belt, and the highest natural point is Mt. Magazine at 2,753 feet," Henry continued.

"Plants?" Lauren posed the question to John Carter, not letting Henry dominate the discussion.

"Pine, oak, hickory, and maple-leaf oaks. There's poison ivy, so … Dad has to watch out." Rowan, as they had learned during a hike in southeast Asia, had developed an extreme allergy to poison ivy in all its forms. He almost went into anaphylactic shock before he'd gotten to the Epi-Pen he carried in his medic-bag on every expedition. He carried two, and it took a second dose to keep him alive until they could get him medi-flighted to the hospital in Bangkok. At one point, the paramedics were discussing intubating him to protect his airway.

A cortisone injection got him off of death's door. From there, he was subjected to medical staff giving him a bath with an anti-urushiol treatment. He was in no condition to object, and certainly in no position to enjoy it.

"I've got my Epi Pens," Rowan said. "I also brought some barrier cream and skin wash, so I should be okay, even in a worst-case scenario."

"Tell them what else you learned," Diana nudged.

"There used to be gangsters here," Henry said. "Pretty Boy Floyd had a hide out and there's some legend about hidden treasure in a cave."

"Your mom told me about that when you were little."

Rowan glanced at his wife. "Maybe we better add that to our list of things to come back to check out."

"Did you take the boys to Heavener?" Lauren asked.

"We went last weekend," Diana said.

"What'd you think?"

"I think the state needs to invest some money in renewing the park there," Henry said. "The runestone is cool to see, but the campsites could use some attention."

Lauren's brow lifted as she glanced at her husband. "But you saw the runestone, right?"

"Yeah," he said. "But Jamie almost fell off the waterfall. No guardrails."

"We'll be sure to send a hazard alert to OSHA," Rowan said, smirking. "So, do you have all your camping supplies ready?"

"Yessir," the boys chorused.

"Did you make a list of what you want your mother to cook while we're in camp?" Rowan asked.

"We did," John Carter said. He got up and went to the living room, coming back with his notebook. "I wasn't sure how long we were going to stay, so we may have more stuff than we need." He pushed the notebook over to his mother.

Lauren took the list, holding it where Rowan could see it, too. She wasn't surprised to see her famous Red Beans and Rice at the top of the list. It was their father's favorite, and it had become their favorite, too. Lauren had become known as the *Queen of Campfire Cuisine*. Her Pinterest board of recipes was popular among the viewers of their television show, and she'd even been invited to appear on the *Chef's Network* and several morning talk shows to share some of her favorites. "Camp bread, huh?"

"Can you make it more than once? It's my favorite," John Carter said.

"I'll have to prep a couple of batches here before we head to camp," Lauren said.

"We'll have a whole prep-day if you like," Diana offered. "I don't mind pitching in."

"Might take two days," Lauren said, as she turned the page and realized there were three more pages of meal-requests. "Remember, I have the whole team to feed, too."

"After feeding you and your six brothers, I think I know how to feed an army," Diana mused. "Besides, I'm back in practice now that I've had these *bottomless pits* to feed for the past few weeks. Do they ever get full?"

Lauren glanced at her boys who peered back at her sheepishly. "Not that I've seen."

"We'll help, Mom." Henry nudged John Carter.

"Yeah," John Carter said. "We'll help."

"Do you have plans for the day?" Diana asked.

"Today is a recovery day," she said, yawning. "So, no. I don't have anything planned."

"If you're up to it, I thought we might go to town and get a pedicure and have lunch," Diana suggested. "If not today, maybe tomorrow."

"That sounds like heaven." Lauren sighed. "I don't think I've had a pedi since my birthday."

"Why don't you girls go do your thing and me and the boys will work on the shopping list and any equipment prep work we can do today."

"Will you play video games with us, Dad?" Jamie asked.

"When our chores are done," he said. "I need to start some laundry for me and your mother. Do you need laundry done before we go?"

"Yes, sir."

"So, how have you been feeling?" Diana asked as they settled back into the massage chairs, their bare feet soaking in the swirling blue waters of the pedicure bowls.

"I've made it to the second trimester sweet spot," she said. Her hand went to the bump beneath her peach and white striped t-shirt.

"No morning sickness?"

"Not anymore. I had some with Jamie. That was nothing compared to *this* one," she said, wondering how much of her morning sickness with Jamie could be chalked up to her encounter with Enlil and the forces of Darkness she'd battled. This one had no such excuse — just the extreme altitude in Tibet.

She hadn't mentioned her role in preventing Armageddon to her mother. They'd come to a good place in their relationship, but she wasn't sure how much her mother would believe, much less understand, and it was easier to keep it on the down-low, for now.

"I had horrible morning sickness with you," she said. "Your energy was stronger than any of your brothers. We were constantly at odds even before you were born."

Lauren cast her a sidelong glance. "I didn't realize our conflicts began that early."

"I'm just glad we've found our way through," Diana said, reaching over, taking her hand. "I always hoped we would."

"I am … I am terribly sorry it took so long," Lauren said.

Diana made a noise in her throat. "Stop. We agreed we would not speak of it again."

Lauren realized her mother was correct. "So, what shall we talk about?" Lauren asked, leaning back in the chair, letting the gentle massaging work on her already aching back.

"You're not going to let Rowan name this one, are you?" Diana reached over and rested her hand on Lauren's abdomen. The baby must have had the hiccups. Her stomach quivered with frequency.

"I picked out Jamie's name," Lauren said. "Of course, I let Rowan think he had a say in it."

"James is a good name," Diana nodded. "Not something from Star Wars, I presume?"

"No, but … something from Star Trek … almost."

"Star Trek?" Diana scowled, laughing. "Almost?"

"James Tiberius Pierce is an homage to Captain James T. Kirk on Star Trek," she mused. "But I'm the one that insisted we call him Jamie."

"Why *Jamie*?"

"After Jamie Fraser in *Outlander*," she said. "Surely you've heard of *Outlander*? James Alexander Malcolm Mackenzie Fraser?" Her voice went misty as she leaned back and relaxed, her eyes closing to slits. The massaging chair had found just the spot in her lower back that needed attention.

"There's a mouthful." Diana shook her head, sniggering. "You're not thinking of replacing Rowan, are you?"

"Heavens no, Mom." Lauren sat up and glanced at her from the corner of her eye. "You haven't read *Outlander*?" Lauren gasped. "Jamie Fraser is the *King of Men*. You have to have read *Outlander*."

"Oh, it's a book," Diana said, with realization. "I thought Rowan was the *King of Men* in your book."

"Well," she said, blushing. "He is, but … every girl needs a *book boyfriend*. I remember you used to like to read."

"I still do. I've been reading Mary Stewart's *The Crystal Cave*."

"I haven't read that since I was a girl," Lauren said as the nail tech pulled a low stool and her small work table over to the basin in front of her. She folded a towel over her lap, before laying one on the pads at the front of the basin. She motioned for Lauren to lift her foot out of the tub of warm water. The woman said something in Vietnamese to the man across the room doing a woman's manicure as she inspected Lauren's foot. Lauren swallowed hard at the snide comment about the dragon scales on the bottoms of her feet but kept her expression neutral. "It's been a while since I had a pedicure," she said to her in Vietnamese. "I just got back from Cambodia and Thailand," she added in English. The woman's complexion flamed, but she said nothing else as she went to work on Lauren's poor feet. Hiking through soggy jungles in protective boots were murder on the soles.

"You have become quite the linguist, haven't you?" Diana arched a curious brow at her daughter. "I shouldn't be surprised. You've always been good at languages. When Ms. Lopez used to babysit you, I wasn't at all surprised to come home to find you counting to fifty in Spanish."

"Me?" Lauren asked. "I don't remember that. I didn't think I understood more than rudimentary Spanish until I was an adult and … studied it *purposefully*." She didn't know how else to say it without explaining to her mother the gift of the Ancient All-Language she'd been given by the gods.

"You were always ravenous in the thirst for knowledge. You loved words," Diana said. "And then you started to learn so much about science and the world that your brain got too full. It's difficult to fill a cup that is already over flowing."

"You are so wise."

Diana shrugged. "I haven't always been."

There was a long moment of silence between them. When Diana spoke, it was in Cherokee, a fact that Lauren didn't even recognize. "I was foolish after your father left me." She swallowed hard. "I was hurting badly."

"Left *us*," Lauren corrected. "But you never talked about it."

"You may not understand this, but I loved your father the way you love Rowan."

Lauren lifted her head from the massaging headrest and turned to Diana. "You never talked about my father. I assumed you were just angry and wanted nothing to do with him. I guess … I just decided you … *didn't* love him … that maybe he'd done something to hurt you."

"It hurt when he left." Diana lowered her tone, gazing

down at their joined hands. Lauren noticed her mother's knuckles showed signs of arthritis and she knew it must be painful. "I internalized all of it. I tried to numb the pain with alcohol. I knew I wasn't a good mother to you, but … I was in such a dark place. I didn't know how to get out of it. You reminded me of your father, even more so than your brothers. That was painful, too. He never got to know what a wonderful daughter he had, and I was so deep into the bottle … I couldn't see it either."

Lauren patted her mother's hand gently. She felt the tears threatening to escape her eyes. "I'm sorry. I was just so angry … I never once thought about what *you* were going through. I thought … it was something I had done."

"Oh, honey," Diana said, holding Lauren's gaze. "It had nothing to do with you. Not one bit."

Lauren fought to hold back a flood of tears, trying to convince herself that her raging pregnancy hormones were making her more emotional than she should be. But then again, she'd held onto the belief that her father's leaving was all her fault for so long, that the sudden epiphany was a huge relief. "I guess maybe that's why my most irrational fear is that Rowan will leave me."

"Honey." Diana's eyes brightened, and an impish grin curled in the corner of her cheeks. "That man will never leave you. He's yours, heart, and soul. Any fool can see that."

Now, Lauren had to fight tears as she forced her expression to remain neutral. "But if …" she started, but she couldn't force her tongue to make the words. "Never mind." A tear tumbled down her cheek. She pushed it away. "You're right. I know that."

"Now, tell me about this *King of Men*."

WHILE THE TECH WORKED, LAUREN PROCEEDED TO TELL HER mother all about *Outlander* and the series of books that followed. When the tech finished buffing and filing away the layers of dried skin off Lauren's feet, she wrapped her feet and lower legs in hot towels and moved her supplies over to Diana's chair and went to work on her feet, which weren't as bad as Lauren's.

The silence returned between them. That comfortable rapport they'd been working to establish seemed to settle back around them. It hadn't been easy, coming to terms with their past, but Lauren's sons had been a bridge between them. It began when Henry was just a baby. Lauren had connected with her on Facebook, and the two chatted from time to time over text messaging. Diana offered motherly advice when Lauren needed it.

"What sounds good for lunch?" Diana asked, when the tech moved back over to paint Lauren's toes.

Lauren pondered this thought for a moment. She hadn't had cravings with this one the way she had with John Carter. "I don't know. What's good around here?"

"Do you remember Kelsey Baker?" Diana asked. "She played piano at the church when you were little."

"Vaguely." Lauren had taken out her phone. One of the boys texted her. She typed back a reply, then allowed her mother to continue.

"She just opened a new restaurant a few months ago," she said. "Everything I've heard has been positive. We could go try that."

"Is she the one who always brought the fried chicken for the church socials?"

"Now that you mention it," Diana said. "She was. You always liked her banana pudding though."

Lauren sat back. "Mmm. I do like banana pudding."

"Why don't we go there?"

"Sounds good," Lauren said. Her stomach growled in anticipation. "As soon as our toes dry."

KELSEY BAKER WAS A LITTLE PLUMPER THAN LAUREN remembered, but at the moment, so was she. By the time they got back to the house, Lauren was stuffed and spent. The fried chicken had been just as good as she remembered. The banana pudding was even better.

"Go lie down and take a nap," Diana said, putting a hand on her shoulder. "I'll see to Rowan and the boys."

"Thank you, Mom," Lauren said, wearily.

Diana slapped her on the behind, sending her down the hall. Lauren yipped but started for the guest room, yawning and ready to peel out of her shoes and maybe her bra. A shriek from the backyard stopped her in her tracks and she turned, hurrying, racing past her mother. At the patio door, she froze, the tension in her shoulders melting as she opened it. "What in the blue blazes is going on out here?" Henry and John Carter had Jamie duct-taped to the elm tree in the back corner of her mother's yard.

"Henry Jones Pierce!" Diana pressed past her. "John Carter Pierce! Where did you get that duct tape?"

Lauren took a step back, letting her mother handle it. She'd faced the wrath of Diana as a girl and knew there was nothing she could do to correct their behavior that her mother couldn't. She started back towards the guest room, but then paused to wonder where Rowan was. She turned right instead of left, and headed to the garage, expecting he might be tinkering with equipment or doing some honey-dos to earn bonus points with his mother-in-law. He wasn't there.

Sighing, she glanced out the front window, not seeing him outside. Yawning, she surrendered the search. She heard the snoring before she opened the door. Rowan was sprawled out in the middle of the bed, like a starfish. He had slipped off his jeans and slept in his t-shirt, boxer shorts and socks, a blanket gathered haphazardly over his body.

~

ROWAN AWOKE WHEN HE HEARD HER COME IN. FROM SLITTED eyes he watched as Lauren slipped out of her jeans — jeans she could no longer button. She had an elastic hair tie as an extender, for now. Her low slung jeans wouldn't fit her hips much longer. Tugging up her bikini panties that had rolled down, she slid into the void between his right arm and right leg, pulling the blanket over herself as she nestled her head against his shoulder and made herself comfortable.

He feigned a yawn and lifted his head. "You're home."

"You were supposed to be watching the boys," Lauren said.

"They're playing *landing party* in the back yard." He shifted, pulling her into his arms.

"And there's a *duct-tape force field* holding our youngest to a tree," she said in his ear.

"What?" He sat up, unsettling her, snagging her braid, yanking it.

"Ow!"

"Sorry." He started to get up, but she caught the tail of his t-shirt and pulled him back down.

"Mother is managing it."

He paused. She appeared as tired as he felt. She had dark circles under her eyes. "Oh." He lay back down, curling into her, tucking her into his body. She rested her head on his arm, making certain her braid was safe from being caught or pinched. "Did you have a good time with your mom?"

Lauren sighed. "Yes," she said. "It was nice."

"You smell like fried chicken." He inhaled the perfume of it in her hair.

"That's what I had for lunch."

"Maybe I'll have you for lunch." He nuzzled her neck, cupping the swell of her stomach in his large paw.

"Hmm …" Lauren sighed. "Yeah, sure."

He stroked her stomach, his hand sliding up under her t-shirt to cup a breast. She sighed again and he could feel her melt into putty. A moment later, she was a limp weight in his arms. "Maybe later," he sighed, as he moved his hand back to her stomach and closed his eyes, letting sleep return.

2

Scotland – 1378 – Rosslyn Chapel

The young prince, Henry Sinclair, sat in stunned silence. He had heard these stories in whispers, spoken behind cupped hands, in rumors shared in dark corners. Now, he had been told the whole *truth* of it. He considered his source most reliable. It was a legend, but one he would play a role in, whether he liked it or not. "But … but," he struggled for words. "How do ye ken *it* came here? And is it really *The Sacred Heart of the Rose*? I thought it was just … a myth."

"Nay, it is no' a myth. My own namesake liberated it from *The Asāsiyyūn's Guild* in France some generations back," the old man said. "It was meant tae be returned tae the Holy Land, along with rest of the treasures of our Order, but the danger was too great."

"Why take it to the Holy Land?" the young man asked, not knowing the full story.

The old man studied him a long moment. As if making up his mind, he heaved a heavy sigh and spoke. "The Book of Daniel … the Book of Revelations both speak of the return of Our Lord, aye?"

"I've read them," Henry said.

"*Thy Kingdom come ... Thy Will be done ...*" William turned to the fire, his gaze going distant. "When Our Lord returns, it will be in Israel ... Jerusalem. In those last days, the Holy Land will not be ruled by Saracens, nor by Franks ... it shall be returned to the sovereignty of the Tribes of Israel. 'Tis one of the reasons the other faiths have fought sae hard for control. But the Christians are not at war with the Tribes of Israel, ye ken?"

"It seems as if they are, Grandsire."

"As it must be, for the safety of the treasures in our keep," William said, rising with great effort, grunting at the pain in his joints. He moved slowly, turning his back to the fire. "A new Jerusalem must be built," he said. "The Revelations say it must be built on the *high cosmic mountain*, as it was in Ezekiel. Here, in the Center of Creation — between Heaven and Earth —the legends say we will be gi'en a sign. We will recognize the path to this new city on a hill by the broken cross and the crown. Here, the foundation of this new world is to be laid by those who will be sent by God to receive it."

"What are these treasures, Grandsire? Are they to be returned to the Holy Land now?"

"Let us speak plainly, lad." The old man moved stiffly, coming over to put a hand on the young Prince's shoulder. "*Our Father, who art in Heaven* is no' a myth, aye?"

"Aye."

"And what great gift did He gie us?" He turned and stared the young man down.

"His only Son, Our Lord and Savior, Jesus Christ," Henry said clearly.

"And that is the gospel, aye?"

"Aye."

"Every word of it?"

"Aye. Every word, Grandsire."

"Our Father in *Heaven* ..." He lifted his eyes to the hearth, where a carved crucifix had been hung generations before. "If our God dwells above, perhaps ye ken it's because our God is ... no' like us."

"How can that be if he made us in His image?" Henry lifted a ruddy brow. "And His Son wouldna he *be like us*?"

"In His image, maybe, but tis no' the same." The old man returned to his chair. "This is a secret the world was no' meant to know, ye ken. A secret the Clan of Saint Claire hae been sworn tae protect for generations."

"Protect from whom, Grandsire?"

"Anyone who would deny the truth for the sake of their faith, ye ken."

"Like ... *The Asāsiyyūn's Guild?*"

"Or the *Holy See*."

"The See? The Church itself?"

"Since the *Schism*, it is hard tae know who tae trust, the pope in Rome or the pope in Avignon. The church, no matter which side, does nae want the truth of the *Sacred Rose* tae be known."

"And *The Asāsiyyūns*?" The young man turned to his grand-father. "Surely, the Saracens will nae come *here*. Will they?"

"Tis the curse o' the Clan Saint Claire, lad. Our enemies are everywhere. They sup at our tables. They listen at our doors. They march at our side, and yet we ken them no'."

"But ... *The Asāsiyyūns...*"

"Aye, lad," William said. "Lang syne past, our clan was chosen to ensure the safe return of a number of relics to the Holy Land. Among them were two hearts ...the Sacred Heart and that of our King, Robert. Your grandsire and his young bride took the Heart of the Sacred Heart, while his brother took the heart of King Robert. William's brother, John was tae arrange for their passage from Spain tae Jerusalem. But William and his party were beset in France by The Asāsiyyūns. The Brothers of his Order ... the Order of the *Sacred Heart of the Rose* ... came to his aid and there was a terrific battle near Aquitaine. Many Templars died. The brothers were reunited in Spain, but neither made it to the Holy Land and their armies were slaughtered at the Battle of Teba. If it were not for one brave squire who escaped the fray with all the treasures he could carry, the relics would have fallen into the hands of our enemies. It was a precursor to the end of the Order. Or so, some would have you believe. The Order has survived. It is our clan's sacred missive. The Order lives on in Clan Saint Claire. But … I fear our sanctum has been compromised. The treasures in our charge are in danger and must be spirited away to safety … and with haste."

"What are we tae do, Grandsire?"

"The treasures are no' safe here, lad. They must be taken tae a place where *The Asāsiyyūns* can nae find them … to the New Jerusalem."

"But if they are everywhere …?"

"Ye must take your most trusted men, travel tae the west. There is a land there *The Asāsiyyūns* have nae ken. Ye must take *The Sacred* Heart tae this land. There ye'll find a sacred place … a cave. When the signs are upon such a place, here will be the entry to the New Jerusalem."

"A cave?" Henry puzzled.

"I've heard of it from a Levite priest I met in my travels." The old man went over to the desk and reached into the bottom drawer, withdrawing a small chest. He reached into a second drawer and found a key tied on a red velvet ribbon. Henry came over as his grandfather opened the box. The sheaf of parchment paper contained within was as ancient as anything Henry could imagine, yellow and crumbling along the edges.

William Sinclair unrolled it, pinning the corners to the desk with a lead weight and other sundry objects he kept on his secretarial for such purposes. The ink was faded and difficult to read. An oil lamp was lit to aid in their effort. "This is the map the priest gae me, in exchange for me sparing his life.

He told me, should I ever gae there, I might no' return for a hundred years and a day, so tae be cautious of such a venture."

Henry studied the markings over his grandfather's shoulder. "Why would you no' send your armies on such a quest?"

"*The Asāsiyyūns* would expect that," Sinclair said. "The armies would no' make it tae the coast before they were assaulted. A clandestine mission requires stealth and agility that armies cannae manage. Ye will need tae make haste … and with great care as well."

"I should take Laird Gunn," Henry said, twisting the whiskers beneath his lip between his thumb and forefinger. "He is the most trusted man I have, but he is also a skilled navigator."

"A wise choice," William said. "And what of your Venetian friends?"

"Nicolo and Antonio?" He queried. "Aye. They would be most helpful."

"Ye ken anyone else?"

"Laird Armstrong would be my next choice, but Lady Armstrong is due to deliver, and I suspect he will no' want tae leave her."

"Still, it would be wrong no' to consult him before you gae."

"Aye," he said. "I'll send word. I'll have Nicolo, and Antonio discreetly inquire for ships, wi' crew," Henry said, studying the map, trying to make sense of it.

"A well paid crew is the most discreet," William said. He took a second chest from another drawer. He pushed the box over. "This should help."

The heft of the chest surprised the Prince. "Grandsire?" He opened it and gasped. The stash of gold and silver coins was impressive. "Is this … my whole inheritance?"

"You are the Earl of Orkney, Baron of Roslin, a Prince …

when my days are done, there is much more to bestow upon you. *This* is Templar gold."

"But … I thought poverty was a caveat of the all Templars …" the young man puzzled.

"Indeed, but the Templars held the gold of kings and popes for safe keeping, ye ken. *This* is allotted tae secure the protection of our sacred treasures."

"I … I dinnae feel worthy, Grandsire." Henry swallowed hard. "I dinnae ken I can do what you ask of me."

"You are Prince Henry Sinclair." His grandfather managed to get to his feet and took the young man by the shoulders. "You will do what you must. This is your calling from God. He will see you safely delivered home. You must see His greatest treasures protected."

THE MEN ASSEMBLED UNDER THE COVER OF A MOONLESS NIGHT as the fog rolled heavy on the moors. "Laird Armstrong?" Henry hesitated, surprised to see the man. "I did no' expect you tae come."

"My Prince, of course I would come." The tall older man bowed with his hand on his heart. "Your servant, my Lord."

"But your wife?"

"Died, childbed fever."

Henry's heart landed in his gut. It was all he could do not to buckle, seeing the pain in his friend's eyes and the weariness etched into his face. "Brother … my sincere regret for such a … tragedy."

"She suffered a terrible labor," he said, his cheeks and eyes growing red. "In the end, it was God's mercy."

"And … the babe?"

"He was born still in death," Armstrong said, swallowing hard. "There was no help for him. There was no help for either of them."

"Surely, this is nae time for you to be leaving your family to undertake this quest," Henry put a hand in the middle of his chest, then glanced down, realizing he wore a tabard of white with a red cross. A single rose was embroidered in gold at the center.

"Wi'out Jennet and our son, I have nae family. My place is with my Prince. I take on this holy quest because I know my beloved wife would want me to. She was a devout believer, and I do this in her honour … and her memory."

Henry's hand moved to the man's shoulder as their eyes met. The Prince nodded. No words were needed.

"Lord Sinclair," James Gunn brought the Prince his saddled horse. "It is a long ride to Stromness. Nicolo has ridden ahead to attend final arrangements for passage. Antonio is in charge of covering our tracks and making sure we're not followed. If we are followed, he will … take care of it. If God sees merciful, he will meet us there in three days' time."

"Is the cargo secured?"

"Yes, my Prince," Gunn said. "You have the map?"

"Aye. I do," Henry said. "My sister made an effort tae retrace the image into something legible, but ye ken, I have the original, to ensure there is no error."

"When we reach the *western coast* …" The men had been instructed to keep everything discreet. No one could name their destination, or their cargo, nor the purpose of their mission. This was one way to ensure there were no spies among the men who would accompany the party. "How will we find our way?" Gunn asked.

"I have a trusted man with me who traveled there some years ago with the French," Armstrong said. "He says he can communicate with the locals and find us a guide. We can make allies in *the west*."

"Such a man is an asset," Henry said. "If you trust him, then welcome, and let us be off."

3

Southeastern Oklahoma

"John Carter!" Lauren stood up from the fire she was tending and scanned the camp site, not finding her sons amongst the crew. Her hands went to her hips as she scowled. The television show host turned as Rowan approached carrying one of the equipment trunks from the trailhead. "Have you seen John Carter?"

"I sent him and Henry to get water from the river," Rowan said.

"Oh," Lauren said, handing a stick to Jamie who sat on a blanket safely away from the glowing flames she was coaxing.

"Momma, what's for dinner tonight?" Jamie asked. The boy was always worried about his next meal. The first night of camp was all about convenience. After an early departure and long drive, and another two hours of hiking with all their equipment, they'd spent the last three hours setting up tents and establishing base camp. While Lauren set to work on the meal, the rest of the team set up alarms, calibrated sensors, and prepared camera equipment.

"Red beans and rice." Lauren announced. "Your favorite."

"Aunt Lauren?" Nyota came over. "Mom said to tell you the perimeter alarms are set, and Papa is setting up the trap cams now."

"Thanks, honey." Lauren stood.

"Want me to take Jamie down to the meadow to pick berries with me while you cook dinner?" Nyota was the same age as John Carter, but she treated all the Pierce boys as if she were the older sister, even Henry.

"Berries? What kind of berries?"

"I found a patch of wild blackberries," she said. "I thought we could make a cobbler for dessert. Will you teach me?"

"Sure," Lauren said, glancing at Jamie' who's face lit up. "Just watch out for bears, okay?"

"Of course," she said. "I have my whistle and bear mace if we have any problems."

"Okay," Lauren said. "I'll mix up some dough for the crust once I get dinner started. I'll heat up the Dutch oven, too."

"Thanks, Aunt Lauren." Bahati and Jean-René's daughter had become Lauren's best assistant, and usually helped her keep up with Jamie and John Carter. Henry was older and contended that he didn't need a babysitter. She made sure Lauren always knew what he was up to, especially when he was up to no good.

Having a child like Henry was always a challenge. He was brilliant and free-spirited, and adventurous, like his dad. But he was never where he was supposed to be, and Lauren often had to rein him in. Just because he could do things the younger children couldn't, that didn't mean his mother liked it, and she struggled to keep him under control, for his own safety and her peace of mind.

Lauren had just put the pot of beans on to simmer, when Henry came running into camp, with his little brother on his heels. She rose slowly, her back already aching.

"Mom! Mom!"

"What is it, Henry?" She straightened.

"We found a cave," John Carter announced. "A big one! Maybe there's outlaws treasure in there."

"Mom, there's something else." Henry caught her arm. "Come on! You have to see this!"

"Bahati, will you keep an eye on dinner? I have to see what Henry and John Carter found."

"Sure thing, boss," Bahati said.

John Carter grabbed her by the hand and tugged on her. "Come on, Momma."

She stumbled but caught herself, straightening. "Slow down! I'm coming." Lauren fell in with her two older boys.

While Henry had the features of their father, with copper hair, and blue eyes, his little brother had the Cherokee features of Lauren's family. Jamie had his father's coloring, but he resembled Lauren's side of the family in the face, despite the freckles dotted across his nose.

Which side of the family the next one would resemble was a tossup. She secretly hoped for a girl, though she'd never said anything to Rowan or the boys about it. Another boy would be fine, of course, but she was about to run out of boys names, and the chances Rowan would want to name the next one Mr. Spock increased with each son she delivered. She had one named after Indiana Jones, one named for Rowan's favorite Edgar Rice Burroughs hero, and one named for Captain Kirk. If the next one wasn't Mr. Spock, it could just as easily end up being named Jean-Luc or Luke Skywalker.

The thought amused her, but her attention was drawn away from the idea as the boys led her up a narrow and treacherous trail, which dead-ended into a small opening.

John Carter turned on his flashlight before Henry could get his out of the pocket of his jacket. He aimed it into the void, so his mother could see.

"Can we go in?" John Carter asked.

"Uhm ..." Lauren hesitated. Her fear of tight spaces made her heart race at the idea. She could see the cavern was large, despite the small opening. She also knew she had to get past this phobia. She certainly didn't want her boys to know she was afraid. She didn't want her fears rubbing off on them. "Maybe you should bring your dad back later. I've got to finish getting dinner ready and we don't have the time or the equipment to explore."

"Come on, Mom," Henry caught her hand. "I won't let anything happen to you. You just need to see this one thing."

Lauren hesitated but acquiesced. "Just a quick peek." She wanted them to be brave and knew she'd have to set an example for them. "You can come back with your father later."

They entered the cavern fully, daylight disappearing behind them as they ducked inside. A bat flew past Lauren's head, and she startled, a yelp erupting from her throat before she could stifle it. Out of reflex, her hand went to the knife she kept at her belt.

"It's just a bat, Momma," Jamie chided her.

"I'm okay," she said. "I just wasn't expecting it." It didn't matter how big a cave was, it was still a cave. Caves terrified her. Still, she followed the boys into the darkness, watching her footing, trying not to think of what might be lurking there, or about getting trapped. At least there was a breath of fresh air that tossed a loose lock of hair across her face. That alleviated her fear of oxygen deprivation. Flammable or combustible gasses weren't likely either. The musty damp assaulted her nose as they crossed into an even larger cavern.

"Did you happen to notice what species of bat that was?" Lauren asked. Everything was a lesson if she took the opportunity to teach it.

"No," Jamie said.

"I can't be sure," Lauren said. "But maybe it was the Little

Brown Myotis. It hibernates in caves like this one. They eat mosquitos so they tend to forage over water."

"Cool," Henry said, using his light to search for more bats.

"Do you see that?" Henry asked, shining his light into the cathedral-like expanse of the cave. On the rock wall, there were symbols carved into its surface.

A gasp escaped Lauren's throat, as Henry's light scanned over the symbols. "Those are runes," she said.

Henry beamed. "Like the ones at Heavener."

"What does it say, Momma?" John Carter asked. "Read them!"

Lauren studied the markings for a moment. Her knowledge of the ancient All-Language gave her the ability to read and understand any language. As she deciphered the runes, her breath caught in her throat. "It's ..." Lauren puzzled. While she could recognize and read the symbols, the letters were a jumble. *A cypher? An anagram, perhaps?* She took a step back, letting the beam of her light join with Henry's as she tried to make sense of it. As she gazed at it, one symbol became clear as the meaning scrolled past the back of her eyes. "That's the mark of … Henry Sinclair." She had seen this mark on a henge back east some years ago while filming their television show, *The Veritas Codex*. She'd learned some about Henry Sinclair preparing for their trip *to Rennes les-Château*. As a member of the Scottish royal family — a Knights Templar — he was often associated with the tales of the Holy Grail and the Ark of the Covenant. His family's role in the drama had been a pivotal plotline in Dan Brown's *The DaVinci Code*. While Sinclair was a historical figure, the legends had blurred the lines between fact and fiction over the centuries.

"The Baron of Rosslyn?" Henry asked.

"And how do you know that?" she asked.

"It was in Mr. Brown's book," he said. "The Sinclair family built Rosslyn Chapel. In his book, that's where the body of Mary Magdalene was buried. Some say the Holy Grail is hidden there, too." Her mother must have let him read the *DaVinci* Code when they were preparing to go to France. The boys were encouraged to do their research and report back if they found any information of interest.

"Does this mean that Sinclair was *here*?" Henry asked, drawing Lauren from her thoughts.

"Why would someone else make his mark here?" John Carter asked his brother curtly. "I don't go into *my* closet and write *your* name on the wall."

"Stop writing on the walls, dork!" Henry snapped.

"Stop wetting your bed and I'll stop drawing on the walls." The boys bickered like most brothers, and the barrage of insults and slams continued as Lauren took out her iPhone and started taking pictures, blinding all of them with the flash.

"Cut it out," Lauren said, without any anger in her voice. "Let's get back to camp before dinner is ruined. I left Bahati in charge."

"But ..." John Carter started to protest.

"That's enough!" Lauren turned to the boys. "Weren't you two supposed to bring water for the camp?" she asked. "Your father was expecting you to get that done without detours, so you'd be wise to go get that water and get back to camp before he finds out where you've been."

"He's going to find out anyway when you tell him about the runes," Henry said.

"Yes, but there will be water and at least he won't be angry about not having any," Lauren said.

The boys took the path to the right, towards the river, while Lauren returned to camp on the path to the left.

LAUREN WAITED UNTIL EVERYONE HAD GATHERED AROUND THE fire to eat before she mentioned what the boys had found that afternoon. "Runes?" Rowan's brow shot up. The boys sat grinning sheepishly in the shadows, outside of the adult's circle.

"But, we're not here to find cave drawings," Jean-René quipped. "We're here to find the skunk ape."

"Sometimes adventure leads you to something you weren't searching for," Lauren said with a shrug, digging in to her dinner. She was hungry and tired and couldn't wait to climb into her tent for a few hours' sleep before their midnight call to duty.

"We're not going to abandon our prime objective though," Rowan said. "Let's go over tonight's plan."

Lauren ate while Rowan briefed the crew on their objective. They were deep in the Ouachita Mountains in Southern Oklahoma. To the south, there was a swamp full of alligators and snakes. To the north, was the famous Talimena drive, home of the Oklahoma ghost lights. That was a story for another day. Tonight, it was all about the notorious skunk ape. The Native American tribes had reportedly sighted the skunk ape as far back as the 1800's.

Lauren had it on reliable authority that the People of Tsul'Kalu's race had no residency in the region whatsoever. They didn't care for the mosquitos or alligators any more than Lauren did, but Rowan and the Network insisted on an episode covering the alleged cryptid. They'd just spent the weekend at the Honobia Bigfoot Festival. Lauren had done a presentation on genetic diversity in presumed populations of the North American Wood Ape, while Rowan had done his presentation on the tech needed for an effective bigfoot hunt. They'd both been part of the panel discussion.

AFTER THE BRIEFING, LAUREN LEFT THE DISHES UP TO THE older kids, and set to work getting John Carter and Jamie ready for bed. Their tent was big enough for all five of them.

Two of the boys shared a joined sleeping bag, while Henry slept across their heads. Lauren and Rowan had a second joined sleeping bag, which left room for a small walkway between them. A battery powered lantern hung from a hook on the support pole.

Jamie was the first to bed, after having washed his face and brushed his teeth. Lauren lay down on her bed and read to him until he nodded off, and she could no longer keep her eyes open. She dozed but woke when Rowan came in a short time later with the older boys. He got them settled for the night, then he lay down next to his wife. He drew her into the curve created as he curled up onto his side. She sighed as she snuggled in, warming to him. She could always count on Rowan to keep the sleeping bag warm. He generated heat like a wood-burning stove, and the night was sure to be cold and dark.

"Hey, Dad?" She heard John Carter whisper loudly. "If you find a skunk ape, will you wake us up?"

"Sure, slugger," Rowan said, with a yawn in his voice.

"Do you think there's more than one?" John Carter asked.

"There has to be," Henry answered, clicking on his flashlight, and opening his book. "Didn't you listen to mom's speech about biological diversity and an adequate gene pool at the Bigfoot festival?"

"I just think it's weird that, if there's a lot of them, that they are so good at hiding." John Carter clicked on his flashlight.

"Just one Bigfoot gets to be good at hiding?" Henry responded.

"I bet they hate playing hide-and-seek." Rowan snorted.

"They're good at hide, but … not so good at the seek part," Lauren mused.

"Good one, Momma," John Carter said.

"Okay guys," Rowan said. "We need sleep. Let's zip it."

Lauren rolled over and tucked her belly up against Rowan.

His hand rested on it. It quivered beneath his palm, and he pressed a thumb against the foot of his unborn child. He sighed contentedly. Lauren knew how much he loved their growing family, and the stirrings of new life made him happier than he could express. She could lay there with his hand feeling every move and squirm beneath it all night long. But, in just a few hours, the crew would begin to stir, and Lauren would take her place at the fire, serving as the base command, while Rowan and Jean-René took the teams out.

Lauren's job was to monitor the cameras and sensors while keeping the kids and herself safe. She would also relay communications between the teams, if necessary. Now, it was time to sleep, and even as the boys hid under their blankets with their flashlights and their books, she let Orpheus have her.

4

The New World

Ko'i Minco was aware of the strangers' presence long before they knew of his. He heard their voices as he approached the river. Here, they pulled their boats ashore and made camp. He listened to them talk amongst themselves. He knew some of the white mans' talk, but he only recognized a few words here and there. Their language was different from the Spaniards he had met.

The Panther told him in a vision where to find these men. He and the panther spoke often, and the panther led him as he wandered the lands alone. He listened to the Panther and trusted him.

The lone hunter's father had been a tribal elder. Before he Ko'i Minco been banished, he was an honored member of the Panther Clan. Perhaps that was why the panther guided him, and why the panther spoke to him.

He approached the clearing, careful to move quietly in the dense forest. The soft soles of his leather boots allowed him to disperse his weight so the damp spring leaves made no sound beneath his feet. The sun shone down upon them, and they glowed with a light Ko'i Minco had never seen. The caps upon their heads were metal and they wore unusual attire. White dresses, softer than any doeskin Ko'i Minco ever saw, covered their clinking shirts.

The hunter encountered white men before, but none like these. His mother's father had told him of meeting Spaniards who sought only fortune — gold. Even his father's people spoke of the white men and their greed. Ko'i Minco spared little compassion for these cumbersome creatures who stomped their way across his land, killing his game, and acting as if they owned everything they saw. It was not hard to find them. They left a wide swath of destruction in their wake. He'd been tracking them since they left the coast. Any fool could track a man on a river. The water only flowed one way. Traveling alone, the hunter traveled swiftly. He finally caught up with the heavily burdened party.

"Gold could be useful," Panther said. "You could reclaim your birthright. Think of the wealth the shining white men must bear in that box."

"I do not know if gold is enough to buy back my seat at the council," Ko'i Minco answered, keeping his voice low. "But, it could be sufficient to buy my pardon."

"See how many of them it takes to move it? How much gold do you think they carry?"

Ko'i Minco considered how many guns and horses he could acquire. He could buy bundles of tobacco and barrels of their liquor with that much gold. "Fifty horses. A hundred guns. Metal blades as sharp as your claws, Panther. That is what I could buy with such wealth."

"Then you must do as I say," Panther said. "These men are guided by *Impashilup*, the *soul eater*. They claim to serve a god, but their god is an evil one, a dark lord of the heavens who will curse any who cross them. You must proceed with care."

"I am your servant, Panther. Guide me."

~

THE DEMON HAD BEEN BIDING HIS TIME FOR YEARS. HE WAITED for just such an opportunity. Banished to the depths of Hell, he was bound to suffer. He was bound to remain where he could not battle for the authority that was owed him. He could not take his seat at the right hand of Anu, the Most High — his father. It gave him a perspective this human could relate to. Ko'i Minco had been banished from his father's side. Murder was a sin among most races.

Enlil was not bound by time, and he could still plant seeds of chaos and destruction. It would take time for such seeds to grow. Time was the one thing Enlil had plenty of. With it, he studied the ripples on the plain of time and followed it back to this moment. Now, he found a weak mind — full of greed and hatred, hungry for revenge. Such corruption gave the Dark One power, and it was a power he delighted in. He intended to put it to good use.

"Befriend the white man," Enlil appeared in the form of a panther, and spoke in the spirit guide's voice. "Learn his language and his ways. Tell him you have been sent to see him to a place of sanctuary where his treasures may be kept safe. I will guide you to this place, and when it is time, you will know. Here, I will give you the power to take their treasure. You will see your rightful place among your people returned to you."

"I will have my name restored?"

"Your crimes will be forgotten, and you will be glorified," Panther said. Enlil offered up the greatest reward. "Your face will be looked upon by future generations. You will gain the attention of your people's progeny. But take warning. These men cannot be trusted. Like the Spanish, they will plant seeds of destruction. The *Apafalaya*, The *Chickasaws*, the *Chakchiumas* — all the tribes of this land — will fall if they are not stopped now."

"I will stop them," Ko'i Minco vowed. "I will be the champion of my people."

"Then you must do exactly as I command," Panther ordered.

"Tell me the ways, Panther. I will obey."

Lauren awoke with a start, realizing it was no longer dark, and Rowan was climbing back into bed beside her. She rolled over and glared at him in the dim light of dawn. "What time is it?"

"Almost seven," he said, warming himself against her. His clothing was cold on her skin, evidence that he spent the night out with the teams and was just now returning for some much needed rest. They often slept in short shifts when on an expedition, and this one was no different.

"What?" She sat up, panicked. "What happened? Why didn't you wake me up?"

"Believe me, I tried," Rowan said, pulling the sleeping bag back up to keep their body heat in. Lauren lay back down, staring up at the shadows of limbs waving above the top of the tent. "You were so tired. I just didn't have it in my heart to press the matter."

"But ..."

"Bahati ran base camp," Rowan said. "Clearly, you needed the rest."

Lauren curled up on his shoulder and ran a hand down the front of his soft t-shirt, shrugging the sleeping bag over her shoulders. She heaved a heavy sigh. "Find anything?"

"Not a damned thing," Rowan said. "Everyone got all excited about a pack of coyotes baying at the moon. Once Bahati got them on the trap cam, we were able to put the rookies at ease and move on."

"How are the new techs doing?"

"They're getting the hang of it." Rowan sighed. "I wish you could be out there to help me though. They're still pretty jumpy. They could learn from you and your calm demeanor."

That made Lauren happy.

"So why didn't you tell me about the runes when the boys found them?" he said, out of nowhere.

"My priority was getting everyone fed." Lauren yawned. "I'm sorry."

"I didn't work all those years to get my archaeology degree just for you to leave me out on an archaeological discovery like that."

Lauren opened her eyes. He was legitimately affronted. "You're right," she said, laying her head back down. "I'm sorry. You worked hard for that degree. It wasn't an intentional slight. I told the boys if they wanted to explore farther, they should bring you up to the cavern."

Having taken a hiatus after having John Carter, they returned before Jamie arrived. The extended break gave them more family time. Rowan got his master's degree, after being accepted into the University of Cairo's archaeology program. Jamie had been an unexpected but welcomed result of their time off work.

Just a couple of months ago, Lauren found out she was pregnant ... again.

Deep in the remote regions of the Himalaya mountains in Tibet, Lauren took ill. In the middle of a blinding snowstorm on the top of the mountains, she suffered morning sickness so severe Rowan gave her IV fluids until the storm abated. Of course, they didn't know it was morning sickness. It wasn't until she got back to base camp that one of the Sherpas' mother asked her how far along she was, that she realized she might be pregnant.

That meant she was in no condition to be climbing on a glacier, much less chasing a Yeti. But Rowan had no choice.

He needed to keep the team working. There was no other option but to leave her in basecamp where there were medics and medicine women to care for her.

In the time they spent interviewing soldiers who claimed to have seen the *snowman*, Rowan had learned that their commander had ordered them to find it and catch it or kill it. Before the weather socked *The Veritas Codex* team in, they'd gone hunting with the soldiers, and in the fury of the blizzard, someone saw something, and shots were fired. Drops of blood had been found on the snow where they thought they saw something. Rowan had taken a sample and was anxious to get back to civilization to have it analyzed.

When the weather cleared, Lauren was in no shape to hike out, and they called for an evacuation chopper to get them down and back to Kathmandu. By the time they got back to the states, the worst of it was over, and they spent several weeks at Rowan's boyhood home for her to convalesce and regain her strength before they headed back to work, leaving the boys with his parents for the first half of the season. His parents delivered them to Lauren's mother once the school year was completed.

This season of the show had followed a theme, to find the mythical great apes: *Yeti, Sasquatch, Yowie, Yerin, tek tek* — and now — skunk ape.

It was fully light when she realized she was alone in the tent. *How long had she slept?* She picked up her phone and found the battery dead. She had a portable charger, and she rummaged through her pack to find it. It would take some time before she could turn her phone back on, and she hoped by then she'd be able to answer the provocative question: *Where was everyone?*

When they camped, she typically slept in a pair of sweat

pants, and a long-sleeved t-shirt. If it got exceptionally cold, she'd add double-layered cabin socks, a hoodie, and a stocking cap. Today, she rose and changed into cargo pants, a t-shirt and a flannel lined plaid shirt, socks, and her hiking boots. She ducked out of the tent, finding the fire had died down, and the coffee pot set to the side of the grill was lukewarm. She scanned the campsite beneath the canopy of the oak and elm trees but found no one.

She heaved a heavy sigh and set to work, adding kindling to the fire, coaxing a flame back to life. Lauren reheated the remaining coffee before going to the chow locker to find something to fix for her breakfast.

With a cup of coffee, some fried eggs, and a cold biscuit, she was fortified, and ready to face the day. She found the wash bucket setting at the edge of the clearing. Lauren washed her dishes, then put them away.

Chance was sitting down the hill next to a fallen log, away from the main circle of tents. He had one of the cameras taken apart with the pieces lined up around him on a canvas tarp.

"Morning, boss." He glanced up as she approached.

"Where is everyone this morning?" she asked, walking over towards him.

"Down at the river, I think," he said. "Rowan said something about a cave though."

Standing with her hands on her hips she debated where to even begin the search for her boys, but then recalled the earlier conversation with Rowan. She knew just where to go. The hike up the narrow trail had seemed easier the day before, when she was trying to keep up with Henry and John Carter. But now, it seemed more rugged — more perilous.

She stood at the edge of the cavern with no flashlight or her phone to light the dark cave. She listened for the sound of boys mucking about in the back of the cave but heard nothing.

"Rowan?" she called. "Henry? John Carter?" There was no answer, just the buzz of some trapped insects high in the walls. It must have been a swarm of cicadas or grasshoppers by the fevered buzz. The echo off the high ceiling became deafening and her head began to spin, and bile rose in the back of her throat as the world tilted off balance.

Her hand went to her belly. The growing roundness of her stomach reminded her that tight spaces were no place for her. When she came out of the cave, she was breathless and light-headed. She worked her way down the trail and found a rock to sit on. That was the first spell of *morning sickness* she'd had in a couple of weeks.

"Well dang it." She sighed. After a moment's rest, she regained her strength and rose to continue the search. She worked her way around camp, going down to the river, sweat peeling down her skin as she found the path. The night might have been chilly, but the day had turned warm.

At the river, she found all four of her boys, buck naked in the cold, clear water. Their clothes were strewn along the banks with no care, and she paused to pick up Jamie's shirt from a damp puddle. "What are you doing?" Lauren said from a rock on the river's edge.

"We needed a bath," Jamie, in his dad's arms, called back.

"Where is everyone?" Lauren called out.

Her answer came from above, as a naked white form flashed from a rock, screaming, "Canon ball!" Jean-René arced over the water and into it with a great splash, drenching everyone, including Lauren who stumbled back from the water's edge at the cold splash on her face.

"Jesus!" she exclaimed as Jean-René came up sputtering, laughing along with everyone else.

"Where's Bahati and Nyota?" Lauren scowled, wiping the water from her skin.

"They are down the river, around the bend doing the

same thing." Rowan grinned, stepping closer to the bank, setting Jamie down. She studied his lean frame with obvious approval as the water came up to the dip in the muscles along his groin. He caught her eye and gave her a suggestive grin that told her he might have allowed her a more thorough inspection had they not been in the company of their offspring.

"Isn't the water cold?"

"Oh yeah!" He sucked in air between his pearl-white teeth. "But extremely refreshing."

"I think I'll go check on Bahati and Nyota ..." Lauren stepped back and turned down stream, leaving the boys to their games thinking there was more swimming and horseplay than bathing going on.

She found Bahati wrapped in a towel at the edge of the river when she rounded the corner. Nyota was already dressed, but had her long braids wound up on her head, wrapped in a towel. "About time you woke up," Bahati said. "Feeling better?"

"I didn't realize I was so tired." Lauren shrugged.

"You should know as well as anyone how pregnancy can drain you," Bahati said.

"True," she said. "I thought I'd be enjoying that 2nd trimester sweet spot, but the exhaustion is lingering, and I got kind of queasy this morning."

"It will pass," Bahati said. "You were just as tired with Henry and John Carter, and Jamie, too."

"So, how's the water?"

"Cold," Bahati said. "You'd be wise to send the boys back with the bucket and let them bring you water to heat over the fire to wash with."

"I think that sounds like a good idea."

～

By mid-day it was significantly warmer than it had been when she crawled out of the tent. Lauren stripped to her boy shorts and a tank top and used a wash cloth dipped in warm soapy water to bathe. The men and boys had made themselves scarce, gone on the pretense of checking trap cams and perimeter sensors. Bahati and Nyota were busy with preparations for lunch. Once she'd washed her body as best as she could, she flipped her long hair over her head and submerged it in the tall pot of steaming water, dunking her head in the process. She used a biodegradable shampoo to scrub her scalp and wash her locks, then took the pan and tipped it over onto her head, drenching her hair, rinsing the soap from it.

She was clean and mostly dry when she heard the clamoring of boys approaching from the direction of the cave. Lauren sat combing her hair at the picnic table. Bahati made her a sandwich and tossed her a bag of chips. Nyota brought her an apple and a bottle of water.

"Mom! We're back," Jamie called.

"As if we couldn't tell." Bahati chuckled. "Lunch is ready." She handed a plate to Jamie, then one to John Carter. Rowan arrived behind them a moment later.

"Hooray, lunch is ready," he exclaimed, snagging a banana from the tub of supplies while accepting a plate from Bahati.

"Did you go to the cave and show your dad the runes?" Lauren asked when Henry sat down beside her with his plate.

"Yeah," Henry said.

"Pretty amazing stuff," Rowan said. "But I am having a hard time believing the Sinclair party made it this far south and this far inland. It's probably a hoax ... modern day graffiti."

"There are validated runes less than one hundred miles north of here. Why couldn't Sinclair make it this far? Someone else did," Lauren pointed out. "How would you find out if it were ancient or modern?"

"I suppose a forensic geologist with a background in archaeology could tell," Rowan said.

"Do you know a forensic geologist with a background in archaeology?" Bahati retorted.

"As a matter of fact, I do," Rowan said. "Did you ever meet Robin Brackett? He did some guest consulting on the Science Channel a couple of years ago."

"No, but the name sounds familiar."

"Do you think it's worth calling him in?" Jean-René asked.

Rowan shrugged. "Who knows?"

"I think that's more interesting than this whole skunk ape hype," Lauren said, trying to sound passive.

"I recorded the coordinates of the cave on the GPS," Rowan said. "We'll be in the area to visit your family often enough, and we can always come back."

Lauren shrugged, and let it go.

"So what are you making for dinner tonight, Momma?" Jamie asked, climbing up to the table with his plate. His lunch consisted of a sandwich, *two* bags of chips and a banana.

"You haven't even eaten your lunch, honey. Isn't it a little early to be worried about what's for dinner?"

"But what if I don't like it? I might decide I need *two* sandwiches to hold me over, Momma."

"Have I ever made anything you didn't like?"

"Never," he gasped. "Which is why I gotta make sure I have enough to hold me ... because the law of averages could catch up with me."

Lauren's jaw dropped and she glared at Jean-René, knowing he'd been instructing the boy about hockey and statistics. "I promise, you will love it," Lauren said with a scowl at her co-worker.

"You don't know what you're going to make, do you?" Rowan asked, grinning, as he joined the argument simply for argument's sake.

"I'm making chicken and dumplings." Lauren thought quickly.

"My favorite." Henry grinned.

"No, it's not!" Jamie's face went red as he glared at his older brother. "It's *my* favorite. Not yours!"

"It can be both of your favorites," Lauren scolded. "Now finish your lunch so we can get your lessons done before I have to start dinner."

"Aw, Mom." Henry rolled his eyes.

"Did you finish your homework, or did you stay up reading all night?"

"I finished the book you told me to read," Henry said. "Erich Von Däniken has some pretty crazy ideas about aliens."

"What year was that book published, Henry?" Jean-René asked.

"Like a million years ago." Henry shrugged. Lauren's brows lifted. "Well, it was before *you* were born," he added.

"Not by much," John Carter piped up.

"Hey!" Lauren and Rowan both scowled and scolded in unison.

"Momma, I read all my book, too," Jamie said with a mouth full of sandwich.

Lauren turned her attention to him. "And what did you learn?"

"There was a dog who saved a whole town," he said. "All the children were sick. They couldn't get their medicine, so this dog ran through a blizzard to carry their medicine to the town because the cars and trucks couldn't get through the storm."

"What was the dog's name, Jamie?" Bahati asked.

"*Balto*," Jamie said.

"Did you read *Balto* all by yourself?"

"Yes, Aunt Bahati," he said.

"What?" She gasped. "That's an awfully big book for a little boy."

"Second grade level." Lauren nodded. "Jamie is a proficient reader. In truth, it's too easy for him."

"Can I read one of John Carter's books?" Jamie asked.

"Which one of John Carter's books would you like to read?" Rowan asked.

"I don't know," he said. "Little kids don't get cool books about science fiction like big kids do."

"I'm sure we can find something like that for you to read," Lauren said. "Now, let's finish lunch so we can get the hard work out of the way and do something fun before we have to start evening chores."

"You know, I think I'd like to go back to the cave with Jean-René and Chance and get some lighting in there so we can get better pictures to send to the forensic geologist," Rowan said. "If you guys have your lessons done, we can go together."

HAVING A MOTHER WITH A PhD IN BIOLOGICAL anthropology and a father with a master's degree in archaeology — as well as Bahati who had a degree in journalism and Jean-René who had a degree in cinematography — came in quite handy when they made the decision to homeschool the children. Lauren had been both mother and teacher to all three of her boys, and to Nyota, too. She was every bit as bright as the Pierce boys. They were all eager pupils, and their world-travels had given them experiences few kids their age had.

While the boys didn't always travel with them, Lauren based their lessons on the destinations they journeyed to and brought the boys back souvenirs related to their lessons as rewards.

John Carter was beginning to learn how to read Egyptian hieroglyphics and had a knack for picking up foreign words and phrases. Jamie, however, loved stories, and when he didn't have a book in his hand, he always had a journal in which he drafted stories he heard along the way.

Henry was good at math, and was starting to pick up physics, while Nyota preferred to observe the rocks and plants they'd encountered along the way, and had become quite adept and identifying medicinal plants, and edible mushrooms and roots.

ROWAN WATCHED HIS WIFE WITH THE CHILDREN AS SHE BEGAN the daily lesson. The kids settled and sat with their notebooks ready for their assignments. *This.* This was everything he'd ever wanted — of course, he still didn't have a dog, but that was okay — for now. They traveled as much as they wanted and having Diana and his parents to help with the kids was priceless. He loved their life, and it was about to get even better. He'd always wanted kids, and soon, she'd give him another son, or possibly a daughter. Of course, he couldn't think about her in this condition without remembering how it'd happened.

The team had been deep in the jungles of Cambodia, searching for the mythical *tek tek*, a smaller version of the Bigfoot, near the ruins of an ancient temple. Traipsing up densely vegetated trails for a week, they found a clearing with a number of rising ancient towers climbing high above the trees towards the bright sky.

One afternoon while they were scoping out filming sites, Rowan waited until he and Lauren were alone and pulled her into him unexpectedly. He'd told her later that he had been watching her from behind all day as they'd worked through the dense jungle, up the steep hillside to the crumbling, moss-covered monolith. The intoxicating sway of her hips had distracted him from the oppressive heat, and the heavy pack on his shoulders. He had to admit that his thoughts had been anything but pure since early in the day. There, in the overgrown temple, he made his move.

She hadn't been expecting it, a million miles from anywhere, but he had her just where he wanted her. He froze when she abruptly turned her head and caught him inspecting her up and down ... mostly down. His starving eyes could have devoured the flesh from her bones, the gooseflesh rising on her skin as the heat of the jungle paled to the fire in his eyes. It had been a long time since he'd hungered for her like that.

A surprised gasp escaped her throat as he pounced. His mouth captured her lips, and he backed her into the temple wall, pinning her backpack — and her body — between the ancient stones, making his intentions fully apparent.

"Rowan?" She broke loose, managing a chuckling gasp. "What's gotten into you?"

"I need you." He breathed on her skin, having to put a hand up on the wall behind her to hold himself up.

"But ... my camera's still running," she protested. She made no move to escape.

"Let it run," Rowan groaned, his lips searching her bare neck. He nibbled on her ear and despite her hands flat on his chest she lacked the strength or desire to hold him at bay. With a skilled hand, he unbuttoned her shorts, and they fell down around her ankles, and he started on the buttons of her shirt. She shrugged off her backpack and let it fall away. "We can delete the video after we review the performance."

Any protests Lauren might have had quickly melted as Rowan stripped her naked, worshiping her body with a frenetic passion she was unaccustomed to. He picked her up, and she wrapped her legs around him, grinding her hips into his as he carried her to a worn stone altar in the middle of the crumbling temple.

In ancient days, Rowan imagined, virgins would have been sacrificed to ancient gods, and matrons would conduct similar rituals to the one he performed now — to honor the goddesses and ensure a plentiful harvest — here on this very altar. Rowan couldn't say for sure that the spirit of the ancient gods hadn't overtaken him, but he hoped to honor his own goddess as he peeled off his shirt and reached for the button on his shorts.

She was more than his goddess. She was his own *Dejah Thoris*, his Princess of Barsoom, and he was her *Jedak of Jedaks* — Crown Prince of Helium. He had longed for her his whole life, even before he wanted a wife. Just the thought of his princess — his goddess — was too much for him to bear, and his knees threatened to buckle as he admired the beauty of her skin, as her lips drank from his, and he from hers.

Lauren's camera had fallen aside when he stripped her, and he left it where it had landed. He didn't care about what it captured as he crawled onto the altar with her, and she opened to him. Their bodies molded in an intimate alliance of desperate, and much needed passion. *God! What a woman she was!*

He prayed to all his favorite goddesses: Aphrodite, Baalast, Cybele, Freyja ... *Oh goddess yes! Freyja* ... Of all the goddesses of love, Freyja was his favorite ... the Norse goddess of sexual activity, to whom the ancient Vikings worshiped. Bride of the god Odr, she ruled over the ninth level of Valhalla and decided where the warriors would sit at her feast. The warrior goddess also road a golden chariot into battle to collect the souls of the dead warriors of the Valkyrie. She was his princess, his goddess, his own *Dejah Thoris*, and his Freyja — all in one perfect form.

Lauren indeed had the body of a Norse goddess, long and muscular, with shoulders much wider than most women, and hips to match. Childbirth had left her with faint marks where her flesh had been stretched to its limits, but given a number of years to recover, her waist had narrowed, and her stomach had flattened. Her breasts were full, her nipples dark and warm. They grew taut as he bowed over them to suckle, all the while, her hips rose and fell beneath his. Her back arched and he could feel her whole body tremble as her muscles contracted around him, and he felt his control fleeting.

Freyja, please...

Within the span of a quickening heartbeat, the goddess brought them to Valhalla together, and Lauren's voice pierced the cavernous monument with a cry that echoed off the stones high above them. Bats erupted from the cracks in the walls, scattering and disappearing through a void into the afternoon sky, squealing as sharply as she had. Her back arched, and she throbbed around him, holding him inside her a moment longer. He buried his face in her damp hair, breathing deeply. He fought to still his racing heart.

"Team one to Rowan." The radio squelched and startled them out of their fantasy. Rowan rolled off the stone altar and was to his feet at once, snatching up his clothes, turning off the camera before reaching for the radio.

"Go for Rowan," he managed to say, still breathless.

"Are you okay? We heard someone scream," Bahati came back.

"Lauren ran across ... a snake, but she's okay," he lied, glancing up at Lauren as she came over and collected her clothes.

"Where are you guys?"

"We were scoping out the main temple to see if we wanted to film here tonight, before we encountered *the snake*," he lied again. "Where are you?"

"We're on the way to the ruins west of you, but we can turn back, if you need help," Bahati said, her voice heavy with concern.

"No," Rowan said, catching Lauren by the waist as she started to pull on her shorts, dropping his clothes. "We're fine now. We're going to see if there is anywhere else we want to revisit later. You go on and let us know what you find. We're okay here." He dropped the radio and pulled Lauren into him, upending them both. She squealed as he caught her and groped her breast, making it clear that he was not done with her.

"Is that another snake?" She giggled, finding his body responsive.

"Same snake." He grinned, chasing her naked across the expanse of the temple.

Rowan had told her later about his prayers, and they blamed — or more properly credited — Freyja for her current condition.

As an only child, Nyota had been fascinated with Lauren's pregnancies and asked lots of questions, which Lauren answered matter-of-factly. Nothing about being pregnant was out of bounds, but she discouraged questions about how she became pregnant. He knew Lauren would have happily explained everything — from a completely scientific stand-point, of course — except that she didn't feel it was her place. She encouraged the girl to ask her mother, and then come to her if she had any questions.

Bahati had later told her that she'd scowled at her mother through the whole conversation about the *birds and the bees*, and when she was finished, had said, "I'm sure glad you don't let Papa do that to you. I don't need any little brothers following me around, telling me what to do." Rowan got the stink-eye every time Nyota saw him for several weeks after that, though he had no idea for the reason behind it until he said some-thing, and Lauren explained it to him.

In truth, the statement might have stung just a bit. Bahati and Jean-René very much wanted more children, but it just hadn't happen for them. Nyota's birth had been difficult, and the couple hadn't had much luck since. At this point, it didn't appear like they'd have anymore.

Bahati couldn't get pregnant. Lauren couldn't keep from it, or so it seemed. She and Rowan both had fond memories about how this baby had been conceived, and had they realized at the time, they might have suggested Bahati and Jean-René try the same technique.

5

"What?" Lauren caught him watching her and saw his cheeks flame at having been caught lost in thought. She could just imagine what he was thinking about. She knew that expression all too well.

"I was thinking about turning in early." He feigned a yawn. "I could use a nap before another long night traipsing in the jungle." He realized his mistake too late.

"Jungle?" Jamie crossed his blue eyes as he wrinkled up his freckled nose at his father. "This is a forest, Dad. Don't you know the difference?"

"Sorry, Jamie." Rowan was now beet red. "My bad."

"You should go lie down," Lauren said, with an arch of her brow, never lifting her head nor meeting his gaze. "Clearly you're tired and not thinking straight."

"Yeah," Rowan hesitated. "Maybe I'll go refill the water bucket before I lay down." He took up the bucket, then turned and started to head in the opposite direction, but Henry and John Carter leapt from the table.

"We'll go, Dad," Henry said, snatching the bucket away as they raced by.

"Keep an eye on your little brother," Rowan shouted after them, when Jamie took off after the older boys.

"No side trips," Lauren added, picking up their notebooks glancing over their homework. John Carter had filled a full page of math problems, each one written backwards The equations were perfectly solved. He did that — wrote things backwards — when he wanted to show off. Homeschooling had been good for them all, but she realized she wasn't challenging him enough even though he was already doing algebra. *Time for a little geometry, perhaps some rudimentary calculus?*

"Alone at last …" Rowan grinned over his shoulder as he ambled towards the tent.

"I'll be right there." Lauren glanced at him. She put their books away in the equipment case and went to ask Bahati to keep an eye on the boys for a while so she and Rowan could lay down and rest, over-exaggerating her exhaustion.

"Jean-René and I were going to go down to the clearing beyond the river to scope out our filming locations for tonight. I'll take the kids — and the rookies — with us, so they won't bother you."

"Thank you." Lauren returned back to the tent.

ROWAN HAD STRETCHED OUT ON TOP OF THE SLEEPING BAGS and lay with his hands folded across his stomach, his face a study of perfect peace as he feigned sleep. Lauren zipped the tent back up and peeled out of her sweater and kicked off her shoes. She caught Rowan peeking at her from under his lashes, turning her back as she reached under her shirt and unclasped her bra. He knew she was tempting him, and it was working. Her hips now were even fuller than they had been that afternoon in the temple when they worshiped all the goddesses. The deities had heard his prayers and brought life into her. She was a beautiful mother. He sighed as she came and lay down beside him and he drew her into his arms.

"Thinking about Cambodia again?" she whispered.

"I will think about that day as long as I live and breathe." He rolled towards her and pulled her into him, tucking her head under his chin, taking a deep breath of her and sighing.

"I figured that had to be it." She smirked.

"Was it that obvious?"

"Only to me." Lauren sighed.

"What about the boys?" Rowan asked.

"Bahati and Jean-René are taking them down to the meadow. I figure we have an hour, maybe two before they come back wanting their dinner."

Rowan's hand slipped slowly down her waist, finding the swell of her stomach, but not stopping there. She rolled back, as his lips traced down her neck. She ran her hands up his hip and under his shirt as he leaned over her and kissed his way down to the *v* of her t-shirt.

Lauren ran her fingers through his hair as he warmed her with his touch. His mind wandered back to Cambodia wishing they could recreate that moment somehow. Romantic interludes were inconvenient when they were on location. Rarely were they alone long enough for even the briefest intimate moments. Fortunately, they'd never been caught, at least as far as Rowan knew. The radio call in Cambodia had been the closest *close-call* they'd had.

Rowan paused in his ministrations to peel off his shirt. A child's cry pierced the silence of the woods, and all thoughts of romance were over. Lauren leapt from the bedroll and flew out of the tent before Rowan even managed to get up.

In haste, Rowan pulled his shirt back on and fumbled with his shoes. He paused at the door, realizing the tent was still zipped. She hadn't had time to zip it back up. Come to think of it, she hadn't had time to unzip it either. *She'd done it again.*

Hurrying, he fumbled for the zipper pull, and climbed out,

tripping over the edge of the tent as he exited, landing hard on a rock as he did. Once he found his feet, he took off in the general direction of the disturbance, towards the wailing cry that abruptly stopped.

Moments later, Rowan skidded into the muddy clearing, finding Lauren sitting on a fallen log, holding their littlest boy, with her hand clamped down over his forehead, blood oozing from between her fingers. Her pale t-shirt was spattered in red, and the expression on her face made his heart break. "What happened?"

"It's all Henry's fault!" John Carter ratted his brother out.

"No, it's not!" Henry said curtly.

"What happened?" Rowan repeated.

"We were walking along the fallen log and Jamie slipped," Henry said in his defense.

Rowan inspected the log, which was at least six feet in diameter, an ancient cottonwood that had once towered above its fellows before the wind caught it and ripped it from the ground, taking its shallow roots with it. It had been laying in the river bottom for some time. It'd rotted and was covered in damp moss.

"Henry, go get your father's first aid bag," Bahati said. Rowan noticed she had blood on her shirt, too. The tail of her t-shirt had been intentionally torn away. If the scraps of it were under Lauren's hand, it wasn't visible for all the blood.

Henry started to protest, but a glare from Bahati prompted him to obey. He turned and took off running, *disappearing* before he even made it over the hill. Rowan watched to see if anyone had seen it, but no one else seemed to see the trick. All attention was on Jamie.

Jean-René sidled up to Rowan with his back to Lauren. "She just appeared out of nowhere."

Rowan cast him a knowing look, his brow flattening. He put a hand on Jean-René's arm, suggesting they would talk later. He knelt in front of his wife and son, trying to take inventory of the injuries. He instructed Lauren to keep pressure on the wound, and the river of blood slowed to a trickle. Jamie had a few scrapes on his face, including one across his nose, and his hands were scraped and dirty as well. He held his wounded hands out in front of him, which suggested to Rowan they were still hurting.

"Okay, buddy," Rowan said to his son, putting a comforting hand on his chest. Jamie sniffled and lifted his eyes to the heavens. The little boy was genuinely distressed. "You're okay. I am a trained paramedic, and this isn't as bad as it seems. I would know. You should have seen the big cut I had to stitch on your momma's head the last time we went Bigfoot hunting."

Jamie swallowed hard, a tear running down his cheek. "Stitches?"

"It's okay, sweetheart," Lauren whispered to him. "Your dad is extremely skilled, and it feels just like a pinch."

"And I have plenty of numbing medicine with me … this time," Rowan said, as Henry returned with the kit. The crew moved away, giving the family a moment's privacy.

"Please don't make me get stitches …" Jamie wailed.

"We don't even know yet if it needs stitches," Lauren said, brushing back his hair. "You are the bravest boy I know. It's okay to cry. No one here will blame you." Lauren's chin rested on Jamie's head. She kissed him. Tears dripped from her eyes as she rocked him gently, trying to soothe him.

"Okay, Tiger. I gotta look at that cut on your eye and see what I'm working with," Rowan explained. Jamie whimpered at what needed to be done, but Lauren whispered soft words into his ear and hugged him gently. He calmed as she comforted him.

"Facial wounds always bleed a lot, so when Momma lets go, it's going to bleed some. I've got some bandages here ready to put over the cut. We have to get the bleeding stopped before

I can do anything with it, and I know you are brave, so … it's going to be okay."

"I … am brave." Jamie set his jaw, his lip trembling in spite of his alleged courage.

Rowan lifted his gaze to Lauren, who cried unashamed. He had never seen her react so in an emergency, but he knew as a *mother bear*. She took anything that happened to her *cubs* personal.

He donned a pair of surgical gloves and unwrapped several packages of gauze, stacking them up, and readying himself for the reveal. He reached up, nodding at Lauren to let him take over, and she reluctantly let go of the wound. Blood coursed from the torn flesh, spilling down the boy's face, onto the leg of his jeans and the front of his shirt, which were already stained with drying blood. Lauren swallowed a gasp and turned away, burying her face in the boy's russet hair.

Rowan covered the wound again, dabbing at the wicked slash that bisected his left eyebrow. Henry shied away, while John Carter stood watching, ready to assist, if needed. Jean-René came in behind Lauren and put a reassuring hand on her shoulder, but in truth he was there to catch her should she swoon. He and Rowan exchanged a quick glance, as Rowan shook his head, and turned his attention back to his son.

"Okay buddy," he said. "That's a pretty deep cut, but I think I can fix it with some surgical glue, so I won't have to do stitches, but we've got to get the bleeding to stop and I'm going to have to wash out the wound with some saline because you've got some dirt in there." Jamie nodded and sniffed, his face remaining a study in courage. "I'm going to have Momma lay you down and hold you like she did when you were a baby, okay?"

His lip trembled. "I'm not a baby," he said defiantly. A tear rolled down his freckled cheek.

"I know you aren't, buddy," Rowan said, patting his arm.

"But I need you laying down, so the blood and saline don't run into your eyes. Can you hold still while I do that?"

"Yes, sir," he sniffed.

"That's a good man," Rowan said, patting his arm. He nodded for Lauren to reposition him. Jean-René came around and sat beside her, supporting Jamie's feet, but keeping an arm free so he could support her as well. The photographer must have seen her sway, too.

It took several minutes for Rowan to flush the wound with bottled saline, then to get the bleeding to stop enough to apply a line of surgical adhesive, then press the flesh together and hold it long enough for the seal to be secured. Jamie grunted and bit his lip, but he never cried out, even though fresh tears escaped his eyes. Rowan knew the surgical adhesive would sting, but he also knew it wouldn't last long, and soon Jamie's tears dried up.

When Rowan sat him back up, his eyelid was swollen, and his hair was matted with dried blood. Rowan commended him for his bravery as he used the rest of the saline and some sterile gauze to clean him up. "You are a credit to your name, James Tiberius Pierce, brave as any captain should be." Rowan saluted him with his fingers spread open in a *V*. Jamie pursed his lips and nodded but nestled himself in Lauren's arms. She made no move to displace him. Rowan noticed she was trembling and pale. Jamie sniffed and ran a dirty finger across his nose. "I don't think I want to go to the meadow anymore," he said, so quietly just those closest could hear him.

"Why don't we go lay down and rest for a little bit," Lauren said. "I'll give you some Tylenol. That'll make you feel better."

"Good idea," Rowan said, rummaging through his triage kit for the bottle of children's Tylenol he always carried. "Think a Superman Band-Aid would help?"

"Not Superman." Jamie sniffed.

"Spiderman?" Rowan held one up.

"Uh, huh." Jamie nodded. Rowan administered the Band-Aid gingerly and gave him the medicine before packing up his kit, wrapping up the debris left behind in a plastic bag for later disposal.

Henry came over and sat down beside his mother and his little brother and offered his hand. "I'm sorry you fell down, Jamie."

"It's okay." Jamie reared up again. "I know you tried to catch me."

Rowan lifted a brow towards Lauren at this new revelation before his gaze met Henry's. "*You* tried to catch him?"

"John Carter was in front, and Jamie was in front of me," Henry explained. "When I saw he was going over, I caught him by the back of his shirt and pulled, but his feet came out from under him, and he went face first into one of the broken limbs on the tree. I thought I was helping, but ... I made it worse."

"The point is, you tried," Lauren said, reaching over, putting a hand on her oldest son's head. "Thank you." She kissed him and mussed his hair affectionately.

"Good job, son," Rowan added.

Lauren shivered, noting the temperature had dropped. A cold breeze was coming from the north. Then she glanced down at her shirt and her hands, and at Jamie's. Rowan saw what little color she had left drain from her face as she did. Apparently, so did Bahati.

"Why don't we go change clothes?" Bahati directed the comment to Jamie, but meant it for Lauren, too. "I will make some hot chocolate and we can make s'mores for our afternoon snack. Doesn't that sound good?"

"Just don't spoil your dinner," Rowan added playfully.

"Then we can lie down and rest for a while," Lauren added.

Jamie nodded and climbed out of Lauren's lap. She slumped back against Jean-René's arm, and he held her a moment. Rowan came over and offered his hand, helping her to her feet. He took Jamie's hand and put an arm around Lauren. Jean-René collected the triage kit, and they headed back to camp.

"You okay?" Rowan asked as they started back up the trail.

"Yeah," she said, nodding. "Thank you."

"For what?"

"Taking care of our son," she said. "I felt pretty helpless."

"You helped." He consoled her, kissing her head.

6

There was no hunt for the skunk ape that night. After dinner, Lauren sent the boys to their tent, but Jamie returned a short while later in his pajamas, dragging his blanket in the dirt, collecting leaf litter and pine needles. Lauren collected him in her lap and shook out the leaves before wrapping him up, snuggling with him. The night was growing cool, and the evening stars had just appeared over the horizon. Rowan sat on a camp stool, tending the fire. A mournful howl in the distance made him lift his head and turn. Lauren's eye followed his as she tried to picture in her mind's eye where it had come from. A second call answered from the west, and Rowan turned, looking to her.

"What was that?" Chance asked, as he skidded down the path into the center of camp. "What *was* that?"

Rowan gave Lauren an inquisitive cock of the eyebrow. "Probably just an owl," she said. "Maybe a coyote." The call echoed yet again. "Definitely a coyote."

"Oh," the audio tech deflated, and returned to his tent across the clearing where his trainees gathered. "Dang it. Never mind guys, just a stupid coyote." Lauren heard him tell the rookies, realizing they'd collected just outside the center of camp.

Poor Chance. He never seemed to get to see the evidence first-hand.

He had been with the team since he was just an intern. Now he was the lead audio tech and he'd been assigned to work with the newer team members directly. It was his job to keep them from bumbling into a shot or contaminating audio. He wasn't all that much older than the new recruits, and they responded well to his patient instruction. It took a lot of the burden off Lauren.

"A coyote?" Rowan asked, using the stick Jamie had been playing with earlier to push a small piece of firewood back into the coals. "Are you sure?"

"No," Lauren said, softly, kissing Jamie's head. The little boy's eyelids were heavy and he was happiest in his mother's lap.

"I thought you said we wouldn't find anything here."

"It's unlikely," Lauren said. "You know I have … *inside information*."

"So, no Bigfoot around here."

"Nope. No Bigfoot. Probably not a coyote, but *definitely* not a Bigfoot. Might as well go to bed."

"Only if you're coming with me."

How could she resist? Lauren ended up sleeping next to Jamie, while John Carter took her spot next to his dad. For a second night, she slept through moon rise, grateful for the comfort of the sleeping bag.

Autumn was usually warm in Southern Oklahoma, but in general Mother Nature was tough to predict and subject to wild mood swings. By morning, it was bitterly cold, and frost kissed every blade of grass. She coaxed the fire back to life and put on a pot of coffee.

All the things they had planned to do the day before had been set aside but would have to be made up today. They didn't have but a few more days scheduled for this project, and they didn't have much to show for it. All they had was some rough video from the rookie crews, still trying to earn their stripes. Lauren hadn't expected as much, if truth be told. They'd had a few episodes like this in the past, where evidence had been sparse and hard to find. The work of the post-production team was the show's best hope, and with Rowan's ability to make a story come together from bits and pieces, they rarely wasted a single expedition.

Lauren decided a hot breakfast would get the day going and rouse the crews from their bedrolls. By the time the perfume of frying bacon and pancakes filled the air, she had four hungry kids at the table.

"Henry, do you think you could go down to the river for some more water?" Lauren asked, pouring Jamie a cup of milk.

"Sure, Mom," Henry said, shoving the last bite of pancake in his mouth.

"Do I have to go?" Jamie asked.

"No sweetie," Lauren said. His eye was much better this morning, though it was still puffy and bruised.

"Come on, lil' Indy," Jean-René said to Henry, his voice gruff with morning. "I'll help you."

"Thank you," Lauren called out as Rowan emerged from their tent.

"Everyone's up early this morning," he observed, sitting down. Lauren brought him a cup of coffee. He nodded in thanks, catching her hand. His touch reminded her of their plans the day before — plans that had failed.

"We have lots to do before tonight's investigation," Lauren said. "Pancakes?"

"Hell, yeah," Rowan growled playfully. "Bacon, too. Don't skimp on the bacon."

Lauren fixed him a plate, setting it in front of him, moving the butter and syrup from the end of the table. She made a plate for herself and came to sit down beside him.

"Sleep okay?" he asked.

"Well enough," she said. "You?"

"Eh," he said. "Not as well as I would have liked. Might need a nap later."

She cast him a sidelong glance nodding. She didn't acknowledge the innuendo, but she didn't need to. They were both sorry for the missed opportunity from the day before, but something told her he'd make up for it eventually. He always did.

"Just don't disappear on me like you did yesterday," he said.

Lauren gave him a perplexed expression. "What?"

"You don't even know you're doing it, do you?" Rowan asked.

Lauren paused, setting her jaw as she considered him. "Remember, it's not just me," she said. "Henry knew I needed to be there. That was my baby's cry. I didn't even realize what'd happened until later." The last of her sentence trailed off as Bahati came to the table.

"So, what's the plan?" Bahati asked, getting a plate of pancakes for herself. Jamie finished his breakfast and went back to the tent to rifle through the stack of his brothers' books he'd absconded with, intent on reading everything in the equipment trunk they'd brought with them.

"I think Rowan and I should take the kids, and maybe one or two of the techs and go scope out the meadow. You and Jean-René can take the rest of the team and hunt for animal trails and figure out areas to get some footage," Lauren said.

"Tonight's the full moon — the Hunter's Moon — so we need to compensate for that with the night vision cameras, but it might also give us some great lighting for regular film, too."

"I need to take some time this afternoon and charge the batteries on all the FLIR cameras," Bahati said. "I'll have Jean-René set up the generator if anyone needs their phones charged."

"I do. My iPad, too." Lauren smirked. Unlike her kids, who didn't have electronic gadgets, other than their walkie talkies and Henry's eReader, Lauren relied on her tech for weather reports, communications, and her occasional fix of Solitaire.

"The sat-phone could use a charge, too." Rowan nodded. "Not dead, but we can't risk it."

"So, when we film tonight, I would like to have a couple of cameras to set up in camp. The kids will want to help run the command post and if we have some footage of them helping out, we could incorporate that into the final production." Lauren was excited about the boys making their debut, officially, though they had shown some brief clips of them saying goodbye to their folks as they headed off on an investigation. They'd also gotten some screen time in Montana in the summer.

"I think I'll do some interviews with them, just to get them accustomed to the cameras," Rowan said. "Too bad we didn't have video of all that yesterday."

"Uhhhh, boss?" Bahati started but was reluctant to speak up. Lauren and Rowan both turned toward her. She folded like a house of cards. "I know you were both too busy to notice, but the crew had the where-with-all to grab cameras and film from a respectful distance. I didn't know if you'd want to use any of the footage, but they did take some."

Rowan glanced over at Lauren. She held her face in perfect tranquility, but beneath the surface, he could see the raging rapids of emotion in her eyes. "I'm not sure how I feel about that," Rowan said, speaking more for her than himself. "I'll have to watch it first."

"That's not something I necessarily need to relive," Lauren said. "The risk of one of them getting hurt is just the reason why I've been selective about which expeditions they go on, and I'm not sure I want to take them on another one any time soon."

"Boys will be boys, whether in the woods or in the Colonel's back yard," Rowan said. "What's a facial lac to a five-year-old?"

"It's a scar he will carry with him for the rest of his life," Lauren clipped. "And so will I."

"But what's important is, it will heal, and a lesson was learned." Bahati put a calming hand over hers. "Besides, if we don't bring them with us, when would we ever see them?"

"She has a point." Rowan put an arm around his wife. "You'll have the final say on whether or not we use the footage." He kissed her head. "Let's hurry up and finish so we can go check out the meadow."

THE DAY REMAINED COOL AND CLEAR. THE MORNING FOG burned off by the time they reached the valley below camp. It was a beautiful location, especially with the sunlight beaming through the dew-damp tallgrass, surrounded by colorful fall leaves.

Rowan, an excellent photographer in his own right, had brought a couple of cameras with them and used them to set up some shots with the boys. He had even used the automatic settings to get a couple of family photos for his personal collection. They'd taken pictures for Christmas cards from every location they'd traveled before the boys were born, and often ended up sending those cards back to the friends they had made along the way. Rowan was so completely extroverted that he could make friends in any crowd, so he did. As a result, there wasn't a country they'd been to that he didn't have at least one person he could pick up the phone and call at a completely random moment just to chat about the weather, and what was going on that might give them an excuse to come back. Rowan had gotten them invited to family reunions, carnivals, great-grandmothers' birthday parties, and even a few weddings. They'd taken up some of those offers, when it worked with their schedules, though sometimes the best they could do was send a card, flowers or a present.

Rowan had said once, that if he chose, he would never have to stay in a hotel, because in every country, he had at least one person who would put him and his family up for a night, if not the whole crew. That's how he liked it.

ONCE EVERYONE HAD BEEN FED DINNER, FINAL PREPARATIONS were made for the night's adventure. The afternoon had warmed little, but as night came crashing down, so did the temperature. Compounding the cold, the skies had clouded over, and a freezing drizzle began just as cameras were set up for the first shoot at base camp.

The team recreated the afternoon's orientation for the sake of the cameras. It was not an uncommon practice. The scene featured Rowan in the center of the group, laying out assignments, discussing potential hazards, and encouraging everyone to be on guard. "Temperatures are falling fast, and Lauren says we could have some heavy rain moving in by morning, so I'd like to wrap everything up no later than 4 a.m., if not before."

"I'll keep the coffee on here. It would be wise to come back in from time to time, and warm up, maybe put on some dry socks," Lauren added. "Don't get wet if you can avoid it. Keep your slickers on and protect your equipment."

Jean-René had the steady-cam rolling and moved behind the crew until he'd filmed the entire 360 degrees of the circle, pausing a moment to adjust for hard and soft focus over a team member's shoulder, or to catch a long angled shot from their ankles. Once Jean-René was satisfied, Rowan wrapped up the orientation and dismissed the teams to their assigned areas.

Lauren watched the camera crews go their separate ways and sent Rowan off with a nod and a longing expression, as she pulled on her jacket, and sat down at the table beneath the rain tarp. The boys were chasing one another around the camp site, playing their favorite game of *Star Trek: Landing Party*. Jamie was Captain Kirk, as always. John Carter was Mr. Spock and Henry was Scotty. Nyota lay on her stomach at the entrance of her tent, the flap open, as she thumbed through a National Geographic, not interested in a single thing the boys were doing.

Chance added wood to the fire before the team left, and it crackled and popped. Rain drops hissed and burned up even before contacting the flames. The camp lanterns had been lit, illuminating the circle of tents around the fire. The light of day faded as the shadow of night was upon them.

Lauren turned her attention to the computer and pulled up each of the trap cams. The baby in her belly was doing somersaults and she sat back, wincing as the kid gave her a swift kick in the bladder. "Pipe down, you!" She poked her belly and found her orders answered by a jab to the side. Her baby bump was still on the smallish side, but after three boys, she was already bigger than she had been at this point with any of them. Had she not remembered the afternoon of this baby's conception so vividly, she might have thought she'd miscounted, but the midwife she'd seen in Bhutan had examined her — not using methods any traditional doctor might — and corroborated her suspected due date while trying to soothe her raging morning sickness.

RUNNING THE COMMAND POST WAS ONE OF THE MOST BORING jobs ever. It was important to watch the video feed for anything out of the ordinary that the teams might not notice, and to watch the trap cams and perimeter alarms. Lauren stood and paced, keeping her eyes on the multi-image screen of her laptop, pausing here and there to stretch out her back or scold the kids.

"Okay guys, time for bed," Lauren said, having had enough of their laser-beam sound effects.

"Aw, man!" Jamie tossed down the stick he'd been using for a laser cannon. "Do we have to?"

"Yes," Lauren said to her youngest. "You guys are making so much noise you'll scare off the skunk apes," she added. "If you want to stay up and read for a while, I won't mind, but you have to be quiet. I can't hear anything in the woods over you hoodlums."

"Come on, Jamie," Henry said. "You too, John Carter."

It took almost a half hour to get them bedded down for the night. The dim glow of their flashlights gradually faded, and by midnight, the tent had gone dark. Lauren walked over and added another log to the campfire, shivering and wishing she had a blanket handy. Instead, she decided to put on a fresh pot of coffee and warm herself by the fire.

Another hour passed, and another pot of coffee had to be made as the teams rotated into base camp to warm up. Other than the mournful baying of coyotes and hooting of a distant owl, the night had been quiet. Rowan's team checked in from the meadow, while the other team reported nothing from the river bottom. One of the permitter alarms went off, but a quick check of the cameras showed a flock of wild turkeys had scattered and had most likely tripped the sensor.

Lauren gave up and surrendered to the cold, having unzipped the tent, and rummaged through their belongings for a wool blanket she'd bought in Scotland. But before she settled in again, she decided a trip to the privy was required.

The privy was a make shift toilet just past the edge of camp under the cover of a stand of trees. Rowan had rigged it up. It consisted of a five gallon bucket lined with a heavy duty trash bag, filled with a layer of kitty litter, and a pool noodle for a seat cushion. A hula hoop hung from the tree above, surrounded by blue polyvinyl sheeting that served as a privacy screen. It wasn't for the boys. They didn't need it, except maybe in the middle of the night when it was too dark to go off into the woods and find a rock or a tree to pee on. This set up was for the girls.

Lauren was glad for it, though she wasn't beyond going in the forest, but this was a convenient way to keep her close to the kids, and the monitors. Once her business was done, she started back to her post, but paused when something rustled in the woods over her shoulder. She chided herself for being jumpy, but a deep rumble made her turn and pause. Then the smell hit her. For a moment, she thought it was from the latrine, but she realized the wind wasn't in the right direction.

The flash of eye-shine caught the moonlight above her in the trees nearby. Startled, Lauren could feel her heart thundering against her sternum. Her pulse constricted her throat. Not one to shy away, she took a step towards the trees shielding the form that hid in the shadows. She hesitated and the grumbling grew louder. The eyes blinked but held her gaze locked.

She knew it wasn't a Bigfoot. It couldn't be. She would have been able to sense it. She had a *connection* with *The People*. Worst case scenario, it might be a bear. Bears weren't uncommon in southern Oklahoma. The black bear population was on the uptick — especially in this part of the state — according to her source at the Oklahoma Wildlife Conservation Foundation. Bears were the least of her worries, this time of year. Most would be preparing to hibernate and preferred to feast on plants, insects and small animals, like reptiles.

Then a thought struck fear in her. *What if it was a bobcat ... or worse ... a mountain lion?*

∾

ROWAN AND HIS CREW WERE FILMING THE MOON GLOW OVER the meadow that they'd captured in sunlight earlier in the day. Spiders spun gossamer webs between the blades of grass. Their heads of seed were so heavy they were ready to lay down. Trees around the clearing blocked the breeze, and the clouds lifted, which meant —for the time being — it wasn't raining.

"See that?" One of the new techs pointed across the clearing as a herd of deer raced across the meadow. "Wonder what spooked them?"

A mournful bawl echoed from the distance, and Rowan pointed in the direction it had come with a nod. "Coyotes."

"That didn't sound like any coyote I ever heard." Jean-René shivered.

A high-pitched scream peeled the skin from Rowan's flesh and he recognized it at once. His wife wasn't one given to flights of fancy and never screamed without a reason.

Without a word to anyone, Rowan bolted from his spot in the grass and raced back towards camp. Jean-René and the rest of the team were hot on his heels. They ran into Bahati's team as they converged at the edge of base camp, finding the kids peeking out of their tents, and the command post by the fire, empty.

"Jesus, not again," Rowan groaned.

"Where's your mom?" Bahati asked the boys.

"I don't know." John Carter rubbed his eyes.

Nyota appeared at the flap of her tent, bleary-eyed. "I'm trying to sleep over here," she barked at John Carter.

"I didn't do it!" he replied.

"Zip it!" Jean-René had the spot light on his camera pointed at the ground, inspecting for tracks. He raised it and scanned in the direction of the privy.

If Lauren had gone anywhere, that's where she would go,

Rowan deduced. He raced past everyone, skidding as he reached the edge of the clearing where Lauren sat on her butt in the mud. Her eyes shown white all around, like those of a frightened horse. The pupils and irises were equally black with the horror that was inscribed on her stunned face. Her eyes were locked on nothing in particular.

Her face was paler than the ashes of the nearby fire. Her hands shook visibly as she held them up, as if unsure what to do with the mud-caked appendages.

"Honey?" Rowan dropped to one knee and caught her by the shoulder. She looked up at him blankly. "What happened?"

Her mouth moved as if trying to speak, but little more than a trembling gasp managed to escape before she successfully got out a few guttural grunts. Rowan reached up and smoothed her hair back away from her face, inspecting her. He prayed the horror on her face wasn't reflected in his eyes. Breathless, she managed a faint gasp. "I ... I ..." she fumbled for words. "I s-s-s-aw it."

"Saw what?"

"S-s-s-skunk ape ..." Her stunned expression took him aback. Her gaze turned away, back to the direction of the trees. Rowan let his eye follow, to allow himself a moment to compose his thoughts and calm his heart.

The medic in him kicked in when he realized there was a trickle of blood leaking from her nose. "Are you hurt?" He inspected her in the dim moonlight. He glanced up realizing the cameras were rolling. He didn't see any injuries on her extremities.

"Huh?" Lauren turned back. Her expression remained blank. It reminded him of the day they'd seen ... *something* ... in the meadow near Mt. St. Helens, when the Bigfoot told her the story of the rabbit being the leader in all the mischief. A cold chill rushed through him, and his copper hair lifted on his arms, catching the light.

"Are you hurt?" he repeated impatiently. "Injured? Wounded? In pain?"

"I ... I don't think so."

Rowan sat back on his heels and inspected the area around her. The ground was soft. It was covered with pine needles, stones, and leaf litter. He dug in his pocket and found his bandana that he used for a handkerchief and reached up to blot the blood away. "Are you sure? What did you see?"

She recoiled and snatched it away, taking over the job as she seemed to regain a modicum of composure. She inspected the bandana, wincing at the blood that continued to drip onto the cloth before she put it back to her nose and applied pressure.

Rowan rose, moving carefully. He took out his flashlight to inspect the ground for prints.

Bahati took his place and supported her friend. "It was ... like ... like ..." She struggled for the words. "Like a Bigfoot."

Rowan turned sharply and walked over, picking her up by her elbows, standing her on unsteady legs. Bahati jumped back, startled by his sudden movements. Jean-René caught her arm and drew her back out of the camera shot. Rowan turned his back to the camera then leaned in and spoke in low tones as he moved her away and back towards camp. "I thought you said you *talked* to them. *Tsul'Kalu* ..." The name felt odd on his lips. She hadn't spoken it in years, and he'd tried to forget the name since. "He said ... I mean ... you spoke to *him*. Right?"

"I have." Lauren's eyes drifted back to the trees. "But this ... it's different."

"How so?"

"I didn't even know it was here."

Rowan inspected her closely, convinced she wasn't hurt, but not sure she was entirely okay. She was trembling and clearly shaken up. He glanced around at the crew. "Okay, cut the damned cameras already," he groused. Rowan had never scolded the crews for filming, but he was as upset as Lauren and knew she wouldn't want video of all this.

Seeing the hurt expressions on the team members' faces, he shook his head. As he turned Lauren around and put an arm around her waist, holding her up by her belt loop, he said, "Check the area for prints. Document anything you find. Pack it in when you're finished. We're done for the night."

ROWAN TOOK LAUREN BACK TO CAMP AND SAT HER DOWN, dumping out the cold coffee from her cup, refilling it with the steaming hot liquid, handing it back to her. "Drink."

He went through a list of questions meant to identify any injuries he might need to triage her — or the baby — for. She answered no to every question but one. "Are you in any pain?"

She took a deep breath from over the cup before she sighed and tipped the cup to her lips, sipping the hot liquid, steadying her quavering hands. She shivered violently. Rowan took the cup. He was afraid she'd spill it and burn herself.

"Look at me," he said, motioning Jean-René to get some lights set up so he could see. Once the entire center of camp was set up, Rowan shooed the kids back to bed, assuring them that their mother was fine, just shaken up. "Where does it hurt?"

"My ..." Her unsteady hand went to her cheek.

A wide red welt had formed across her face. Blood still oozed from her nose, though it no longer bled profusely. There were spatters and splotches of blood drying on her plaid flannel shirt. Her lower lip was starting to swell, and it trembled as he ran a hand down her arm. "Did it ... hit you?" he asked in low tones, dabbing the blood away with a clean piece of gauze Jean-René handed him from his kit.

"I'm not ... not sure ... what happened," Lauren admitted, wrapping her arms around herself. She still seemed stunned. *Was she in shock?* With ample lighting now to assess her, he decided she was still pale and probably was in shock after all.

"Bahati? Can you get her a blanket? Jean-René, come get some pictures of this," Rowan instructed, tossing a nearby log onto the fire to help warm her as Bahati laid her wool camp blanket around her shoulders. "It looks like …like … a large hand print."

"Sorry, boss," Jean-René said to Lauren, as he picked up his digital camera and moved in close. Lauren said nothing in protest but glowered at him and raised a hand with one finger unfurled over her face.

"Come on," Rowan said sternly. "This is evidence."

She couldn't argue that. Lauren put her hand down and closed her eyes, enduring what had to be done, no matter how much she hated it. Once Jean-René was finished, she threw off Rowan's hand on her arm and stood. "I'm fine," she said, pulling the blanket around her shoulders even as she swayed.

She glanced over at the three worried faces peering out from their tent and softened. "I'm fine," she said.

"You have mud on your booty," Jamie said.

Lauren turned a hip and to inspect her backside over her shoulder, unable to see anything. She wiped it off. "Just a little dirt," Lauren said. "We'll do laundry in the river tomorrow."

A chorus of groans answered her, and the boys disappeared to their beds. Lauren turned back to Rowan, reaching for her cup. He sat back on his heels, watching as she took it and drained it, her hands steadying. With a deep breath, she seemed to relax, and even her color seemed to improve.

"Something tripped the perimeter alarm just before midnight," she said, by way of explanation. She returned to the spot by the fire where she could see Rowan, and where Jean-René could film the scene. "Wild turkeys tripped the trap cam earlier in the evening — something must have disturbed them from their roost I thought — and I thought perhaps they'd come back."

Rowan shook his head. "Hey, Chance, go check ...?"

"North three," Lauren said.

"Go check the perimeter sensor north three," Rowan said. "Take Nate with you. We know there's something out there, but we don't know where."

As if in answer, a klaxon sounded on one of the monitors. Rowan rose and jumped over the wood pile to get to it. "South two! Jean-René, Brandon, you're with me!"

The three of them darted off, leaving Lauren and the remaining crew standing in the center of camp. She turned in the direction of where she had been ... *attacked*. That seemed too harsh of a word. She didn't feel *attacked*. She felt like she'd cornered an animal and the animal had inadvertently knocked her down as it darted to safety. She might have done the same had she been cornered.

"Find anything?" She turned to the team. "Shawn? Todd?"

"Some smudged tracks in the mud," Shawn said. "I came back for the casting kit."

"I want to see it." Lauren started to follow but Bahati caught her arm.

"You need to stay here with your children."

Lauren stopped, opened her mouth to protest, then closed it. She seemed to deflate, and she returned to her chair at base camp, trying not to think about what Rowan and Jean-René were doing. She returned to her computer on the table and pulled up the camera in the direction they were headed, but there was nothing in the shot but waving vegetation. With that, the skies opened, and rain began to beat down on the canopy over her head.

The team crowded in around her, seeking the protection of the tarp. She all but leapt out of her skin when the radio squawked. "Rowan to base camp." He sounded out of breath.

"Go for base camp." She wrestled with the radio.

"We're hearing heavy foot falls and this deep grunting," he whispered.

Lauren shook her aching head. "I smelled it before I saw it," she said, realizing it as she spoke.

"Do you smell anything?" Rowan asked. She heard Jean-René's response. "No, no smell."

"Head toward the trap cam in that sector," Lauren suggested. "I'd feel better if I had eyes on you."

"Will do." Lauren did feel better when she could see their ankles. Rowan kept his finger on the radio button, and she heard the entire conversation.

"Who set these cameras? Tyrion Lannister?" Rowan groused.

"Probably Jamie," Lauren said. "I don't know."

"We'll hang out here and see if we run across anything," Rowan said into the radio before setting it aside. He reset the camera, gazing into it as if to send a silent message to her. "I'll check in on the half-hour," he said once it was fixed, and he could take up the radio again.

"Make it the quarter hour," Lauren said. "You know how I ... worry."

"Will do," Rowan answered.

"So what do we do?" Shawn said to her. "Rowan said to pack it in, but he's out hunting."

"Pack up the equipment so it doesn't get any wetter than it already has," Lauren said, probably a bit more curtly than she had intended. She was tired and her head was now throbbing, and she was in a mood.

"We'll wait for them to come back in before we turn in," she said. "In this rain they shouldn't be out long."

"You should go to bed." Bahati nudged her. Lauren appeared as if she might protest but didn't. She nodded, stiffly and moved to get up. Bahati went over to Rowan's bag and found a bottle of pills. She took out a couple and handed them to Lauren. "Take these. You'll regret it in the morning if you don't."

Lauren did protest the Tylenol, but it was a battle she would not win.

LAUREN WAS VAGUELY AWARE OF BEING AWAKE WHAT SEEMED like just a few minutes after she'd lain down. It took her some time to figure out what had brought her to this state of being. She had a mad sense of pressure in her face, and her right eye was swollen shut when she tried to open it. She moved to get up but realize there was a small boy nestled in the sleeping bag between her and her husband.

She reached over Jamie and poked Rowan in the ribs. He came awake ready to fight. He realized it was Lauren who'd stabbed him with her long, narrow finger.

"Holy crap, Lauren," he gasped.

"I can't open my eye," she said through a fat lip.

Rowan sat up and gazed down at her, wincing. "You gotta see this." He fumbled in his pack for a camera and sat up. He fired off a few shots then turned the viewfinder so she could see.

"That would explain why I feel like …" Jamie stirred, and she stopped.

Rowan got up and pulled on his shoes before hoisting her up. He led her to the center of camp where Jean-René was nursing the fire back to life so Bahati could make breakfast.

"Hey," Rowan drew their attention as he led Lauren to a chair. "Ever seen anything like this?"

Jean-René turned and took a step back. "*Saperlipopette!*"

7

Jean-René handed her the ice pack. "Our best evidence of Bigfoot to date, and it's on your face." He shook his head, sitting down at the table across from her. He had the pictures pulled up on his iPad, and he scrolled through them, zooming in on the best shots. A distinct outline of a handprint, albeit an exceedingly large handprint marked her face. It was a print left in welts and bruises.

Lauren pressed the pack to her face and leaned her elbow on the table. "I've been hit harder," she mumbled through a fat lip. "And by bigger."

"Easy to say in the light of day, isn't it?" He quipped. "You were scared to death last night." Normally, she would have flipped him off, but she knew he was right.

"*Saperlipopette?* I don't think I have ever heard you use that expletive," Lauren said to her director of photography.

"My mother's favorite swear," he said. "It means little more than *gadzooks* or, *fiddlesticks*." Like Lauren needed him to translate for her. She also knew it hadn't always been such an innocent oath. Like other such expressions, they were invented to avoid swearing. The well-known *sacrébleu* was a similar innocuous variation used to avoid taking the Lord's Name in vain. "I've been spending too much time with her on Facetime since my father died."

"How is she holding up?" Lauren asked, forgetting about the words rolling around in her head. It had been six months since he lost his father, but clearly, his mother wasn't coping well. She wasn't sure he was doing any better.

"She's a strong woman," he said. "She just doesn't have anyone to fix the sink or check the oil in her car. She relied on my father to do it all. I made some calls and found some friends to help her. Several of the men in her church have agreed to check in on her once in a while."

"Your father was handy?"

"He could do basic things, but he was no mechanic or carpenter."

"Do you need to go home?"

"To France? No." He stood. "I don't. My mother will adapt. It won't be easy, but if I go running every time she needs me, the Network will be down a cameraman and quite frankly, it's been good to have the team back together. I don't want to ruin it."

Lauren turned at a rustling of leaves that signaled the approaching teams returning from their mission to reconnoiter the area. Jamie came bounding into camp, breathlessly. He started to throw himself into Lauren's arms, but Jean-René reached out and hooked an arm around his waist, spinning him out of his trajectory. "I don't think your *Maman* is up for any rough-housing today, *mon petit chou.*"

"We found prints!" He squealed, trying to get loose. When he did, he paused at Lauren's elbow. "Momma, we found prints! Great big giant footprints. Dad says to bring the casting kits. He says to hurry."

Lauren glanced up at Jean-René. Jean-René gave her a hand up, and she moved slowly, unable to turn her head. She rose, moving with a stiff gate as the crew in camp rounded up the materials they would need. "He said to bring at least four, maybe five packages," Jamie added.

Jean-René's brow went up and he collected five of the boxes, handing two to Jamie, and another to John Carter, who came trailing in behind.

"Dad says you don't have to come if you don't want to," John Carter announced, taking his mother's hand, stopping.

"I want to," Lauren said. "But I might need an arm to lean on."

John Carter was nothing, if not a gentleman. He gave his arm willingly and patiently walked at a pace Lauren could manage. Jean-René stayed close. He watched his boss apprehensively as Jamie ran on ahead.

The mark on her face had gone from bright red last night, to black and blue today. She had dark circles in the corners of her eye, and he suspected her nose might be broken, but he kept his suspicions to himself. He was no medic. *What did he know?*

~

ROWAN MET THEM AT THE EDGE OF THE RIVER, WITH A BROAD grin on his face. "You're never going to believe this," he said, taking her arm and leading her over to where the crew knelt over a massive footprint in the mud.

"Holy ..." she stopped. "That's huge."

"I found it," John Carter said proudly. "I get to keep the cast, right?"

"We'll take two," Rowan said, patting his son on the back. "The first one goes off to be analyzed. The second one is for your collection."

"Cool!" John Carter said. Rowan had a collection of casts — as well as souvenirs and mementos from his decades of travel — adorning his office back home in Hilo, and John Carter had been fascinated by them since he was little. Of course, they hadn't spent much time at the house in Hilo since John Carter was born, and Rowan regretted that. Maybe when this season was over, they'd take some time off and go home before the next baby arrived. Lauren had complained about being cold, which he read as code for *take me home*. John Carter and Jamie were both big enough now to take to the beach, and Henry was keen to go surfing and scuba diving with his dad. Rowan watched Lauren, who was busy supervising the mixing of the casting material, standing with her hands on her hips, coaching Henry on the correct water to casting powder ratio. Her poor face broke his heart, and he was seriously close to packing it all in, telling the network to suck a lemon. He wanted to take his family home once and for all.

But then, there was that damned handprint on her face, and these prints in the mud, and he knew, he couldn't give it up — not when they were this close. He turned and gave directions to the crew on how to preserve the casts, how long to let them dry and what was important to photograph and document. The rookies still had a lot to learn, but they were earning their merit badges on this trip, which was for certain.

"A FEW DAYS HERE, AND THEN A COUPLE OF WEEKS AT HOME — this time my mother's house — while we do some pre-production research for the next episode," Rowan overheard Lauren telling Bahati.

"Where are we off to next, boss?"

"Back up to the Pacific Northwest," Lauren said as they sat by the fire that evening while everyone was getting ready for the night's filming. "Mount Rainier for the investigation, but also a drive down to Boring, Oregon to the *North American Bigfoot Museum*. We're helping the owner break ground on a new auditorium and doing a fund-raiser to help them with the construction costs."

"Do you think that's wise?" Bahati watched the children gathered nearby, fighting over marshmallows.

"Because of *our history* with that region, I think the boys should stay with my parents in Denver," Rowan said. "I wish you'd stay with them, too," he added to Lauren. "But ... I know better than to ask you not to go."

"I know I am a mess, and yes, my face hurts, but I didn't get attacked," Lauren explained her theory on the wild animal defending his territory. "I should have backed off, but I didn't. It's as much my fault as anything."

"No one is blaming you, but you," Rowan said. "You take things personally, and I wish you wouldn't do that."

"I'm not taking it personally," Lauren said. "I'm just reminding myself of what needs to be done differently, so it doesn't happen again."

Rowan nodded and stuck out his lip. "Fair enough. I'm going to leave Chance with you tonight at base camp," he said. "He can run ops, so you can go to bed whenever you're ready."

"Rowan," she started to protest.

"This is not negotiable." He took her hand and held it in his, pressing it over his heart. "I couldn't bear for anything to happen to you, or ..." one hand went to her bump. "Or our child."

Lauren couldn't argue with him after that. "I promised the boys I would take them up to the cave before we leave," she said, glancing up at the gray sky. "I don't think there's time tonight, but if I turn in early then I'll be ready to get up and go when they are. We can check it out in the morning and be back in time to get ready for the last night of filming. While you are out with the teams, I can start packing up anything we don't need tomorrow night. After everyone's had a few hours' sleep and a hot breakfast, we can break camp before the weather goes afoul."

Rowan's brow lifted. "Weather coming in?"

"NWS has put out a couple of Twitter posts indicating a chance for rain later in the week. Nothing severe, but if the temperatures drop it could get miserable. I'd prefer to be out of here before it hits."

Rowan nodded. "Sounds like a plan."

"You should go to bed," Chance told her for the fifth time, but Lauren resisted. She rummaged around in the chow locker, trying to find something to snack on, but after a week at camp with four hungry kids and a fully staffed crew, the offerings were meager. A small bag of potato chips and an apple served as a midnight snack.

She was ready for another hour or two when Chance turned to her and said flatly, "I know you are the boss, but I have my orders. You have stayed up much too late already and Rowan insisted I send you to bed when the boys went. I didn't because you are a grown woman, and I am not your father." In truth, Chance was at least ten years her junior, but the seriousness in his tone and the narrowing of his brow gave him an air of someone much older. "If you are still up when Rowan comes in, *I* will be in big trouble and I don't particularly care to be in trouble, especially not with your husband. He's twice my size and he'll kick my butt."

"He wouldn't kick your butt." Lauren scowled. Chance had been with the team over ten years and had grown from a boy into a man right under her nose. The lanky frame of a nineteen-year-old intern had been replaced by lithe muscles. Finally, he managed to grow something akin to a scraggly beard, though it was nowhere as majestic as Rowan's.

Chance's hair was brown like the bark on an elm tree, and

his eyes were greenish gray with just a hint of blue around the edges of the irises. He'd finished his degree a few years before they'd gone on their sabbatical when Jamie was born. He could have gone to work anywhere he wanted, but he followed Jean-René like a puppy dog and was twice as loyal. A brilliant photojournalist in his own right, the young man had a couple dozen trophies for his mantel at home.

"He told me he would, and I believe him," Chance said. "So for the sake of my hide, I am asking you one last time, would you please go to bed?"

Lauren shook her head, not so much mad with Chance, but frustrated at how over-protective her husband was being with her. She heaved a deep breath and let it out slowly, then yawned. "I'm tired," she announced, standing. "Think I'll go to bed." By the time Lauren lay her head down on the pillow, it was near midnight. The night had gone cold, and without Rowan to warm her sleeping bag, she shivered even in her little nest. The baby inside her stretched and rolled before settling down for the night. Lauren lay listening to the hoots of owls in the trees, and realized she was listening for any sounds made by the teams. She never made it to the next radio check.

"Is this not the largest cave you've ever seen?" John Carter asked as Henry led the way into the cavern. Each of them had a flashlight, and all the torches aimed at the rock walls above them.

"I've been in one that we spent a week in and never saw all of," Lauren said, moving into the cavern. This one was nothing compared to the cave in Peru. Though this one had a high ceiling, the cave itself might be fifty meters in diameter, except it wasn't perfectly round. The cave in Washington State might have been about the same size, not counting the lava tubes that led to it.

Henry glanced back at his mother. Lauren stopped in her tracks. "Don't worry," he said. "It's perfectly safe." Henry's enthusiasm was overt, and she could tell he was trying to be protective of her and his siblings. She also sensed his concern, too. Her phobia of caves had been something she'd always tried to hide, though he seemed more in tune with her than even Rowan was. Lauren moved after the boys, keeping ahold of Jamie's hand. "Here are the glyphs." He stopped, walking over to the damp rock wall. Henry aimed his light on the marks high above his reach.

Lauren shone her light on the wall and stood studying in detail than she had the last time she'd been here. There were other marks she hadn't noticed before, worn, and fading. Jamie glanced up at her. "What is that?"

"See the single line with the two legs?" She analyzed aloud as she focused her light on the mark. "That is the symbol for cup or chalice," Lauren said. "The straight line with the two wavy crosshatches, the one that looks like an F? That means of God."

"Chalice of God?" Henry turned, arching a brow like his father often did. "Does this mean ... the Holy Grail?"

"I'm not sure." Lauren shrugged. "It's a good guess," she said, re-reading the full inscription aloud. "This next line is confusing. It's similar but the word isn't *chalice* ... maybe ... *heart of the rose? Sacred relic?*"

The runes morphed into something in her mind she could read. She could comprehend the words. She found herself reading it in the language it was written in. It surprised them all when she spoke the ancient words aloud. "Mom! That's cool!" Henry chirped.

She stopped and went back to the beginning, reading the entire inscription in the ancient language. "That doesn't make any sense," she muttered to herself, certain she wasn't interpreting the language correctly. *But how could she not know it when she could read any language known to man? That had to be right.* She read it again.

"Mom can read runes!" Jamie cheered and the excitement seemed to swell in the small space around them.

The boys were giving one another high fives and turned to give her one. Lauren reached out her hand — her mind still on the inscription. As she read it again, she missed John Carter's hand, slapping the cavern wall with her palm. With that, a bolt of lightning shot up her arm and turned to sparks behind her eyes. She felt the world spinning out of control around her. Her knees buckled and she could hear the voices of her children piercing the ceiling. Bile rose in the back of her throat and a high pitched hum filled her core, and then there was nothing.

8

"Momma?" Jamie gasped, shaking his mother. "Henry! Do something."

"Mom?" Henry dropped to his knees beside his mother, taking her hand. "Mom? Wake up!"

"Henry? What happened?" Panic filled the smallest boy's voice. "What did you do?"

"I didn't do anything!" Henry whined. "We're all okay. Mom's breathing," he said, doing a quick assessment. "We'll figure this out. Just stay calm."

Jamie started crying as he lay with his head on his mother's chest. "You killed her!"

"She's not dead!" Henry insisted. "Listen."

Jamie did and felt the thumping of her heartbeat beneath his ear.

"You know you're not supposed to do stuff like this," John Carter scolded his older brother. "Mom's strong, but she wasn't ready. Take us back."

Henry shook his head. "I can't," he said. "I didn't do it!"

"Daddy's going to be mad at you, Henry," Jamie barked.

"No," Henry said calmly. "He won't."

"Yes, he will. Why did you bring us here?" John Carter asked.

"I didn't do it," Henry insisted.

"Who did?" Jamie demanded.

"Mom did."

"Mom?" John Carter's brow narrowed. "She can't do that by herself. You told me that!"

"*She* read the … incantation," he said. "I barely had time to *direct us*, or it would have been a lot worse."

"So, how do we get back?"

"I don't know," Henry said. "Mom doesn't do well with trips like these." Obviously. She was unconscious and Henry thought she appeared pale. He patted her arm trying to stir her. It didn't seem to help.

"What happened to the markings?" Jamie asked, shining his flashlight up.

Henry stood, scanning the rock face with his flashlight. "They're gone."

"Truth seeker?" Lauren could hear the whole exchange between her boys, but the voice of Tsul'Kalu startled her. She thought for a moment she could bring herself into consciousness, but the effort drained her. She could feel the threads of her life unraveling, loosening her conscious from her body. "Have no fear, little one." A warm calm came over her, and she could smell a familiar and comforting perfume of flowers, herbs, and beast. "Rest now. I will see to your boys." She struggled toward the sound of his voice but realized it was of no use. She took his advice and surrendered to the void.

It was sometime later when Lauren's eyelids lifted, and she scanned the dark above her. Unable to focus, she swallowed hard and rolled to her side, forcing herself up onto one elbow.

A large soft hand found its way beneath her arm and aided her in the effort. A cup was pressed to her lips, and she drank greedily. The liquid was warm, with a bitter tang and floral aftertaste. "Thanks," she managed, as he helped her lie back. The kind eyes of the shaman gazed down at her, but something wasn't right. It was the same kind eyes, but the beast's fur was darker, and he appeared ... younger.

"I did not expect to find you in this *now*," he said, setting the cup aside.

Lauren reached for his hand, and he took hers and held it. "Tsul'Kalu, I have missed your voice."

"You have changed little, child," he said. "What happened to your face?"

"I ran into a ..." she hesitated. "A skunk ape ..."

Tsul'Kalu considered her for a moment. "Pesky beasts," he sneered. "Nothing like our ilk."

"You know them?"

"Of them," he said. "They are as insignificant to the People as a monkey would be to your kind," he said. "They are a step lower on the evolutionary scale. They are much like Neanderthals, if you will. Not unintelligent, but ... *unenlightened*."

"Oh." Lauren's mind raced to process the encounter, her hand mindlessly floating to her cheek, feeling the sting of the mark on her flesh. "Where are we?" She asked, still unable to focus on anything beyond him.

"The correct question would be *when* are we." He had that same all-knowing countenance she remembered so well, and her heart seemed to lighten as she realized he truly was right there in front of her.

"When?"

"Precisely," he said. "You are in the same place, but not *in* the same time."

"Where are my sons?" She bolted abruptly, and immediately regretted it. The world spun around her, but her gaze came to focus on the three frightened boys cowering against the cavern wall nearby.

"Momma!" Jamie started to bolt to her, but John Carter held him fast.

"Mom, are you okay?"

"Let him go, John Carter," she said. "This is Tsul'Kalu. He is a friend. He will not hurt you."

Tsul'Kalu put a hand behind her shoulder and lowered her back down. "Lie still," he ordered. "Your son wasn't prepared for the sudden time change. He did his best to shield you, but he has not yet reached his full power."

"Henry did this?"

"No. Not exactly," Tsul'Kalu said, glancing down at Jamie who crept up at his elbow. John Carter came around to the other side of his mother. Henry remained steadfast. He stood frozen. "You spoke the spell. You caused the tear to open. Henry kept you from falling … farther."

"How do you know the skunk ape again?" Lauren's hand was in his. Firelight flickered in his deep eyes, and he sighed. She felt sluggish and disoriented.

"There was once a war between *The People*," he said. "A time when our tribes were split, a schism between the clans. We warred against one another, and then each went our separate ways. *The People*, the ones you know, went north and west, leaving the battling tribes to their primitive war. We lived in harmony with the ancient gods, and with the universe in which we dwelled. But our cousins, whose mark you bear, they lost touch with their gods and their warring led to chaos and kept them from growing in wisdom. They forgot the old ways, and before a generation passed, they knew nothing but war."

Lauren's head was swimming, and she could feel the herbs from the drink taking effect. "How did we get here? In this *now*?"

"You know, there are places in this world where the veil of time is thin. Only those with great power can bridge the gap between one time or another. You have done this yourself before, with the aid of your son."

"I feel so dizzy." Lauren swallowed hard. "I must have hit my head ..."

"Temporal displacement often causes disorientation," Tsul'Kalu put a hand on her shoulder. "You have experienced this before. It is important that I caution you. Leaving your place in time and space is a danger to your body as well as your mind. There are those who can sustain themselves in other time-places for long periods. Eventually, it will take a toll. The best thing you can do is decide if the toll is worth the price."

"A toll?" Lauren swallowed hard, fighting to keep her lids open.

"The mind is a fragile thing, little one. It does not take much for it to suffer the effects of being outside your own place in time."

"Are you boys okay?" She caught Jamie's hand.

"We're okay, Momma," John Carter said.

Tsul'Kalu's eyes twinkled. "You and the Protector have done well. You, however, need to rest. I will make sure your boys are fed and cared for. When you wake you will be hungry and there will be food. That which you carry is safe, and you need not fear, so long as I am here. Rest now and we will talk later."

Lauren was in no position to argue. Tsul'Kalu's large hand was warm on her shoulder, and she could feel the warmth radiating through her body. Her lids closed, and she was lost to dreams for hours.

"And when your father saw me, he screamed like a frightened otter and passed out cold on the ground," Tsul'Kalu said, prompting the boys into peals of laughter. "In his defense, he had been injured, but it was amusing none-the-less. All *The People* thought so."

Lauren sat up on her elbow, feeling much more clear-headed than earlier. Her boys sat around the fire in the middle of the cave on furs, with empty bowls beside them. Tsul'Kalu was telling them stories and he paused when he noticed Lauren.

"Your mother was much more brave," Tsul'Kalu said. "It is because of her courage that you each have your gifts, bestowed upon you through her by the ancient gods. One must prove themselves worthy in order to receive such gifts, so I know you must each be of good character."

"What gifts, sir?" Henry asked.

The Bigfoot shaman's brow tightened. "Your gifts," he addressed Henry. "Are your command of time and space. More gifts will find you when you are ready," Tsul'Kalu said to him. He turned to Jamie. "You will know truth in all things, though you may not always be able to speak it. You are also blessed with the wisdom to share what you know only when it is wise to do so."

"What about me?" John Carter asked. "I can't do any of the stuff Henry can do."

"You are the son of a mighty wizard and the Jedak of Jedaks." Tsul'Kalu's eyes brightened. "*This* Earth cannot hold you, when it is time for you to go. You will take your place among the stars. You will travel far in your days, which will be many."

"Jedak of Jedak is from an old book," John Carter said. "It's one of my dad's favorites."

"All stories of men are grown from a seed of truth," Tsul'Kalu assured him.

"Do I have gifts?" Jamie asked.

"You will … in time. Not everyone's gifts find them so early in life as your brother's. I can assure you, your powers will be great, if you are wise."

"What are our momma's gifts?" Jamie asked.

Tsul'Kalu turned to Lauren as she sat up. Lauren glanced down at her belly, and he could hear her thoughts as she contemplated how much she had grown in so short a time.

Tsul'Kalu continued. "She has the knowledge of the ancient gods, and the knowing of the All-Language," he explained. "Her powers continue to grow as she brings new life into the world. The gods have chosen her to serve as their hand. It is a task she has performed well."

Lauren rose and came over to sit beside her boys. Her hand went to her stomach and the life growing there.

"Momma said the ancient gods told her she'd have a lot of kids." Jamie moved to sit closer to her.

"And she shall," Tsul'Kalu said. "They will be seekers of truth, like you. They will bring light to the world and become scholars and peacemakers. Her sons and their sons will bring her honor and she will be exalted among women."

His words were comforting, but also surprising. "Do you know how many we'll have? Can you tell me?" Lauren asked the shaman.

A light passed over his countenance. "Suffice it to say, there will be enough."

Lauren scowled, pursing her lips, wrapping her arms around her stomach. She was nearing the age where having babies would be impossible, not just dangerous. She was already dreading the lecture from her doctors that began with, "Because of your *advanced maternal age*..."

"Now we just need to get back to their father. He's going to be worried." Lauren swallowed the words.

"It is not possible to return, yet," Tsul'Kalu said.

"Why not?"

"The runes have not yet been put in place," the shaman said, pointing with his chin at the blank cavern wall. "The time is coming, but you must bide a while. You are here for a purpose."

"But —" Lauren started to protest.

"Fear not," Tsul'Kalu said. "Time does not pass the same in this time-place. A day is but a second, a week but a day, a year but a month. Rowan's heart will know you are safe with your sons. Though ... his brain may not be so moved. You, *Truth Seeker*, must trust this for the sake of your children ... and their future."

"Tsul'Kalu, you said we were here for a purpose. Do you know what that is?"

"It is not for me to say," he said. "To everything there is a season. There is a purpose. You must find your way in the proper time."

"So what are we going to do, Momma?" Jamie asked.

"We will wait until the runes are restored," Lauren said. "While we are here, we will learn as much as we can from Tsul'Kalu. He is quite old and exceptionally wise."

John Carter leaned on his mother's shoulder and gazed up at her with dark eyes. "You never told us you were friends with a *Bigfoot*."

"Not just one Bigfoot," Lauren said. "All the Bigfoot ... well, all the ones who call themselves *The People*."

"Can we meet the rest of the Bigfoots?" Henry asked.

Tsul'Kalu lifted a hand in consolation. "Perhaps another time," he said. "Now, your mother is hungry and needs food."

"I'll get it." John Carter rose. He took one of the wooden bowls by the fire and filled it with what appeared to be soup and brought it to her. Lauren thanked him and drank greedily, finding the food delicious.

"Why don't you tell them the story about the rabbit?" Lauren suggested.

Tsul'Kalu nodded. "Yes, that is a good one. They will like this tale."

"I know this one," Henry said, leaning forward. "It's a good story."

~

ROWAN SAT AT THE TABLE AT BASE CAMP, TRYING TO CALIBRATE the timing relay on one of the trap cams. It'd malfunctioned after Lauren's episode with the skunk ape, and he was convinced if the timing of the aperture had been right, it would have caught something, anything, but every picture on the digital device came back blank.

The screwdriver slipped and jabbed him in the wrist, and he dropped everything. It was just a scratch, but it must have hit a nerve that left his fingers tingling. He shook his hand. "Son of a ..."

"Are you okay?" Bahati came over to check on him.

"Yeah," he grumbled, showing her the faint puncture wound. Blood oozed from it.

"Aww, poor baby. Do you need a Batman Band-Aid?" She cooed at him playfully.

"No," he snarled. "I do not need a Batman Band-Aid. I am a grown man. I am not five."

"Of course." She chuckled, returning to the job of getting all the equipment ready for the night's investigation. He watched her for a few seconds, then shook out his tingling fingers and went back to his work.

He picked up the screwdriver and pressed it into the narrow slot, turning the calibration pin ever so slightly. He heard a click, and hesitated, laying down the screwdriver, fumbling with the controls. Nothing happened. Then he thought to change the batteries. Batteries could be drained dry by a spirit during a ghost hunt, but he'd never seen one drained during a Bigfoot investigation. They always put new batteries in all the devices before sunset each day, so they didn't usually have one die after a single night's hunt. Rowan popped in the new battery and closed the cover, flicking the switch. The device hummed to life, and the screen came up, with pictures that hadn't been there before.

He scrolled through them, tapping the button, thumbing through the image log. Each picture was stamped with the hour and minute. Rowan stopped when he came to the time stamp that coincided with Lauren's scare the night before, and his jaw dropped. "Well, that can't be right," Rowan muttered to himself. "Hey! Hey, Bahati!"

She rose cautiously, not sure what to make of his tone. She moved over to him, noticing his gaze fixed on the camera screen. He flinched when she put a hand on his shoulder, but he recovered before he could drop the camera. Numbly he peered up at her and handed her the camera, pointing at the screen, unable to get out even a simple order like, "Look."

Bahati took the camera and sat down beside him, staring at the screen. "Is this ...?" She started.

"Uh, huh."

"Did you ...?" She struggled for the words, but he didn't wait for her. He knew what she meant.

"Yeah."

"Have you ...?"

"No, not yet."

"Jesus, Rowan." Bahati got to her feet. "Jean-René! Chance! Everyone, come see this!"

The crew stood around the laptop where Rowan had uploaded the pictures. Chance zoomed in on the image, and sat at the screen cocking his head sideways, as he examined it. "Is that what I think it is?"

"You see it, too?" Bahati said.

"Yeah," Nate said over Chance's shoulder. "That's definitely a face."

"Not just any face." Rowan paced behind him and chewed on his thumbnail. He crossed his arms over his body as he watched everyone's reactions to the image. "That's a Bigfoot face."

"Technically, that is a skunk ape face," Jean-René corrected.

"It's not a face," Nyota said, leaning in and glancing at it as she walked by. She took a bite of the apple she'd snagged from the chow locker. "Your brain is programmed to find faces where they don't exist."

Rowan turned to the girl. "You don't see a face?" he asked.

"Oh, I see it, but it's not a face." She came back, moving past Rowan, leaning over Chance's shoulder. "That's a tree stump." She reached over and pointed at the screen. "See, that's a knot hole, and a branch. Those things that you think are eyes are just patches of moss."

"Nope," Brandon called out the debunker. "Can't be moss. Moss *only* grows on the north side of trees."

"That's a myth, too," Nyota said, denying him a victory. She set to work preparing herself a sandwich for lunch. "Moss *mostly* grows on the north side of trees in the northern hemisphere. They like to be moist, so they tend to stay on the shady sides of logs, and usually that's the northern side, but any shady spot will do."

Brandon screwed up his face, defeated. "How do *you* know so much about moss?"

"Aunt Lauren taught me."

"Speaking of …where is your Aunt Lauren?" Jean-René furrowed his brow. "I'm sure she'd like to see this."

"She took the boys to the cave this morning," Nyota said. "I haven't seen her since breakfast."

Rowan glanced at his watch. It was well after noon. He'd expected her back much sooner than this.

"Maybe they found something interesting." Bahati lifted a brow.

"Am I being over-protective?"

"With *your* wife?" Chance chortled, then cringed, realizing Rowan might take offense.

Rowan's gaze turned on the audio tech, his lips pinched tight.

"Come on." Jean-René leaned in, slugging him in the shoulder. "Let's go see. Maybe she's found something better than what we found."

Chance snorted. "Better than a picture of a Bigfoot?"

9

R owan sat on a rock outside the cave with his chin on his fist and his elbow on his knee. They'd spent hours searching the cave and the area around it. He sent the crew to search the meadow, the river and back to the camp site, but there was no sign of Lauren … or the boys. God knew, he loved that woman, but some days … she tested him. Today, she was testing him.

Having a wife like Lauren would be a dream come true for any man, and he counted himself as the luckiest bastard to ever walk the face of the earth. Lauren was smart. She was brilliant even. She was strong. She was beautiful. She was sexy to the Nth degree. It was a bonus that she was a great mother, an amazing executive producer, and a brilliant researcher. Her endless curiosity was one of her greatest strengths, as well as her greatest weakness. She was stubborn, willful, and prone to wandering off whenever it suited her, usually to her own detriment.

Jesus, Lauren. Where are you? He rubbed his eyes. It was growing dark, and the entire crew had exhausted themselves searching for their boss and her kids. Their allotted time in the area was running out, and they'd just gotten a picture of a skunk ape on trap cam ... allegedly. The team was also anxious to get out and hunt for it again, but Rowan was a hot mess, and he knew it. He also knew it wasn't likely to change until he knew where Lauren and his sons were.

"Maybe she went back to base camp," Bahati said optimistically, but concern was written all over her dark features. "Come on. Let's see." She took Rowan's arm to help him up, but he didn't budge.

"Chance and Shawn are at base camp," he said wearily. "They haven't found any sign of them."

"You don't think they got lost on the far side of the meadow, do you? We haven't explored that area yet." Bahati was doing her best to keep his spirits up. Rowan recognized that fact.

"She wouldn't take the boys toward the swamp," Rowan said, assured. "I'm going to go back in the cave ..."

"Rowan." Bahati sat down beside him and put an arm around his shoulders. "We've searched every inch of that cave, all the way back to the spot where it narrows too thin to get through."

"Jamie could get through," Rowan said, choking back his words.

"He's a smart boy, Rowan," she said. "He wouldn't go any farther than he could go safely, and Lauren couldn't possibly go in after him. You and I both know, wherever the boys are, Lauren isn't far behind."

Rowan stood, pacing a few feet down the trail, standing for a long moment turned away from her. His back spoke eloquently of his distress. When he turned around, his eyes were red. Bahati stood and took four steps to cross the span between them, pulling him down into her arms, holding onto him with a ferocity she rarely showed. She kissed the side of his head and let him weep on her shoulder.

~

Rowan and Bahati sat at the table at base camp. If she'd had a Valium to give him, she would have. It was everything she could do to keep him from wandering out of camp in search of his wife and children. They'd use the sat-phone to call in search and rescue, and the county sheriff and his teams were combing the woods, along with Jean-René and *The Veritas Codex* team. They had their thermal and night-vision cameras and were aiding the search.

All thoughts of finding the skunk ape were forgotten when the sun went down and there was still no sign of the missing members of their family. Rowan had worn himself to near exhaustion and sat with his arms folded on his knees trembling, his face buried in his hands. Bahati could hear his tears hitting the ground and occasionally, he would twitch and sniffle. Bahati reached over and put a hand on his back, in silent solidarity. A crackle of lightning illuminated the sky and a rumble of thunder followed. Rowan shivered and rose and disappeared inside his tent.

The rest of the search teams began returning to base camp as storms moved through the area and the night air went cold. Lightning and thunder made it hard for anyone to get any sleep.

Morning came bright and cool, with birds singing and a happy yellow sun lifting over the campsite. Rowan greeted the sunrise at the entrance of the cave. His mood was less cheerful, in fact, he was downright brooding. He was angry, and terrified. "*Laaaauuuu-ren?*" He cupped his hands over his mouth and let his voice echo across the valley below. Birds erupted from the trees, but he didn't give a rip about birds. He didn't give a rip about anything except finding his wife and sons. "*Jaaaaa-mie!*" he called, holding out the name long and clear. "*Joooooohn Carter! Heeeeeenry!*" He repeated the boys' names with forte, but when he got back around to Lauren's name, his voice failed him as his knees buckled. He stumbled back and found himself sitting on his rump just inside the cave, with his elbows on his knees, his hands holding his face as he sobbed. His voice echoing in the high cavern disturbed the bats that took to wing and screeched pitifully.

His tears were all but spent when Jean-René and Bahati found him. Jean-René sat down and put an arm around him. Rowan sucked up his courage and dried his eyes. Bahati sank to her knees and leaned on them both. Jean-René spoke with a tone of measured calm. "Search and rescue is back on-scene this morning and they're bringing in a helicopter to assist the ground search. They have dogs and they're starting at camp to see if they can get a scent on Lauren and the boys."

"What kind of dogs?" Rowan asked, his eyes red and his voice weak.

"Bloodhounds," Bahati said. "Biggest ones I've ever seen."

"Good," Rowan said. "Better than German Shepherds."

"They've brought in a task force from the *National Center for Missing and Exploited Children* to aid the search. The lead investigator wants to talk to you," Jean-René said.

"Me?"

"Routine procedure," he said, assuring his boss. "They have to rule out the possibility that Lauren might have taken the kids and run."

"Why would she do that?"

"They're not used to dealing with international adventure travelers who deal in cryptid research," Bahati said, trying to lighten the mood, but it was of no use. She sobered up. "They just want to make sure there wasn't any kind of marital discord or family trouble that might have precipitated her taking action to remove the children from an unsafe situation."

"Am I ...?" the color washed from Rowan's face, and he swayed. "Am I a ... *suspect?*"

"Everyone is a suspect until they are ruled out," Bahati said. "That's how you want it, and you know it. We have new people on the crew, so don't think you'll be the last one they'll want to talk to."

"I don't want the media," Rowan said abruptly as it came to him that they might run Lauren's name through the mud as the researcher who'd been kidnapped by Bigfoot … *twice*. That kind of press would completely ruin any integrity they had as researchers and have them labeled as hoax-mongers and charlatans. "No interviews, no news stories."

"You'll have to take that up with the investigators." Jean-René shrugged.

Rowan's face hung haggard and angry. Bahati was taken aback by how wiped out he appeared. She knew he wasn't dealing with this whole situation well. He'd been through this before, and it didn't make things any better. If anything it made it worse. "Believe me, I will."

Rowan's imagination wasn't helping anything because he always assumed the worst-case scenario. In Washington State, he'd assumed the worst, and of course, it turned out to be much worse than he'd imagined. It wasn't just that his wife was missing. Now, so were his sons.

Later, he sat on one of the camp stools with a cup of coffee between his hands, and a stern expression on his face. The lead investigator from the county sheriff's department sat across from him with a notepad in her lap. The lead investigator for the Center for Missing and Exploited children sat beside her, also taking notes. "Tell me how you met your wife, Mr. Pierce," she said.

"She was working as a paranormal researcher and was filming a show in Estes Park, Colorado. I was a paramedic there. Lauren got pushed down the stairs and broke her leg. It was love at first sight ..." His voice faltered.

"I understand this isn't the first time you're wife has been reported missing."

Rowan bit his lip, dreading the question, as much as the answer. "We were on a case in Washington State nine ... no ten years ago. Maybe it was twelve. I lose track of time."

"I understand you work together," she said. "I've seen your commercials on TV, but I confess, I don't watch your show."

"You know the premise, though, right?"

"Uh, huh. You're ghost hunters." She nodded. "Tell me about when she disappeared before."

"Paranormal investigators," he corrected. "We were hunting for Bigfoot in the Pacific Northwest." He told the whole story just as he'd told it a hundred times before.

"Some hoax-monger in a Bigfoot suit took her and kept her for ten days before she escaped. She came back injured and unable to remember anything that happened to her. It was," he choked back a sob. "It was the worst ... the worst ten days ... of my life, until now."

The investigators sat back and considered him for a moment, allowing him time to regain his composure. Rowan stood and paced, turning his back to them. It took him a number of minutes before he could turn around and take a seat. "This might be the worst ... now my sons are gone, too." He hesitated, struggling to continue. "My boys ..." He lost it.

She fished a package of tissues from her jacket pocket and offered him one. He took it and dabbed at his eyes with it, fighting for control. The second investigator took up the questioning. "Mr. Pierce, is there any chance Lauren might have left with the boys and gone home?"

"Our home is just outside of Hilo," Rowan said, the idea that she might have used her abilities to take them home hit him in the face. "We have family here in Oklahoma, but no ... I don't think that's what happened."

"Have you tried to contact her family here?"

"Yes," he said. "Her mother hasn't talked to her. Neither have her brothers. Her mom has been trying to call her cell phone, but there's been no answer. She wouldn't go anywhere without telling someone."

"Anyone she would call if she needed help? Anyone outside the team?"

Rowan shrugged. "It's not like her. I need the media to stay out of this," he pleaded

"We are doing everything we can to help find them," she said. "We might need the media's help."

"No," Rowan said. "Please? They can't know it's Lauren and our boys that are missing."

The investigator nodded. "For now, the media won't need to be included. I can't promise we won't need them eventually, but I will talk to you before that happens," the man said. "Now, can you think of any reason why Lauren would leave without you?"

Rowan was leaning his elbows on his knees gazing down at his hands, shaking his head. "She's pregnant with our fourth," he said. "She has been so happy. She loves being a mother and Lauren is a great mom. She homeschools our boys and they are ... they are so ... so smart." It was everything he could do to hold it together, and he wasn't doing it all that well.

"Tell me about them?" the sheriff's investigator asked.

Rowan talked about them like any proud father would. He bragged on how clever they were, how much they liked to travel, and how much they loved and cared for one another. He raved about how good they were at taking care of their mother. "Do you have pictures?"

Rowan nodded and got up and went over to the equipment table and picked up his camera, bringing it back over to her, turning it so she could see the shots he'd taken in the meadow on the view-finder. "Jamie fell just after this was taken ... split his eye open. I thought it'd need stitches, but a little surgical adhesive fixed him right up." Rowan's lip quivered, and fresh tears threatened to flood his eyes. "He was so brave."

She nodded, a hand going to his arm. "I need you to be brave, too." She stood. "We'll do everything we can to find your wife and your boys. I just need you to hold it together and let our team do their work."

Rowan nodded, turning away again. "I want in the chopper. We've got thermal imaging cameras."

"Rowan, our teams are experts ... and we have all the equipment ..."

"Please." He cut her off. "I have to help. I have to be ... *useful.*"

"Send me a copy of one of those pictures, and any individual shots you have of each boy. That helps."

"I want in that chopper," he punctuated each word, speaking through clenched teeth.

She considered him for a moment, glancing at her partner.

He nodded. "I'll call the pilot and have them pick you up in the meadow."

～

ROWAN STUDIED EVERY VOID BETWEEN TREES, EVERY SHADOW from two hundred feet above the hilly terrain. The chopper was using the same standard grid pattern the searchers on the ground had followed and made several passes before the pilot came over the radio announcing they were getting to the end of their fuel reserves and would have to let Rowan off in the meadow and return to McAlester to refuel. "We can be back here in less than an hour and give it another pass before we lose daylight."

"FLIR doesn't need daylight," Rowan said, his thermal imaging camera scanning the ground below.

"Yes, but we do," the pilot said. "I won't risk flying over uneven terrain at night even in good weather, but we're getting reports of an approaching storm front from the National Weather Service forecast office in Tulsa."

Rowan tried every argument in the book but in the end, he found himself standing in knee-high grass, watching the chopper lift off over his head. The wash of wind and debris kicked up by the blades battered him, and he raised a hand to shield his eyes as the sun faded and the helicopter raced off into the sky.

Rowan stood for a few minutes, scanning the horizon, half-expecting her to come over the hill with the boys bounding down past her, but the vision in his mind's eye faded and his heart sank into his boots.

He walked on, with no direction in mind. Going back to the cave was futile. He'd spent most of the night in there, scouring the narrowest of passageways, almost getting himself stuck in the process.

He crossed the meadow and found a narrow trail down into the woods along a jagged edge of rock. He skidded along the loose gravel and followed the S-curves that led into a valley below. Here, the tree cover was less dense, and the ground muddy and damp. The farther he walked the more it became like a bog than a forest. The knobby knees of the cypress trees gave him a handhold as he struggled through the quagmire and over the roots that ran underwater.

By the time he reached the opposite side of the clearing and into the shelter of the wide-bottomed cypress trees, there was more water than land. He forged ahead, mindless of the hazards and oblivious to the dangers lurking in the dark swamp.

Soon, he was hip deep in the muck and even when something brushed up against his leg, he never faltered from his course, even though he wasn't sure where he was going. He didn't care. If he found Lauren and his sons, so be it. If the snakes got him first, oh well. At this point, any life without his *Deja Thoris*, or their off-spring, wasn't a life he wanted to live.

"Damn you, Lauren," he muttered, feeling the heat rising to his face. Against the chill, his eyes burned with anger. "Damn you! Why won't you stay where you belong?" He screamed into the night sky. "Some days I want to shake you until your eyes rattle and roll out of your head! Why do you have to be so … stubborn? So … pig-headed!" He kicked at a root, and it stung all the way up his foot. The pain made him even angrier.

He wanted to hit something … not Lauren. *No, he could never hurt her.* She was his heart. He'd rather die than live without her. That was a truth of which he was certain. *But Christ! That woman!!*

He calmed himself a little, standing with his hands on his hips. He took a deep breath and made up his mind. He would find her … or die trying. "Come and get me, gators!" He grumbled and soldiered on into the swamp.

10

Lauren stood at the entrance of the cave gazing out over the dense forest. The vegetation seemed even thicker than she'd remembered, and the needles were bright green. The red maples were ablaze while the cottonwoods had gone golden. The sky above was blue, and the day was cool and clear.

Tsul'Kalu stood behind her and sighed. "It has been too long since we have spoken, Truth Seeker," he said, his voice resonating in her head, rather than her ears.

"I have missed the comfort of your counsel," Lauren admitted as the boys ran past her legs, giggling and chasing one another down the path. "Your voice has been silent for so long, and I was afraid for you."

"You know I have lived on this world for many *b'ak'tuns*. This is a truth we cannot change," he said as she started down the narrow path, following the peals of the boys' laughter. Lauren felt stronger this morning than she had since they arrived in this time-place. "But I am not immortal," he added, following her, catching her arm when her balance seemed to falter. "I gain time in the passing between *time-places*, but even that is not infinite. I may not always exist in your *time-place*. My *time-place* calls to me, and like the trout in a stream, I must return to the time of my birth, or die trying."

Lauren didn't understand how it worked, but she found comfort in knowing all these years, he wasn't really gone. He was just *in a different time zone*, so to speak. She basked in the comfort of that thought as they walked, her hand resting on the swell of her stomach. Her back ached. Sleeping on the hard ground, even with a mat of furs, wasn't easy — even when she wasn't pregnant.

"It won't last long," Tsul'Kalu said knowingly. He could read her thoughts, somehow and she blushed.

She nodded, sad in the knowing that there would be a time when the child wouldn't be safely guarded beneath her heart. "I know," she said.

"You are worried." He stopped. "About *the Protector*."

"Yes." She sat down on a rock and stretched out her back, as he lowered himself to the ground and sat in front of her. The boys could be seen chasing one another in the field just beyond. "When I was lost ... *before*, he was terrified. I just pray to God that he isn't going through the same torment now."

"I had hoped that his faith would be stronger, but ... he is not coping well," Tsul'Kalu said, taking her hand.

"You can sense him?" Lauren's eyes lifted.

"Yes," he said. "I have come to know him through you. You have long channeled him to me, even though I could not return the knowing."

"Somehow, I always sensed you were there."

The corners of his eyes lifted into what might pass as a smile. Then he furrowed his brow. "I fear I must bring him *here* or risk his heart truly breaking."

"You can do that?"

"I cannot. But *we* can try," Tsul'Kalu said, glancing up at the sound of approaching voices. "Ah, here we are ..." He stood.

Lauren took a moment longer to get up, and when she stood, the ancient hairy beast beside her wasn't the same. He was the old Cherokee Grandfather that reminded her of her Great Uncle. She gasped as he cautioned her with his eyes. He stepped out into the clearing, calling the boys over to him. They came and didn't seem to notice anything different.

He turned back to Lauren and held out his hand, motioning for her to join him. As she did, she glanced down and realized her clothing had transformed into something her ancestors might have worn. Her ensemble included a calico dress in navy blue, belted above the swell of her abdomen, and a pair of beaded buckskin boots. She glanced up to question the magic, but a group of men approached from the opposite direction. Lauren straightened, stunned by the presence of others. She glanced up as the boys ran towards her. They were now attired in homespun pants and calico shirts, just like the outfit the old man beside her wore.

Lauren froze, the air sucked from her lungs as she inspected the strangers. They weren't men of *her age*, clearly. They wore clothes that appeared like something out of a historical costume drama. Beneath their cloaks, they wore white mantles with a red symbol she couldn't quite make out.

One of their group — clearly not a European — had on a leather coat, lined with furs, despite the warmth of the day. The sun crested over the tree tops, cutting like knives into the canopy. He had a pock-marked face that was pinched, and his head was shaved along the sides. His scalp lock was adorned with a headpiece made of porcupine quills, which fanned out in a circle around his head like a halo. Feathers draped over his shoulder. A white painted arrow was also included in his headpiece. His bare forehead was painted red. A band of black crossed his face over his eyes. His chin was painted with eight vertical lines from his lower lip to his neck. Lauren thought he must be a Chickasaw warrior. His sour expression changed when he caught her eye. She took a step back closer to Tsul'Kalu and lowered her gaze.

"*Ah-yook-pah-che*," she addressed him in his language, keeping her eyes down cast. Then, she greeted him — formally — in her native tongue. "*Osiyo. Dohejunihi.*"

"*Ee-hoh*," he grunted, staring past her to Tsul'Kalu. "*Ah-yook-pah-che e-moh-she.*" He addressed the man. *Greetings Uncle.* It was a term of respect, without resorting to calling him *Grand-father*, lest he slight the shaman by making him feel old.

Tsul'Kalu bowed, as Lauren translated for him. "Male chauvinist pig," she muttered under her breath in Slovenian, just to make sure no one in the group could understand her. Tsul'Kalu put a hand on her arm and bowed to the warrior.

"Tell him I said hello. Pretend you're a diplomat making first contact with an alien race," he said, bemused. Lauren recoiled, trying to control her face, but not having much luck. She translated the greeting with a saccharine sweet smile.

His brow lifted as he studied her up and down. "*Ya-koh-ke,*" he responded. He did not bow to her but continued to address his comment to Tsul'Kalu.

"I am called *Wesa dotlado'hv,*" Lauren spoke. If this warrior would not address her, he would at least have to listen to her. She didn't give him the honor of her real name, but instead, said the first thing she could think of. She knew his tribe respected women, so this man had to be an aberration. "*Koh-e ĭsh-toh* in your language." The name was literally *cat who walks through the mountains*, or *cougar*, perhaps *jaguar* in other climes. She could think of no word in his language for *jaguar*.

"You speak *Che-kah-shah* well, for one of the *Aniyunwiya.*" He spoke for the first time to her. He spoke the Cherokee name with disdain. "My name is *Ko'i Minco,*" he said, once again speaking to the tall man beside her. Lauren was taken aback. That wasn't a Chickasaw name. It was Choctaw! *Had she made some horrible assumption?* Worse, his name meant *Panther*

Chief. Had she known that, she might have invented some other name for herself. She should have let him introduce himself first. "I am a guide and translator for these men from across the *Great Water Where The Sun Rises.*"

Tsul'Kalu said something to her. "*Uncle* wishes to know how a Chickasaw warrior has come to bear a Choctaw name," Lauren said. "And how you speak the *Che-kah-shah?*"

"My mother was Choctaw," he said. "My father is Chicka-saw." He glanced over Lauren's shoulder at the boys behind her. They'd found a clearing and were collecting sticks and rocks, using them like Lincoln Logs to build small houses. "Your children?"

"*Hoh-me,*" she said. *Yes.*

He eyed them a moment then inspected her, his eye going to her swollen stomach, then to Tsul'Kalu. The Choctaw Guide lifted his chin to the old man. "Uncle or husband?"

"Uncle. It is a term of respect among my people. He is a wise teacher," Lauren said, fighting to compose herself. "My husband is … hunting."

"Your husband is not of your tribe." It wasn't a question.

"No," she said, glancing over his shoulder at the tall red-haired man behind him. "He is one of *them.*"

The guide stepped aside as a Scotsman — clearly the leader of the group — stepped forward and gave her a cour-teous bow. He repeated the gesture to Tsul'Kalu.

"*Osiyo,*" Tsul'Kalu said.

"Your servant …" he bowed, but Lauren sensed he real-ized his words might not be understood.

"I speak English." Lauren startled him, then realized she couldn't give all her cards away. "If you … speak slow." She feigned limitation. It was to her advantage though — speaking English — it meant the translators services would not be needed, and it took away any authority he thought he might have over her, and over Tsul'Kalu. But the Templars didn't speak English, she realized quickly— not as it existed in her time. Their speech was a mix of true Gaelic and an older version of Middle English. It mattered little to her, thanks to the Gift of the All-Language.

THE LEADER EXTENDED A HAND TO THE OLD SHAMAN. "BY THE blood," the man said to Tsul'Kalu, removing his helm as his hand was accepted. Tsul'Kalu shook his hand in the Cherokee manner, clasping his wrist. The leader's hair was a vivid auburn red, slicked back and tied neatly in a queue. It was redder than Rowan's, but not by much. "My name is Henry Sinclair."

Those who followed appeared to also be Templars, though she couldn't see all their tabards. One bore a flag with a white banner, emblazoned with a red cross. He used the pole to lean on as they stopped. Most of the men in their company dressed in the same fashion as the leader. They lingered behind, so Lauren couldn't quite make out their details. She had learned from their recent investigation to the South of France that Templars had fifteen official ranks. Grand Master was the highest, followed by Seneschal, Commander of the Kingdom of Jerusalem, Commander of the City of Jerusalem, Commander of Tripoli, and Antioch, Drapier, Commander of Houses, Commander of Knights, Knight Brothers, and on down to Standard Bearer, Sergeant Brothers, Turcopoles and Elderly Brothers.

She also had an idea of the *when* they had traveled to. The Knights Templar were established in 1129 to protect pilgrims journeying to Jerusalem, but in 1312, the Pope suppressed them, under pressure from King Philip IV of France — primarily because the church perceived they had become too powerful. In truth, they had grown too wealthy. The King of France was bankrupt and wanted their holdings for himself.

Still, 1129 to 1312 was a long span of time, and there was a chance they were even later. While the Knights Templar were officially disbanded with the Friday the 13th massacre in the early 1300's, the traditions of the Templars continued some 400 years later in the form of the Poor Fellow-Soldiers of Christ, and later by the quasi-Templar order of Freemasonry.

"We have been traveling long, and are low on supplies," the ruddy man said.

"You are far from your homeland. Are you lost?" Tsul'Kalu asked, with a twinkle in his eye. Lauren translated.

"We are explorers," Sinclair said.

"Not all who wander are lost," Lauren said, in Cherokee.

"Is it fortune and glory you seek?" Tsul'Kalu could give as good as Lauren, and his humor was not lost on her, though how the Bigfoot shapeshifter knew of Indiana Jones was beyond her. Lauren's translation wasn't verbatim.

"Our conquests are … holy," Sinclair said. "We are on a quest from God."

"Then the Great Spirit has brought you to us that we may serve. We have a fire. There is food." Tsul'Kalu stepped aside, as Lauren translated. There in the clearing where the boys were playing, was a fire with a pot hanging from a tripod over it. Lauren might have gasped, but she knew the shaman had magic she could never understand. "Come," he said. "Eat and we will tell of our journeys."

The man nodded and waved his fellows over to join them. As she served up the bowls of stew, she was convinced there wasn't enough for all the hungry men, but the kettle never seemed to empty.

"Thank you," Sinclair said, as Lauren passed him the bowl. He seemed to purposefully keep his hand from touching hers — a move that did not go unnoticed. He was close enough, however, that she was able to make out the symbol on his mantle, a red cross. It was a crusader's cross. All the pieces fell together as she stepped back and returned to her place beside Tsul'Kalu, watching as the men said grace over their meal, then settled in to eat in silence. She knew they would not speak while they ate. They would not ask for seconds, and none would eat more than their leader. It was all part of the Templar's strict code. This was not some costumed drama. She was not in some comatose vision. Before her sat Prince Henry Sinclair and his men. This was the stuff of legends and she wished Rowan were there with her to see it.

When Lauren rose to collect their empty bowls, the leader spoke directly to her. "And where is your man?" *Could he read minds?*

"He is nearby," Tsul'Kalu said in English, before she could answer. He'd given up his cards, but it would make the conversation easier. "He is hunting."

Lauren watched the man in the furs out of the corner of her eye, her hackles rising at the way he was staring at her. Tsul'Kalu's eye met hers. She turned away. Ko'i Minco did not.

"Tell us of your journeys. Your people are from the north. How did you come to travel with Sinclair?" Tsul'Kalu asked the guide.

The man's gaze shifted to Tsul'Kalu, and he eyed him warily. He spat on the dirt just inches from Tsul'Kalu's knee. He sniffed, wiping his nose on his sleeve.

"The White Men asked me to show them the way to the middle of the earth," Koi' Minco said. "They are on a quest."

"And what is it you seek?" Tsul'Kalu turned his question to Sinclair. Lauren translated it.

The Templars shared guarded expressions between them. Lauren noticed the leader tense, thought he tried to maintain his composure. "That remains our business, good sir." The red-headed man said.

"Did I understand our guide to say you were Cherokee?" One of the men asked. Lauren had to assume he was Sinclair's High Marshal. His tabard had red and black bands across the bottom, much like Sinclair's but there were fewer of them. "It was my understanding Cherokee lived in the southeast, high in the mountains."

"We are all travelers," Tsul'Kalu said. "My daughter and her husband have come to trade with the tribes to the west. These are my grandsons by *Alisdelisgi*, her husband." Lauren didn't bat an eyelash at the lie. She knew he was being deceptive, and she knew why. He didn't hold a great deal of trust in these men. She didn't either.

She stood, to refill Jamie's bowl, and Lauren noticed the translator leering at her. His eyes went once again to her protruding stomach. She felt a chill wash through her, and she fought to control her face. She knew it often betrayed her. He was filthy and probably hadn't seen a puddle, much less a bar of soap, in well over a month. His teeth were yellow, those that hadn't rotted out completely, and the stench of him turned her stomach. His sour expression never seemed to soften. It made his face appear like a rotting squash.

She turned, taking Jamie's bowl to him, sitting back down beside him. She watched them as Tsul'Kalu asked questions about their journey, where they were from and how they came to be there. Lauren listened intently, surprised at how quiet and still the boys remained as they sat enraptured by the strangers' story, even though there was no way they could understand the mix of languages being spoken, other than English, of course.

The Templars answered the shaman politely, but she could tell they were holding back. She wasn't sure why they needed to be deceptive, but perhaps a measure of trust had to be earned on both sides before an accord could be reached. She wished Kitty were here to broker a treaty.

"We come from a place called Scotia, or Scotland. My men are my clansmen and sworn Protectors of the Faith of the One True King, Jesus Christ, our Lord, and Savior." Lauren's eye went to the white banner leaning against the tree. "We are the last of *The Order of the Heart of the Sacred Rose*." He moved his coat to show the gold embossed rose at the junction of the cross.

"You honor us with your presence," Tsul'Kalu said. "Welcome to our fire. Let us smoke and be friends." He produced a pipe and a pouch of tobacco.

A jovial and relaxed parlay began at that point. Tsul'Kalu recognized she was growing tired, knowing the time-shift had taken more of a toll on her than he'd initially suspected. "You should rest, daughter," he spoke to her in Toltec. "Your furs in the cave await you."

Lauren had no desire to go back into the cave, but she didn't argue. Instead, she nodded, then rose. She spoke back to him in Mayan, not sure what his game was, but willing to play along. Clearly he wanted to make sure the men didn't understand the dialogue. It was a clever rouse. "First, I'm taking the boys down to the river to wash before dark."

"Have the boys fetch back water and I will make a tea for these men. They will sleep well while we work our magic tonight." He responded in the same language.

"Our magic?"

"We will call to the Protector and see if he can be freed from his bonds of time."

Lauren's heart fluttered, but it was not with love or longing, but fear. Even if they could bring him to this now, what effect would that have on him, and to what purpose, except to ease his suffering. He'd be trapped here like her and the boys. Tsul'Kalu was up to something, but she couldn't figure out his game. Lauren lifted a brow and picked up the empty kettle at the edge of camp and handed it to Henry. The boys fell in behind her without a word, and they headed for the river in silence.

Lauren sent Henry back up to the camp along with the kettle and instructions not to speak to the strangers. She clued them in on the game, even though they couldn't participate the same way Lauren could.

Henry was tall and gangly for a boy his age, but he was strong, and he had no problem with the vessel, which he sat by the fire. He gave a nod to the shaman. Henry turned and started back for the river where his mother was waiting for him. He stopped mid-stride, all but running into the translator. He tried to side step him, but Ko'i Minco blocked his path, his hand on the butt of his knife, as he stared the boy down. Henry wasn't as tall as the man was but was half his mass. Henry lowered his head and made to pass him once again, but the man threw a shoulder into him and knocked him down. Henry landed with an audible *oof.* His expression was one of anger, his color rising.

"Where are you going?" The man challenged, lifting the weapon out of its scabbard, flashing the polished blade with the wicked sharp edge. "You are not very friendly," he grunted. Henry had strict orders from his mother not to speak, and he obeyed much to his credit, but also to his own detriment. "You don't look like your mother." The man kicked dirt on his boots.

Henry scrambled to his feet and managed to dart past him on the trail. Three steps into his stride, a rock caught him in the shoulder, stinging with a fire unlike anything he'd ever experienced. Henry turned with a wicked scowl, his fists balled up, ready for a fight.

Tsul'Kalu appeared at the clearing on the path above him and Henry's gaze lifted to him, averting the aggressor's attention. "Leave the boy alone," Tsul'Kalu said, in a stern voice. "You do not want to anger his father, but you certainly do not wish to arouse his mother's ire, either."

Henry stood, breathing heavily, but relief spread through him when the shaman intervened. "Go along, grandson. See to your mother."

Henry nodded and gave the man one last wicked glare as he turned to go.

BACK IN THE CAVE, A FIRE BURNED BRIGHTLY, AND MORE FOOD had been set out for them. There were corn cakes with maple syrup, roasted meat, pumpkin, corn, and squash. The boys pounced on it, as if they hadn't eaten in a week. Lauren sat back, leaning against a rock, finding little room in her lap for the growing belly that seemed to have swollen even more since this morning. A foot, or possibly a fist, sucker punched her in the ribs and her breath caught in her throat.

"Momma," Jamie said, with a mouth full of food. "Did you get bigger? Your belly is as big as a watermelon." Lauren glanced down. She had grown, much quicker with this one than she had with any of the previous three. She tried to chalk it up to previously stretched muscles and loose ligaments. *What other explanation could there be?*

"She was even bigger with you before you decided to show up," Henry said to Jamie. John Carter chortled. "She was bigger with you, too, dork."

"I am not a dork!" John Carter slugged his older brother in the arm. Henry set his bowl aside and snatched John Carter's away, then the two went tumbling in a mass of arms and legs, squealing, and growling as they wrestled.

"Enough!" Lauren scolded impatiently.

"Here, Momma," Jamie came over with a cup of tea he found by the fire. It was still warm. Lauren held the cup and inhaled the sweet floral perfume. "You seem tired. You should rest."

"Thank you, sweet boy." Lauren sipped the tea. Henry brought over more of the furs that would serve as bedding. He made a pallet for his mother, and one for his brothers to share.

Soon, she found herself nodding. Feeling euphoric, she got the boys to settle into sleep before she lay down on the pile of furs and curled up by the fire. "Tell us a story, Momma."

Lauren yawned. "Which one would you like to hear? Why the buzzard is bald? How the bear lost his tail?"

"How did you meet Tsul'Kalu?" Henry asked.

"Oh, that's a good one," she said. She told the tale, omitting details she didn't feel they were prepared to know, but it didn't seem to matter. They were soon fast asleep before she even got to the part about catching a diamond thief. Her story ended when she realized they'd fallen asleep. She rolled over onto her side and watched them. It didn't take long for her to doze off, too.

Rowan stumbled and fell to his knees, lingering for a long moment in the mud. He was filthy and wet, and exhausted beyond measure. He was hurt and angry to the point that he no longer cared about anything.

Rowan had no idea how far he'd gone, or even where he was. The night had gone dark, and a heavy bank of fog hovered over the marsh. His watch said it was near midnight, but it was caked with mud, and he was certain it was much later. He considered the watch had stopped.

With muscles quaking in his legs, he collapsed to the ground and rolled over onto his back. He took a deep breath, pinching his eyes closed as he fought for the strength to keep going. Rowan was soaked and the cold crept deep into his body. His joints and muscles ached. He shivered violently as he lay, watching his breath hover over his face. He was ready to surrender. They'd find his frozen corpse here — eventually.

A loud shuffle in the branches and leaves prompted him to his hands and knees. Rowan forced his eyes to focus in the dark. He strained to see whatever had made the noise. His heart galloped in his chest. Earlier he'd had one run in with an alligator and he wasn't ready to repeat the encounter. A flash of eye-shine from higher up than an alligator caught his attention. The branches shook violently as whatever it was, darted off, making a run for it. Normally, Rowan would have bolted after it, but his muscles refused to comply with his brain. If it had been Lauren, if he had known it was her, he would have found the energy, but if this was the skunk ape, or a wolf or a bear ... it wouldn't matter. He didn't care anymore.

Wearily, Rowan managed to get to his feet. But there was no enthusiasm in his efforts. He plodded along behind the thunder of crashing leaves like a zombie. The flash of something caught in moonlight, and he froze. The form appeared human, female. *Lauren?* A rush of adrenaline carried him further and faster than he ever thought it could, even as the swamps gave way to meadows and the forest rose up around him. Despite his exhaustion and the screaming in his muscles, he continued. *Maybe he did care after all.*

He was chasing the shadow along a path he recognized. He froze at the edge of the woods, gazing up the rocky trail towards the cave.

Just as suddenly as it had begun, the clamor abated. He was breathless, leaning on his knees and struggling to hold himself up. He tottered up the trail from the clearing to the now-familiar entrance of the cave, where he slipped down to the floor, and leaned heavily on the wall, trying to catch his breath and stop his muscles from shivering.

A fire had been built in the middle of the empty cavern, and the embers glowed and popped, creating a peaceful vision of hearth and home. He found his feet again and made his way weakly to the warm fire, where he collapsed on a pile of furs left there presumably by the same person who had built the fire. Perhaps made by the same shadow he'd been chasing.

Normally, he might have been cautious, but at the moment, he was in no condition to guard himself. He sank into the blackness of exhaustion that sucked him down into the abyss.

11

Lauren moved effortlessly through the shadows, feeling at one with the mist. The shade of her soul felt light, free from her corporeal shell. The bonds of time and place had no hold over her. She found him lying in a heap by the fire, a knot of tense muscle and troubled mind. He was covered in mud, his clothes torn and disheveled. She ran a loving hand along his weary cheek and whispered soft words into his ear. His troubled brow seemed to ease as she set to work undressing him, washing the dirt and grime from his skin with a soft cloth and water she heated with stones from the fire. He warmed to her touch, melting into a fitful state of peace. She could feel his soul unknotting, along with his muscles.

As she bathed him, she drew one of the furs up over the clean body when gooseflesh prickled on his skin. Once she was done, she added another log to the fire, and crawled under the furs beside him, pressing her swollen belly against his back as she held him. She wasn't sure what Tsul'Kalu had in mind, but it seemed the right thing to do. He rolled over in his sleep, and he tucked his head into the nest of her hair, inhaling deeply, sighing with contentment. She could feel the thrumming of his heart against her hand as he melted, content in her arms. Her shade slipped away just as peacefully.

THERE WAS A WICKED THUNDERING, AND A CRACK OF lightning pierced his skull. Rowan rolled over onto his back, clutching his pounding head between shaking hands. He struggled to get his eyes to open, and then to focus once they did. The world around him was dark with a dim glow that illuminated the visage that came to hover over him. Long soft hair brushed against his arms as he removed his hands from his head and shielded himself defensively.

"Rowan?" His vision blurred but his focus righted itself.

He bolted abruptly awake. "Lauren?" His hands caught her arms, finding her in the flesh. This was not the *ghost* he had dreamt about. "Lauren. Oh my God," he gasped, tears building in his eyes and flooding back into his hair as he pulled her into him. "Where have you been? I've been worried sick? Where are our boys?" He was sobbing, and completely unashamed. He held her tightly, compressing the air from her lungs. She could feel him trembling and she lingered long enough for his grip to relax, and moved to sit beside him, leaning against his body.

"I'm so sorry, honey," Lauren said, her brow knitted tightly. "I don't know what happened, but the boys are here. They are safe. You're safe."

Relief flooded over him as his hand went back to his head. "I feel like my brain is going to explode," he groaned, but reached for her, pulling her into him, needing to feel her arms around him, and the weight of her head on his chest. She recognized the symptoms of *temporal displacement*. When he let her go, she rose, and brought him back a cup of the same tea Tsul'Kalu had given her. She helped him, lifting his head, holding the cup to his lips. "What's wrong with me?" He pleaded as she sat the half-empty cup aside.

"Don't worry, my love." Lauren rested a hand on his chest. "It will pass. You just need to rest."

His lids were growing heavy, but his hand wrapped around her, the other finding the swell of her belly. "I'm afraid to sleep," he admitted, his words slurring. "What if you're just a dream?"

"I will be here when you wake up," she said it like an oath, then leaned down and kissed his cheek.

"Promise?"

"I swear it."

Lauren paced the cave most of the day while Rowan was lost to dreams. She could only hope his body was just adjusting to the change of time and place. The boys had gone with Tsul'Kalu to talk with the Templars. Her back was aching and nothing she did seemed to bring any comfort. Even a cup of Tsul'Kalu's tea didn't ease it, though it did soothe her enough to allow her to lie down next to Rowan and rest for a short while.

Late in the afternoon, the boys returned. "Come see what Henry found," Jamie said, coming over to her. In his arms, he held the largest rabbit Lauren had ever seen. It seemed perfectly tame. It didn't flinch when Lauren sat up and reached to pet it.

"What did you think of Tsul'Kalu's story about how the rabbit was the leader in all the mischief?"

"It's my favorite story," Henry said, petting the rabbit.

"I like why the buzzard is bald, too," Jamie said.

"Is Dad *still* asleep?" Henry scowled, glancing at the lump beneath the furs beside his mother.

"Yes," Lauren said. "What about Sinclair and his men?"

"Tsul'Kalu has made them stew and sent us to bring you down to eat," John Carter said.

"I can't leave your father," Lauren said.

"He says Dad will wake up soon and you should come down," Henry said. "He said there are clothes for him in a basket at the back of the cave."

Lauren nodded and gave the bunny another scratch behind the ears. "Go on then," Lauren said. "Eat your supper and help Tsul'Kalu. Dad and I will be down later."

Lauren lay back down beside Rowan, yawning. It was a long while later when she realized Rowan's eyes were open and he was staring at her. She rolled over inspecting him.

A drowsy curl lifted the corner of his lips. "You're still here," he said, his voice gruff.

"I promised," she answered. "How's your head?"

"Better."

"Good," she said. "Are you hungry?"

"Uh, huh." His hand snaked over the swell of her belly, as he pulled her into him, his lips capturing hers. He hesitated and drew back, lifting the covers to inspect her. "Did you get ... bigger?" His hand spread over her swollen abdomen, as if taking measurements.

"Uh, hello. I am pregnant."

"You weren't *this pregnant* the last time I saw you," he said.

Lauren sat up on her elbows. She drew the calico taut over her stomach. Her navel protruded overtly beneath the cloth.

"Rowan," she started, but hesitated. "I don't know how to explain this ..."

"You can start with telling me where you've been the past few days," he said.

"I've been *here* the whole time," she said, her hand going to the cavern overhead.

"What?" Rowan scowled, throwing off the covers, realizing he was naked. He snatched back the furs to cover himself. "I searched this cavern for hours. I called your name until I was hoarse."

"There are clothes in the basket there." Lauren nodded to a dark corner. Rowan rose taking the fur to cover himself. It took a moment for his legs to steady. Once he had his feet under him, he went to retrieve the basket. He returned with a pair of homespun breeches, and a blue and red calico shirt. There were boots in the basket, too.

"It's not about where I was, or where we have been," she said as he dressed. "It's more like ... *when*." Rowan sat down a lot harder than he had intended to, his mouth open. He stared at her.

"I don't know if Henry did it or if *I* did," she continued. "But ... those glyphs were like an incantation written on the cave wall. I read it aloud for the boys ... and *something* happened. Tsul'Kalu says this cave is a place where the veil of time is thin and we ... just sort of slipped through."

"Like Chichén Itzá ... the stone circle?" He gulped.

"Yes," Lauren said. "Just like Chichén Itzá."

"You slipped through it?" He chewed on the idea for a long moment. "Through ... *time*?"

"I know it sounds like ..." She shrugged, trying to behave as if was a perfectly normal thing to do.

"Like Outlander?" He gazed at her with trepidation.

"Me Claire. You Jamie." She feigned a laugh, still trying to read his reaction. She was certain he thought she was crazy. Lauren wasn't so sure she wasn't.

"And who told you this?"

"Tsul'Kalu," she said. Lauren swallowed hard when his brows knitted into a scowl.

"Not *him* again," Rowan groaned.

"What?"

"Your Bigfoot spirit guide?"

"I thought you understood ..." she said, stopping. His reaction stunned her, and in truth, it stung. "You say it like it's a bad thing."

Rowan wasn't one to anger easily, or to fly into fits of rage, but the expression on his face made her uncomfortable. She made the effort to get to her feet and moved away from him for a moment. When she had a bit of space between them, she turned around, hoping he'd had enough time to process. "I thought you'd come to accept him ... I thought you understood ..." she sputtered.

He turned away, staring down at his thumbs, still processing. "I ..." he started but paused. "I want to ..."

"Come meet *him*." Lauren's eyes brightened. She realized he would never believe until he saw it for himself.

"Tsul'Kalu?" Rowan remained stone-faced.

"Please?"

He deflated and shrugged, getting to his feet. "You did get bigger." He scowled, inspecting her.

She just shook her head and shrugged. "Tsul'Kalu says time moves *differently* here," she said, as if that was enough. It would have to be ... at least for now.

LAUREN AND ROWAN PAUSED AT THE EDGE OF THE CLEARING where an old man sat with the boys by a dying fire. He spoke with his hands as he told a story. The party of crusaders was nowhere to be found.

"I thought you said he was ... a *Bigfoot*," he said, leaning into her. Rowan's hands went to his hips as he watched the scene unfolding before him.

"He didn't want to frighten anyone," Lauren said, keeping her tone equally low. "Especially the children."

"He's a ..."

"Shapeshifter?" Lauren put words in his mouth. "Yes."

Rowan let out an exasperated sigh, rubbing his temples with one hand. "This just keeps getting better and better."

"Come talk to him." Lauren took her husband's hand and led him into the clearing. Rowan hesitated but surrendered when the boys saw him.

"Dad!" The boys swarmed him, hugging him. Relief washed through him. "We missed you, Dad."

"I missed you, too." He hugged them, each again, realizing how terrified he had been for them.

"Boys, why don't you go gather some firewood," Lauren suggested. "It could be a cold night." She wrapped her arms around her expanding middle, unable to cover her protruding belly.

"Sure, Mom," Henry said.

"Keep an eye on Jamie," she called, as they scattered into the woods.

Tsul'Kalu stood and waited for Rowan to turn to him. He bowed deeply, offering his hand.

"Hi," Rowan said, accepting the handshake. "Rowan Pierce."

"I know you," the old man said in his deep voice. "*The Protector*. Husband of *Truth Seeker*. Father of her Children."

"Tsul'Kalu, I presume."

"It is one of the names I have used in my travels. I am also known as John Gray Wolf's Son," he said, his eye going to Lauren.

A gasp caught audibly in her throat, and Rowan saw the color wash from her face as he did a double-take. His hand found its way to the small of her back as she seemed to sway.

"Would you ..." Rowan gulped. "Would you also be known as ... *John Grayson?*" Rowan's brow lifted.

Lauren's expression dropped and her knees buckled. Rowan caught her arm, holding her up. He turned back to the old man. A wide grin of disbelief crossed his face and nervous laughter peeled off the tops of the trees. "*Unfreakingbelievable!*" Rowan sounded on the verge of hysteria. "*You* are Lauren's … *father?*"

Tsul'Kalu acknowledged the statement with a calm nod. Lauren stood stunned, while Rowan inched closer to the verge of completely losing his mind.

Lauren seemed to fold into herself, her eyes darting to first one side then another. Her eyes raced from side to side before they locked on … her father. Disbelief burned in her cheeks and stung in her core. Rowan's reaction wasn't helping anything.

"Your *father* is … *Bigfoot!*" He pointed a finger at Lauren. He mocked them both as he paced, then bent into his hands. He dragged his face back as he caught his hair in his fingers. "Now I get it! It all makes perfect sense! No wonder your brother was called *Sasquatch!* Why you're all so tall! Are *you* a Bigfoot, too?" His voice rose in pitch as he began laughing hysterically.

Lauren's gaze turned stone-cold. A dark fire burned visibly behind her eyes as her ire rose. He wasn't completely oblivious to her reaction but in his current state, but he couldn't seem to help himself. Rowan staggered away, laughing, and muttering to himself.

Lauren stood with her gaze locked on the kind eyes of her mentor, her friend … her *father?* Her anger at Rowan washed away as she came to grips with the truth.

"I could not tell you before, daughter," Tsul'Kalu said. "Not that you would have understood … or believed me."

"But …" Lauren fought to find the right words, her mind racing. "How did *you* know? *When* did you know … it was *me?*"

Her father reached for her hand, but she snatched it away. "I know I have much to explain. I also know that nothing I can say or do will make up for the years we could not be together." He caught her hand.

This time she didn't shy away, but her gaze lingered on the toe of his shoe. She refused to lift her eyes to meet his. "But ... how could you ... how could you leave *us?*" she asked but stopped. "What do you mean you had *no choice?*"

"I *am* a powerful wizard," she heard him through her anger. "But even my powers have limits. My gifts are from the ancient gods, like yours, but it is not something I can sustain indefinitely. I grow weaker each time I travel from my own time-place. The longer I stay away ...the farther I go ... the weaker I become. I must return to my *time-place* and regain my strength. Your mother understood the need for me to go, but ... it didn't make the leaving any easier, for any of us."

A thought hit Lauren between the eyes, and she scowled at the pain of the realization. "You didn't fight in Vietnam, did you?"

He shook his head no. "It was a lie that bought me some time. Everyone thought I was overseas, and I was able to return once my strength was restored. Still, I could not stay forever... and we both knew it. It was as if a cancer were eating on every organ of my body, and I knew if I did not leave, I would die."

A tear rolled down her cheek and slapped against the dry ground. "Did *our mother* know ... know what you were? What you are?"

He considered his words a moment. "Not at first," he said. "It was my mistake ... to fall in love outside of my own time-place. You and Rowan are fortunate to have found each other as you did," he sighed. "Your mother had her *magic*," Tsul'Kalu continued. "Her powers were strong, too. I think that was how we found one another. Her soul recognized mine, and I hers. But her magic couldn't help me, and she knew it."

"Wait, my mother has *powers*? Like me?"

"There are different kinds of power in the universe. Hers are unique to her. She comes from a family of healers." John nodded. "She insisted I go."

"She knew where … when … where you went?"

"She did," John said.

It took a moment for Lauren to realize what that meant. Her mother had loved him and let him go. She wasn't sure she could ever let Rowan go — not in a million years. But then again, if it meant his life or her love maybe — maybe she could. "You truly loved her," Lauren stated, setting her jaw.

"I did," he said. "I should have left her before it went as far as it did, but I wasn't strong enough. I loved her and I married her. We made a life together. We made a family. I thought I could sustain myself in her time-place, that our love would be enough. I thought the power of it could keep me. But, I was wrong."

"She turned into a horrible person after you left." Lauren scowled, her lip trembling. "You did that to her."

"I did." He nodded. "The problem with magic like ours, is that it must be answered. You cannot have a love so strong and deny it without dire consequences. I tried coming back, and I do visit your time-place when I can. I did not abandon you completely, daughter."

Lauren searched his eyes finding regret. "Were you looking for me when I found you in Washington?"

"I was not," he said. "I never abandoned you. Your mother, however, forbade me from having any contact with you, in fear of hurting you the way I hurt her. I found my way to be near you … a way she could not know about." The image of the old raccoon came to her mind and her heart flipped in her chest again. "By the time you were grown, I had to return to my own time-place for much longer than I would have liked. I lost you. I didn't know where to find you … *when* to find you. I suffered the effects of time shifting and wasn't myself for a long time. You brought me back when you found me in Washington. My soul knew you, even when my mind did not."

Lauren fought to keep her face from twisting into a sob, but it was in vain. "How ... how could you leave?" His hand went to hers, and she drew it away angrily, fury flashing in her eyes.

"I didn't know your mother was pregnant when I had to go. My energy was waning, and I would have died if I hadn't gone when I did. I didn't want to leave your mother. I loved her. I still do. But I know she will not have me, and that is her right. She threw out all my belongings and told me to leave. I knew she didn't want me to go, but she knew I had no choice."

Lauren blinked back tears, still struggling for control over her emotions and her face. "You sent me money when I graduated high school." Lauren's voice broke.

"I did not," he said.

Lauren chewed on this for a long moment, realizing that must have been her mother's doing. She was just bitter enough to have done something like that. "I have been angry at you my whole life. I couldn't understand how a man could go off and leave his wife and children without so much as a word."

"But I didn't leave without a word," he said. "My parting was carefully planned. We made the most of our time together. I made as much money as I could so I could leave her with funds to keep my family safe. I promised I'd return when I was able. *If* I could. I did return. I was not ignorant of the cave in Washington, or its importance. I provided for my family in the simplest of ways. It was all I could do." Tsul'Kalu's regret shown in his eyes.

"You brought our mother … diamonds?"

"A few times," he said. "I provided in other ways, too."

"Oh?"

"It gets harder and harder to sustain myself in different time-places as I grow older. I've struggled to find my way back to her ... and you. If it wasn't for Henry ..."

"Henry?" Her brow narrowed.

"When I couldn't come to you, he came to me," Tsul'Kalu said. "His magic is extraordinarily strong. He has a command of place and time that is far beyond his years. He has since he was an infant. You know this."

"I mean, we figured out the whole *Momma-go* thing when he was about a year old. I thought I was doing it, but I didn't know how. We've struggled to keep him from misusing his abilities."

"He has never misused his powers," her father said. "When the world was in jeopardy from the Dark One — Enlil — he did what he could to ensure history would be written as it should. While you could never take credit for saving the world, neither could he take credit for his role. He did not do it unbidden or untrained. Michael was there to guide him."

"You know about Michael?" Lauren gasped.

A knowing expression crossed his face. "I am pleased that you two found your path through ... together."

A lump formed in Lauren's throat, and tears sprang into her eyes unbidden. She held them at bay. "You have been there the whole time?"

"I have never been more than a dream away," he said. "However, if we do not find a way to help your husband, I fear for his mind, and for your future."

Lauren turned and saw Rowan in the distant trees, pacing back and forth. He seemed to be carrying on a one-sided conversation.

"I better go talk to him," Lauren wasn't sure what she would say. What *could* she say?

"Best think of something," her father said. "Our guests are returning with dinner." His dark eyes darted in the opposite direction and Lauren had a mental picture of Sinclair and his party returning with a large deer tied by its legs to a long pole. She could sense the hunger for fresh meat in all of them, but also a desire to offer it up as a sign of peace amongst them.

Lauren nodded and went to try and calm her husband.

12

B ahati sat on a tree stump and opened a bottle of water, catching her breath and checking her GPS. It had gone from ice cold a few days before to sunny and seventy-five, with no wind. The search parties had spread everywhere searching for the missing Pierce family. Rowan had gone off in the night and had not returned. He wouldn't come back without his family, she knew that. She suspected he'd gone into the swamp searching for them.

She was angry at the local sheriff for his handling of the search and rescue efforts. He wouldn't let *The Veritas Codex* team help, at least not officially. So she'd slipped off from camp intent on her search. She'd gone in the opposite direction, heading north into the mountainous terrain and thick oak forest. Pausing, Bahati brushed off a tick that was crawling on her sock and felt her skin prickle as she convinced herself she was covered with them.

This was futile, she sighed to herself. If the experts couldn't find them, with search and rescue dogs and helicopters, who was she to think she could do it alone? She glanced at her watch and decided to turn back.

She had just gone a few steps when she heard a familiar

hum. She followed the noise and found her way to a clearing near a precipitous cliff. Here the trees had died off, their *skeletons* standing tall and bare. Jean-René stood with a device in his hands that reminded her of a video game controller. She glanced up in the sky, following the hum to a small drone that hovered over the valley.

"You've been following me," Bahati stated the fact.

"I've already lost my bosses," he said, without taking his eyes off the sky. "I'm certainly not going to lose *my* wife."

"Where's Nyota?" Bahati asked.

"Right here, Mom." The girl came up behind her. "I brought lunch."

It was well after noon and Bahati's stomach growled, reminding her she had a couple of bottles of water and a granola bar in her pack.

"Any luck?" Bahati asked, finding a warm rock to sit on, turning her face to the sunshine as Nyota came to sit beside her, handing her one of the plastic-wrapped sandwiches.

"No," he said. "The Network has ordered us to pack up and go home."

"What?" Bahati protested. "We can't just leave them."

"Lauren and the boys have been gone for over a week. Rowan's disappearance adds to their concern that there's a hazard here that we're all just a few feet from stumbling into."

"What's the latest from the search and rescue teams?"

"Nothing." He brought the craft back to the ledge and landed it a few feet away from where Bahati and Nyota sat. He walked forward and retrieved the drone, sitting with them, as he pulled up the video feed on the drone's display. He studied it while the girls ate. Nyota leaned against her father's strong bicep watching the video feed, which was an overhead view of the colorful fall foliage.

After they'd had a sandwich, and a chance to watch the video, Jean-René rose and packed the drone back into its case, and they returned to base camp together. They hiked in silence, thankful for the downhill trek.

They arrived at camp to find a dozen reporters gathering at the edge of base camp, setting up tripods and camera equipment. "Chance? What's going on here?" Jean-René asked.

"The search team found something." Chance had a troubled expression on his face. Jean-René started past him, but his hand went up and landed in the middle of Jean-René's chest, stopping him in his tracks. "It isn't good."

"What?" Jean-René's brows knitted, and his balding head wrinkled up.

"They found ... *remains*," Chance said, as Bahati approached. "That's all I know. The sheriff is waiting for the medical examiner before they move the ... the uh ... the body."

Bahati slapped her hand over her mouth as she gasped into a wail. Her knees wouldn't hold her, but Jean-René caught her before she sank to the ground. "*Ma chéri.*" He lifted her up. "Don't panic. We don't know that it's one of our people."

"But ..." she started. She gathered her wits and took a deep breath, wiping her eyes and regaining her composure.

"Where's the sheriff?" Jean-René demanded. Chance raised a hand, pointing towards the swamp.

Jean-René ordered his daughter to remain in camp, and started for the swamp, with Bahati right behind him. They found the scene a mile south, surrounded by crime scene tape. Several of the sheriff's men milled about outside the barricade, while he knelt down in hip-boots, examining something under a sheet.

"I need to talk to the sheriff," Jean-René's said, scanning the crowd for someone in charge. His eye found his mark. He marched over to the man in the flat-brimmed hat. "Excuse me!" He started to lift the barrier tape, but a deputy stepped into his path, his hand going to his weapon. "I need to talk to the sheriff," Jean-René insisted.

The deputy stepped aside when the sheriff came over and put a hand on his shoulder. "I've got this, son," he drawled in his deep southern Oklahoma accent. "I told your folks I'd let you know when I found something. This isn't anything you need to see."

"Please," Bahati's voice broke as she came up behind her husband. That's all she managed, a desperate *please*. Her eyes spoke the volumes her voice couldn't manage.

"The body's in bad shape," he said. "Been here a *long* while." He scratched his chin. "Too long to be Lauren or the boys ... or Rowan for that matter."

"You'd be able to tell, if it was, right?" Jean-René asked, as desperate as his wife.

"You'd think," he smirked. "Couldn't tell you if it was a man or a woman, if the truth be told. Honestly, I don't need a medical examiner ... I need an ... an archaeologist."

"That old?" Bahati asked, as Jean-René put an arm around her.

"Rowan is an archaeologist. He has a Master of Science from the University of Cairo."

"Well, we better get back to work trying to find him. I could use a fella like that," the sheriff said, with a twinkle in his eye. "This mess here is just an old mystery for someone a lot smarter than me to try and solve. When we find Rowan, we'll give him a crack at it."

ROWAN SAT WITH HIS BACK AGAINST A LARGE POPLAR TREE. HE had his legs crossed. His arms were folded across his chest, tucked under his arm pits. He was hunched over, hunkered down with his brow drawn over his eyes, narrowed tightly over his nose. He sulked like an angry lump, dressed in calico and homespun.

Lauren hung back, leaning against a walnut tree, rolling a fallen nut beneath the toe of her doeskin boots. She said nothing, but stared at her foot, having to stick her toe out to see it over her belly. She rolled the nut again and cracked it, disrupting the silence of the woods. Rowan lifted his head to meet her gaze, his façade lightening ever so slightly. She took a few tentative steps towards her husband, stopping a few feet in front of him.

He squinted at her in the fading light of day as she gazed down at him. "Rowan," she started, but he stopped her.

"You don't have to say anything," he said. "I'm the idiot here. I realize that. I've been a complete fool and I've belittled you and your experience because I refused to evolve and understand your position … and what you've been going through." He rose and came over, taking her hand, pressing his stomach to hers. "I'm sorry. Can you ever forgive me?"

"Forgive what?" Lauren asked through the tears that rolled down her face. "You haven't done anything that needs forgiving. I know all of this is so fantastical, anyone would have a hard time believing it. I mean, if anyone just accepted all this on face value, I'd think they'd gone crazy, too."

Rowan leaned his forehead onto hers, and she could feel his breath meld with her own. She closed her eyes and held onto his belt to steady herself. "So, if we're in a different *time-place*, as Tsul'Kalu puts it, how do we get home?"

"We have to wait for the glyphs to be restored," she said. "Which reminds me …" she lifted her forehead off his. "There are some people you're going to want to meet."

"More Bigfoot?"

"Crusaders. Knights Templar," Lauren said. "Henry Sinclair, most notably."

"Henry Sinclair?" His brow lifted. "Wait. *The* Henry Sinclair?"

"In the flesh." Lauren affirmed.

"What in the hell?" he said emphasizing each word as she turned towards camp. He fell in behind her. "Now, this I gotta see."

~

THE CRUSADERS AND THEIR GUIDE WERE SITTING WITH Tsul'Kalu by the fire when Lauren led Rowan back into the clearing. The party had returned with a deer and had the animal spitted over the fire. The perfume of onions and herbs joined the aroma of the roasting meat. Lauren's mouth watered in response. Rowan stood studying them as he hesitated to enter the clearing. Their cloaks and tabards might have once been white, but they were soiled and the men appeared weary, even at first glance. Their beards were even more full than Rowan's, which hadn't been trimmed since before the trip to Everest.

Lauren nudged him and he realized everyone had turned to stare at him. He smoothed down his beard and straightened his shirt before he approached.

"Gentlemen," John Grayson said, glancing up at Rowan and Lauren as they approached. "My son, Rowan Pierce." He introduced him as Rowan hesitated. It was hard for him to believe that Tsul'Kalu, — this old man — this shape-shifting Bigfoot — was his father-in-law. The hand on his arm was reassuring but it made him sway. He felt the flutter of an echo against his ear drums. *You will understand*, Tsul'Kalu's voice filled his head.

The men rose off their haunches and turned to greet him. Henry Sinclair appeared startled to find a white man — a Scot, no less, —in the midst of natives, though the copper-headed children should have given it away.

Sinclair gave a polite bow. "By the blood," his brogue was thick and his tongue unfamiliar. But Rowan realized, *he understood*. He glanced at his father-in-law. The shapeshifting shaman of the Bigfoot Tribe gave him a knowing gaze. "I am your servant, sir," Sinclair had said.

Rowan wasn't sure how to respond to the greeting. Then he realized, if the story was true, this was Prince Sinclair, so Rowan returned the bow with equal formality. "Yours as well, m'lord."

"Ye're a Scot, good sir?" Sinclair asked. He seemed puzzled by Rowan's lack of an accent.

"Some generations back, yes," Rowan said. He hesitated to give them his whole ancestry. "I'm anxious to hear how you've come to this place." Rowan thought it best to deflect the attention from himself.

"Allow me to introduce my fellows," he said. "Then we'll tell the tale after we feast." He turned to the man on his right. "May I present, Laird Armstrong and Laird James Gunn, my most trusted men?" He continued, introducing the men who traveled with him. Not all wore the Templar garb.

"*Feasgar math.*" Armstrong bowed.

"Are ye kin tae the Bruce? Clan Pierce did ye no' say?" Gunn narrowed his eyes as Rowan extended a hand of friendship.

"Robert the Bruce?" Rowan lifted a brow cautiously.

"Aye." Sinclair eyed him a moment. "He does bear a striking resemblance tae the Bruce."

"I am told he is of some relation to me," Rowan said. "On my father's side." He glanced at Lauren nervously. "A ... distant cousin, I think."

"Were ye at Bannockburn then?"

"No," Rowan shrugged. "I've been here a while ... apparently." He exchanged sheepish glances with John, then his wife.

Lauren said something to her father Rowan couldn't understand. He had no gift for languages, despite all their travels. He could manage some broken Spanish and even a bit of Farsi, but not all the words he knew were nice ones.

"What does she say?" Gunn asked.

"She says," Rowan hesitated a moment and sensed the deception was for their benefit. "She says we should find our sons. They'll be hungry."

The native man in the furs made a snide remark. Rowan turned on him sharply. "Excuse me?" Rowan asked, certain he should take offense even though he hadn't heard the exact words.

He said something in his native language. Lauren's head whipped around, fire in her eyes. Rowan scowled but waited for answers. He knew he was offended. He just wasn't sure why. One of the crusaders said, "Ignore him."

A wicked grin showed the man's rotted teeth. Rowan had an idea that whatever the man said had been salacious and he wouldn't like it if he had understood it. Rowan turned on him, but Tsul'Kalu raised a hand, and Rowan stood fast, though his color took a moment longer to fade. "Go, find your sons. That one is a man of low moral character, unworthy to carry the garbage of these men. Do not let him goad you into anger. They will be judged as all creatures must be." Rowan was already turning to find his boys when he realized Tsul'Kalu hadn't spoken the words aloud. He'd heard them in his head. Now he knew what Lauren was talking about. Not only was her father a shapeshifting, time-traveling Bigfoot, he was telepathic. *Unfreakingbelievable.*

ROWAN FOLLOWED LAUREN TO THE EDGE OF THE RIVER, where she stopped and leaned over with her hands on her knees. "Are you all right?"

"Yes," she said. "My back is killing me though." Rowan came over and pressed his thumbs into the dimples just above her sacrum, knowing the right spot, even though he couldn't see them for her clothing. A deep sigh escaped her throat as he began to work his thumbs in radiating circles. He'd learned to do this from the midwife in Tibet, and found it provided her relief from several of the symptoms of pregnancy — from morning sickness to an aching back. "Oh, that's wonderful," she cooed as he worked his way up her spine.

"If I had my triage bag, I could give you a warm compress and some Tylenol to help, but this is the best I can offer."

"It will have to do," she said, straightening as his thumbs ran back down her spine and gave her hip bones one more circle, hearing the bones of her vertebrae popping back into place. "Though I am not excited about sleeping on the ground another night."

"How much longer will we need to stay here?"

"Just until the runes are restored." She'd said that before, but it provided him with little to go on.

"How long will that be?"

"They are the marks of the Sinclair, so perhaps that's what he's here to do," she said. "We just need to give them time to do it."

"Can't we just ask him to …" Rowan started to ask but stopped. "Not that easy, huh?"

She shook her head. "No. Not that easy."

"It never is." He sighed. Rowan took her arm and led her over to one of the large flat rocks that was just about right for her to sit down on, and then sat beside her. He glanced up at the tall sycamore tree that shaded him, thinking how much it was like the fallen tree Jamie had taken the header on just days before. "If they don't get on with it, I'm going to go in there and carve the runes myself," Rowan muttered under his breath. "I'm afraid to say this, but you look like you're ready to deliver any minute. I don't like it and I swear to God, I'm not prepared to deliver a baby in this … *time-place*." He used Tsul'Kalu's words.

"Don't be silly. I've still got several months to go." Lauren's hand went to her stomach. "Surely by then, we'll be out of here."

"So, do we know what they are doing out here?" Rowan asked.

Lauren had been eavesdropping on their conversations with Tsul'Kalu and she had an idea of what they wanted, but she didn't have enough details to understand why. She went on to explain to Rowan what she had heard. "They are on some kind of a quest," she said. "They didn't mention any details."

"Lauren, do you know the legends about Henry Sinclair?"

"That he was a Knight's Templar?" Lauren said. "We learned some of the Templar legends when we were preparing to go to Rennes-le-Château. I've read *The DaVinci Code*."

"I read it, too," Rowan said. "And what were the Templars trying to hide in the DaVinci Code?"

"The Holy Grail," Lauren said. "But according to Dan Brown, it wasn't the cup from the Last Supper, it was a child. He got the idea from a book called Holy Blood, Holy Grail. It said the child was the offspring of Jesus." She had read books on the subject. "It's a provocative theory, but the timing is all wrong. Henry Sinclair lived in the time of Robert the Bruce. He and his men returned from the Crusades in time to fight at Bannockburn. If Jesus had a child with Mary Magdalene, it would have been at least a thousand years before."

"You didn't happen to notice any of them drinking from a particular cup, did you?" Rowan said in jest.

"Haha," Lauren smirked. "Like in Indiana Jones."

"Come on," Rowan stood, and offered her a hand up, which she took. "Let's go find the boys."

THEY FOUND THEM A SHORT WHILE LATER, COMING OUT OF the cave. "Just what do you three think you're up to?" Rowan scolded. "You scared your poor mother half to death."

"We wanted to see if the runes were back," Jamie said.

"They weren't," Henry added.

"I hope it won't be much longer." John Carter yawned. "I'm ready to go home."

"Me too, sweetheart," Lauren said.

"Come on, boys. Dinner is waiting." Rowan rounded them up and herded them back down to camp.

AFTER DINNER, A BOTTLE APPEARED FROM KO'I MINCO'S PACK. When it appeared in front of Rowan's nose, he recognized the comforting burn of corn liquor. The boys were drawing in the sand with sticks, playing tic-tac-toe. Lauren was watching the storyteller. Rowan took a generous swallow of the proffered booze, thinking himself clever that no one was watching as he did. The burn hit the tip of his tongue and raced through his mouth and down his throat as he swallowed. It burned all the way into his gut, but it was a good burn.

When the bottle appeared in front of Lauren's nose, she recoiled, and passed it to Gunn, who declined. A fully pregnant woman in their day might have downed the whole bottle, but Lauren had been a tea-totaler since long before Henry was born. She didn't count the one margarita she'd allowed herself on her last non-pregnant-birthday. But Rowan noticed the Templars passed on the booze, too. It did little to dampen the jovial spirit of the evening, which turned out to be pleasant, albeit chilly.

Tsul'Kalu began the evening's story-telling, and Lauren sat back against the fallen tree to listen. Her mind's eye followed the story of *Uktena*. Tsul'Kalu pronounced it *Ook-Tay-Nah*. It was a legendary creature, a water serpent.

"Long ago, the Sun became angry at *The People* on Earth and sent a sickness to destroy them. The *Little Men* changed a man into a lake serpent — *Uktena*. They sent him to kill the Sun, but she would not die. They sent the rattlesnake to finish the job that *Uktena* could not complete, which made him so jealous and angry that *The People* became afraid of his wrath." The strangers — the boys, too — leaned in as he wove his tale. "Many warriors were sent to find and kill *Uktena*, but he always eluded them. To this day, the monster hides in the deepest waters of the lake, coming out in the pale light of the moon to consult with wise men and women who seek the magical beast for conjuring a spell to heal the sick or mend the injured. This is a story of the *Ani yun wi ya* as my grandfather told it to me." Tsul'Kalu ended.

The bottle came back to Rowan. He took another swig, tipping back the bottle again before handing it back to Ko'i Minco. Henry Sinclair across the fire nodded prepared to weave his tale. "Lang syne past, we too hae a grand beastie such as this," he said, his face glowing amber in the firelight. "The Kelpie."

Rowan nodded. "The Loch Ness Monster."

"Ye ken the tales of the water horse?" Sinclair seemed surprised.

"They are extraordinarily old legends," Rowan said. He didn't dare mention that he'd gone scuba diving in the loch trying to find the old kelpie, whose legends were much older than any of those sitting around the fire. The story of the Scottish cryptid was told long before it became known as the tale of the *Loch Ness Monster*. While more modern tales referred to it as something closer to a plesiosaur or sea dragon, the folk tales of the water horse were completely different. The horse was said to haunt the forests near Loch Ness, with its own saddle and bridle. The objects had great magical powers and kept the demon horse alive. Riders who thought they could catch it and tame the beast, were often drowned while trying to ride it. A Highlander decided to slay the monster.

"When he caught the beast and cut off its saddle and bridle, the beast begged for mercy and begged the Highlander tae give him back his magical items. When the man refused, the black horse chased him tae his home and gloated that he could no' take the items through the door," Sinclair told the tale. "Being clever, the Highlander threw them into the house through the window. Unable tae take revenge on the man, the beast fled, cursing, and swearing as it awaited death."

"Did he die?" Jamie asked, his lower lip stuck out.

"Ack, aye," Sinclair said. "And nay. Some said it transformed into a dragon and slipped beneath the waves. Others believe the demon beast wandered the forests and cursed anyone who tried tae catch it."

"Can a man catch it?" Young Henry eyed the Prince dubiously.

"There are ways," Sinclair said. "If ye come across the Kelpie wi'out tack, it is said ye can capture it with a halter stamped with the sign of the cross. But the beastie is a wiry one, and may appear as a dragon, or a horse, or even a pretty lass."

"Ew!" Jamie wrinkled up his nose.

"Some say the beast is the devil himself," Armstrong said curtly.

"Still, it's a good story," John Carter said. "Tell us another one."

"We have a legend about the wee folk, too," one of the men added, his brogue had the subtle lilt of the neighboring isle of Erin. "Lusty capricious beasties, they are. They stole m' shoes once."

"Ack, Paddy, he just took them tae mend," Gunn teased. "Leave a *bodhran* or a tin whistle on the stoop when ye get home, and he'll bring 'em back."

Rowan listened but was busily watching his wife as she leaned, her hand going to her growing stomach. The boys huddled around her, now attentive. They were laughing at the wild stories, having a high time listening to the tales. He'd told them about the Loch Ness Monster, of course. Henry had written a poem for one of his homework assignments about the beast. Rowan kept a copy of it in his wallet, though he didn't know where his wallet presently was. If it had been in his hip pocket — before he came to this *when* — he couldn't say for sure.

He glanced over and noticed Tsul'Kalu — John — gazing at him. Firelight danced in his eyes, and he had a beatific expression on his face as he chuckled at something one of the Templars said. Almost imperceptibly, his eyes darted to Lauren, as if directing Rowan's gaze. Rowan eyed his wife and notice her shifting uncomfortably. Jamie had curled up between her feet and lay with his head in what was left of her lap. Her hand went to her stomach again and she seemed to wince. Jamie's hand joined hers and rubbed her belly as if she were a pet.

Lauren seemed to melt as Jamie did, and he noticed both appeared to be growing drowsy. "The hour is late," Rowan said, as he rose with a nod to the Prince and to Lauren's father, before he collected his smallest son, then reached down to offer Lauren his hand.

She seemed surprised to see him standing over her. "What?" She blinked back the exhaustion engraved in her features.

"It's late," he said. "Time to turn in."

"But ..." she protested. "It's such a lovely evening ... and the stories are just getting started."

Rowan just gave her a knowing gaze, and she surrendered as Henry and John Carter popped up. "Come on, Mom," Henry said, taking her arm. It took all three of them to get her to her feet.

She turned to the company. "I'm sorry to leave you," she said. "Thank you for the stories."

The Templars rose and Prince Henry bowed. "Good night, Mistress Pierce. May God keep you and your family."

She returned the gesture. "Thank you, Lord Sinclair."

13

"That's it," Jean-René said, shaking his head. "We've done all we can. The Network is pulling the plug and we've been ordered out."

"Just because one camera man lost his footing and broke his arm?"

"He fell ten feet off the side of a cliff. It's a compound fracture, and he broke three ribs, too," Jean-René retorted. "Chance is going to be out of commission for months. They're taking him to surgery, and he's going to need months of physical therapy."

"But ..." Bahati was not happy. "We can't just leave the bosses here! What about the children?"

"They're not *here* anymore," Jean-René said, shaking his head.

"What do you mean?"

"They can't be *here,* or we would have found them." He scowled. He knew what he'd seen when Jamie had fallen. Lauren had *powers*. They all knew it, even though they never talked about it. He'd never seen her use those powers before, but now that he'd seen it, he was sure of it. He just wasn't sure the extent of her *abilities*. "We have to trust they will find their way to the road, flag down help. They'll make their way home or find a way to call."

"Where will we go, Dad?" Nyota had been silent through the whole crazy turn of events.

Jean-René realized his daughter had a point. California was too far. They needed to stay close. Lauren had disappeared before. He had to trust she would return when she could. They'd need to be here when that happened.

"Lauren's brother lives north of here," Jean-René said. "We'll go there. If Rowan and Lauren are able, they'll find their way to her family's home. I'm sure of it."

"How can you be sure?" Bahati asked.

Jean-René scowled and shrugged but did not answer. He turned and walked away, his shoulders slumped as he hung his head, and left his girls in the hospital waiting room.

THE TEAM PACKED UP ALL THE EQUIPMENT, AS JEAN-RENÉ HAD instructed. It would be sent back to headquarters in San Diego. The Network would sign for it, and move it to storage, along with the hundreds of hours of footage.

The weather had been nothing short of pleasant since Rowan had disappeared. It felt like summer again, and several members of the team bemoaned the fact that they were leaving just when the weather had cleared. "It'd be the perfect night for a Bigfoot hunt," someone said.

"Maybe we can come back …" Jean-René said, optimistically. "Someday."

The media storm around the disappearance of Rowan and Lauren Pierce and their sons wasn't the type of press the Network cared to receive, and they'd done as much as they could to downplay the mystery. There had been a press conference and one reporter was bold enough to ask if this were some kind of a glorified hoax to drive up ratings for the

Exploration Channel. Jacob, the head of the Network, had arrived that afternoon in a helicopter. He assured the media it was not a hoax, but it didn't seem to do much to soothe the suspicion amongst the cadre of reporters from every news outlet — reputable or not.

When the reporters became hostile, Jacob walked out from behind the mic and stopped in front of Jean-René and Bahati. "Get your stuff and get out of here. Don't talk to reporters. Don't answer any questions."

~

GEORGE — LAUREN'S OLDEST BROTHER — MET THEM ON THE porch, and welcomed them in, as if they were family. They were, as far as he was concerned. "No word?" he asked, somber-faced.

"None," Jean-René said.

"Come on." George waved them towards the kitchen. "I just made a pot of coffee." George always had a pot of coffee on. Folgers was the official drink of the Cherokee Nation's Tribal Fire Chief. He could drink it 24/7.

"Do you have any Coke?" Nyota asked, making a face at the thought of coffee. George reached into the fridge, handing her a red can of soda. She thanked him, as she took a seat at the table. Once the adults all had a cup of coffee, they sat and stared into their cups, silent and lost.

"Lauren ran away from home once," George said. "When she was six."

"Oh?" Nyota perked up. Her Aunt Lauren was one of her favorite people, but she rarely heard stories about her when she was a kid, so this was a rare treat.

"She didn't want to go to private school," he said. "Our mother had bought her a backpack, and all the supplies on the school's list, she even bought her a new dress and shoes."

"Aunt Lauren wore a dress?" Nyota wrinkled up her face.

She had just seen pictures of Lauren on the red carpet once, and she'd convinced herself the media had photoshopped them. She'd never seen a dress in Aunt Lauren's closet, not that she could remember.

"All the girls did," George said. "School uniform."

"Oh." Nyota had no idea what that meant, but she didn't question it further. Her Aunt Lauren had been her teacher for as long as she could remember, and the concept of going to school wasn't completely foreign to her but it was … different.

"She decided schools were where *evil wizards* tried to poison young people's minds, and that the Catholic teachers who ran them, were trying to steal Cherokee girls to sell them as brides. She ran away, vowing she would never go to their school."

"I found her down the river at the grocery store," he continued. "She'd broken open her piggy bank and had used the money to buy a couple of bottles of strawberry soda and a bag of chips. She planned on surviving in the woods, using her slingshot to shoot squirrels, but she needed a snack until she could get enough squirrels for a decent meal."

"How did you convince her to come home?" Nyota asked.

"I told her I would go to school with her and place a curse on anyone that tried to sell her as a bride. I would put a spell on any teacher who tried to poison her mind against her own People."

"And that worked?" Jean-René arched a brow.

"That, and I had to buy her some candy. She didn't have enough money for a chocolate bar, and she decided she'd rather have that than squirrel."

"That sounds like Aunt Lauren," Nyota grinned. "She'd do just about anything for a chocolate bar."

"So, what are you going to do?" George asked, directing the comment to the adults.

"There's not much we can do." Bahati sighed, her voice turning to a sob. "We have our orders."

"Which are?"

"Abandon the project and leave the search and rescue efforts to the experts."

George thought about this for a moment. "Who's leading the efforts?"

"The county sheriff," Jean-René said. "But the weather is supposed to turn again, and I'm afraid they'll call off the search."

"Well, that'll suck," George said, scratching his head. "But the sooner they call off their search, the sooner I can make some phone calls to my friends at the County Emergency Manager's office, and we can take over the search. We have a mutual aid agreement."

"Take over?"

"I'm the fire chief for the Cherokee tribe," he said. "I am the experts … and I have friends … friends with resources … and a mutual aid agreement. That means my friends at the Emergency Manager's office will help us."

It took a moment for Bahati and Jean-René to process the information, but the expression that spread across Nyota's face proved she'd figured it out before her parents had. "Can we come help?"

George shook his head. "No," he started. "I don't think so. I think its best that you follow your orders. My kids are all grown and out of the house, so there's room for you. You stay here, and if Lauren and Rowan do find their way out of the wilds of Southern Oklahoma, they'll come home."

"That's what we thought, too." Jean-René nodded.

"You should meet them here," George added. "If I find anything, I'll call you right away."

"Thank you, Uncle George." Nyota jumped out of her chair and tried to wrap her arms around the large mountain of a man. He put his arms around her, resting his head on hers.

"Of course, *Usyona*," he said.

"What does that mean?" She took a step back.

"It means *little star*," George said.

"My name means *star* in Swahili," she said, clearly delighted.

"Now you have a Cherokee name, too," George said.

"Thank you!" She beamed.

"Come on," George said, standing. "You can have my daughter's room. It used to be your aunt Lauren's. Jean-René, Bahati, you can have my oldest son's room. It's just down the hall. I'll help you with your bags and we'll get you settled."

14

Prince Henry sat across from the fire, inspecting his own hand. Lauren watched him covertly as she worked on weaving a basket. It was a skill her father had taught her. He had brought her stacks of green rushes and showed her how to bend and bind them. If she were doing it right, the basket would be tight enough to hold water.

Sinclair held his middle two fingers together and drew the forefinger of the one hand up his pinky, down between the middle of the two joined fingers and back up, then down the pointer finger. There seemed to be some meaning to this gesture, but Lauren's eye was drawn to his serious expression. His brows were clamped and his ruddy moustache twitched.

She studied his hands as he continued to trace the M over first one hand, then the other. His knuckles were cracked, and a bright red scar bisected the back of his hand. It must have been deep, and it couldn't be more than a few months old. Her eye went to the silver ring he wore. It was a *cross pattee* — a cross through a crown — inscribed with the words *In Hoc Signo Vinces*. It meant *in this sign thou shall conquer.* Lauren had seen a ring like that before. It was a Templar's ring from the time of the Crusades.

Prince Henry had the visage of a man who'd known the horrors of war, though he wasn't born until after the Crusades were over. He must have fought for his own life and almost lost. By the grace of whatever God — or gods in the universe — Fate had preserved him. The scars on his brow and across the back of his hand spoke of valor and strength. His strong brow and high Frankish nose spoke of his heritage. It occurred to Lauren for a moment that his bone structure was not dissimilar from her husband's, if not a bit more pronounced. His hair was lighter, more blond than ruddy, but clearly they were cut from the same cloth. Both were big-boned, hearty men of muscle and sinew weathered by labor. He wasn't at all what Lauren had expected a Prince to be, but he was every bit a Scot.

Lauren lowered her lashes as he lifted his head. She turned to find her children. The boys were playing nearby. Tsul'Kalu and Rowan had gone with the men to hunt, leaving Lauren and Prince Henry essentially, alone. She caught him watching her and a blush came to his cheeks. "Do ye ken the significance of the letter M, Mistress Pierce?" he asked, seemingly out of nowhere. Lauren realized the way he held his hand — his two middle fingers together, with his forefinger and pinky spread away. It was like an *M*. That was what he'd been tracing with his finger.

She wondered if she could make her own hands do that. She had no trouble with the *Live Long and Prosper* hand sign Mr. Spock had made so popular, but that seemed to be the opposite. "I've seen the statues and artwork in France and Scotland with the depiction of Jesus and Mary Magdalene with their hands like that, forming an *M*," Lauren said, as she worked on the basket. "In my husband's books," she corrected. A woman of this age would never have traveled to Europe. There were no pictures of these things, but there were etchings and drawings, and it would not be uncommon for a man like Rowan to have at least one book, maybe several. "But ... what does it mean?"

He held his calloused hand out and she could clearly see the *M* in the form. "*M* is the first letter for Mary ... and Magdalene." Lauren remembered the painting of George Washington in his masonic apron, his hands formed that same *M*. "It's the 13th letter of the alphabet. Do ye ken your letters, Mistress?"

"I do," she said, miffed that she had to find a way to explain why a Cherokee woman in antiquity would know the alphabet. *Should I tell him the truth*? she debated. "My husband taught me to read and write. I have learned many languages in our travels. My father has also learned this magic."

"You are a rare woman, Mistress Pierce," he said, admiration evident in his voice. "Did your husband tell any of the stories of our people?"

Lauren nodded. "Yes," she said. "Many of them."

"We serve an order called the *Sacred Heart of the Rose*. We are holy warriors committed to protecting an ancient secret."

"I know of your God," Lauren said. "Of the Son He sent to be a teacher."

"This is not the whole story," he said. "There is more the Pope in Avignon did not want revealed. It was a secret that gave my brothers and those who came before me a power over Kings and even the Pope himself. You ken what a Pope is, aye?"

"Yes. He is the chief of your church."

"On a day called Friday, the 13th ... many years before I was born ... in the age of my grandfather, the leader of our order was arrested and most of our brothers were slaughtered. Since, this day has been considered cursed."

"Ancient Sumerians have their own legends about this date, too," Lauren said before she could stop herself.

Sinclair lifted a brow. "Do tell, Mistress Pierce."

"The Sumerians considered the number thirteen to be a

perfect number, and that thirteen was most certainly not unlucky." Lauren glanced up at him from under her lashes. "Yet, some say an ancient book of law," Lauren hesitated, deciding not to mention that it was called the *Code of Hammurabi*. It wasn't discovered until the late 1800s. The Templars wouldn't have known about it. "This ancient law may or may not have omitted a 13th rule from its list. I have not seen this book for myself, so I cannot say if this is true."

She had, in fact seen the book for herself, but he didn't need to know this. "This is a story we learned from a traveler we passed some years ago."

A cautious grin spread across Sinclair's bearded face. "Aye, ye are a rare, learned woman," he said, beaming. "When our Order's leader — Jacques De Molay — was taken hostage, he was tortured for months. His hands were bound so tightly that the blood pooled in the tips of his fingers. He was placed into a pit no wider than his feet." Lauren cringed but Sinclair continued. "He was stretched on a rack until his joints separated and his ligaments tore. His feet were dipped in oil and held over a fire until the flesh fell from the bones. It broke this man so badly that he confessed to false charges, but he never revealed the sacred secret he carried with him to the pyre."

"Horrific, Lord Sinclair." She shook her head. "My heart breaks that such cruelty exists in your world."

"They might not have suffered such fate had the King not owed the Templars so much money," he said. "Or had they not held the secret over the King ... and the Pope. By 1307, when the Templar Order fell, the *Sacred Heart of the Rose* had already been secured but was thought lost when it was taken by an order of Saracens called the *Asāsiyyūn's Guild*. They vowed they would capture our treasures. The promised to take them to the Holy Lands ... to have them burned ... destroyed." The words seemed to hurt. The pain was present in the lines on his face, and deep in his blue eyes.

"The Sacred Heart? The heart of ... Mary Magdalene?"

He shook his head and lifted his eyes to her. "No, Mistress Pierce," he said. "Not the Heart of Mary ... the heart of her child ... the offspring of Mary and Our Lord. They had a daughter ... called Sarah."

Lauren hadn't been expecting that. It startled her so much her breath sucked in audibly before she could stop herself, a foot catching her in the ribs at the same moment. Her hand went to her side as she recovered her composure.

"Aye." He was silent for a moment. "I dinnae ken why I even told ye. But ... I sense ye can be trusted."

She held his gaze, as if to assure him she could be trusted and that his faith was well placed. "Tell me more," Lauren said. "What happened to your Order's chief?"

"After seven years of suffering, Sir De Molay wasn't just burned at the stake ... he was roasted alive like a stag." He swallowed hard. "All to extend his suffering." He took a deep breath and let it out in a trembling sigh. He picked up a stick the boys had been using the night before. He used it to make a mark in the sandy ground beside the fire. "Do ye ken this symbol, Mistress?" Lauren did, but she didn't want to admit it. "It's a sign from an ancient language, 'tis called the *hooked X.* Some would translate it as a sacred symbol. This line is for our Lord, this line is for his Bride ... and this line?" He pointed to the hook. "This ... is for the Lady Sarah, who was raised in secret outside the Holy Land ... by my own ancestors ... in Scotland."

Lauren nodded, not sure what to say as she tried to reconcile his words with the different versions of the story she'd heard. "Safe from the *Asāsiyyūn's Guild,*" she said, taking up her basket again, to divert the conversation while she processed. She fumbled with the strips of grass as she tied off the last row of her basket, tucking the ends into the row before it, weaving the tail into the layers so it lay hidden. She shifted and got to her feet, with great effort. Sinclair rose and started to reach for her catching her arm but stopped short. "Thank you, I'm fine," she retracted her arm from his grasp, in respect of his Templar Code.

"Mistress?" His eyes searched hers. "Are ye well?"

"I'm fine," she assured him. "I grow restless as my time to deliver grows closer. Shall we walk, my Lord?"

"Of course." He nodded.

She stretched her sore back, then turned to the boys who played nearby and called them over. "Come with us, you can play in the meadow." The boys ran on ahead as they left the camp. "Tell me more about your ancestors," she said as he allowed her to pass along the narrow trail.

"There were a line of kings in ancient times," he began. "The Kings of the Franks. They ruled in Europe from the borders of the Visigoths to the Kingdom of the Lombards, and all through Bavaria to the Saxon borders in the north."

"The Merovingians defeated the Visigoths in the year 507," Young Henry said, running back to the Prince and his mother. "They conquered most of Gaul."

Sinclair seemed a bit taken aback by the boy's knowledge. "The sons of Merovech were sometimes referred to as the long-haired kings," he said. "They could not cut their hair if they were to rule, ye ken."

"I've never cut my hair," John Carter said, running around the adults in a circle. "Have I, Momma? I'm going to grow it out until it is as long as my Uncle Michael's." John Carter admired his Uncle Michael, though he hadn't seen him since he was little. Lauren's brother had been called to serve the gods, and to prepare for a great conflict between the forces of good and evil. Enlil, also known as *the Dark One* had been bound and cast into the pits of Hell, but Michael had not returned. Lauren could only assume the threat might still exist, even though she'd been the one to bind the demon, thanks to Michael's divine intervention.

"Remember the tail of the *water horse* I told?" Sinclair asked the boys.

"My dad saw the kelpie!" Jamie chirped. "He said it was a nice beast. Didn't try to eat him or anything!"

Sinclair exchanged a glance with Lauren who rolled her eyes, as if that explained everything. Boys were boys after all. Even a prince knew that. The Prince continued his tale. "There was a book called the *Chronicle of Fredegar* that told of the founding of the Merovingian line of kings. It was said they were descended from such a sea-beast. King Chlodio was staying on the seaside one summer when his wife went to the sea to bathe at midday. There a beast called a *Quinotaur* found her, and she was made pregnant by it. She gave birth to a son who was called *Merovech*. From him, came all the kings of the Franks and were called *Merovingian*."

The boys raved about how cool that was, then ran off without asking for details, much to their mother's relief. "That was in 496," he said to Lauren. "But there are tales told behind hands and in whispers that are much older. To be spoken aloud within earshot of the Church would be considered ... *heresy*."

"There is no need to whisper here, my Lord," Lauren said. "You are among friends. Your secrets are my secrets."

Henry seemed relieved. He reached up and moved a branch for Lauren to pass along the narrow trail. "When Our Lord was nailed to the cross, his wife wept at his feet, alongside his mother. Months later, her *condition* was growing difficult to conceal." His eye went to Lauren's belly. She blushed, as her hand ran over the swell. "The Disciples feared for the Bride's safety, as well as the safety of Our Lord's Blessed Mother. They escaped, first to Ephesus in Turkey. Here, they lived, and the Magdalene gave birth to a daughter. Some years later, Our Lord's Blessed Mother took her last breath and she ascended into Heaven to be reunited with her son. The Bride, under the protection of the last disciple took her child and fled to Cypress. Our Lord's Bride is mentioned in the Bible thirteen times," he said, as if it was an afterthought. "Did ye ken that?"

"I did not," Lauren said, her hands going to her aching back as she waddled along the path.

"She was considered the thirteenth Disciple. *Mary Magdalene* has thirteen letters."

This significance was not lost on Lauren. She knew from her own recent investigations that thirteen was a significant number. The Free Masons considered it significant as well. There were thirteen original colonies, thirteen stars on the original US flag, thirteen red and white stripes on the flag. Even on the back of a one dollar bill, there were thirteen levels of stone on the pyramid, thirteen oak leaves, thirteen stars over the eagle, thirteen arrows in the eagle's clutches. There were thirteen stripes on the crest and thirteen letters in *E Pluribus Unum.* It was a common theory that the Templars and the Masons were one in the same.

Sinclair studied her for a moment. She could feel his eyes drilling into her soul. *How could she say what she wanted to share? How could she do it without him thinking she was a madwoman?* "The People," she started, but hesitated. "Among my people, we believe signs and *visions* are gifts of the spirits, and that the heavens and the earth are two sides of the same world. I have seen a vision of an eagle with thirteen feathers, and thirteen arrows in its talons. I have seen a shining city on a hill, with a temple that is thirteen levels tall. There, mankind will make peace ... and war. Here, a flag with thirteen stars will come as a symbol of this land." She nodded towards the white banner with the red cross leaning against the tree. "There will be red and white stripes of the same number."

Sinclair stopped and froze as they stood at the base of the trail that led to the cavern above. "Red and white, ye say?" He glanced down at his own tabard, his hand clutching the middle of it. His long thumb stroking the gold embroidered rose centered there. Lauren glanced up and realized what had caught his eye. One of the trees on the rise had a branch that had broken and fallen sideways, creating a cross. The sky beyond the rocky slope had turned red as flame as the afternoon faded into evening. "So ye're a *seer* then, a *charmer?*" His voice had taken on an air of wonder. A beam of sunlight broke through the clouds, illuminating his face with what some might describe a holy light. His blue eyes glistened as tears seemed to well within.

"Something like that," Lauren said, glancing back up at the broken tree.

Lauren wondered if he had been searching for a sign. If he were, she had to believe this could be it. He dropped to one knee and crossed himself, bowing his head. His prayers weren't audible, but she caught bits and pieces as he prayed. She recognized it as a prayer of thanks — in Latin.

"Mistress Pierce," he said. "*Ye shall remember all the ways in which the Lord your God hath led ye in the wilderness these forty years, that He might humble ye, testing ye, to know what was in your heart, whether ye would keep His commandments or no'.* Aye, it seems forty years since we left our home …"

Lauren recognized the Bible verse. Deuteronomy 8:2. "*I have humbled you, and in your hunger He gave you manna to eat, which neither you nor your fathers had known, so that you might understand that man does not live on bread alone, but on every word that comes from the mouth of the Lord.*" It was another section of the same book but seemed like the appropriate answer to his verse.

Prince Henry turned, still on his knee, taking both of her hands in his, though he'd avoided touching her before. "*And an angel appeared to him in the wilderness of Mt. Sinai, in the flame of a burning thorn bush* … for surely you are the angel we seek, Mistress."

Lauren took a step back, her hands slipping from his as she realized what he was implying. "I am no angel, my lord."

"I hae been a faithful and obedient servant these years. When m' grandsire gae me my missive, I asked few questions beyond how. He assured me God would provide. I have kept my fears and doubts to m'self, even when we were hungry, and thought for sure our God had abandoned us. We were promised a land of plenty, where we would find a safe place where God would provide for all our needs. I was told an angel would be here to show us the way."

"Please," Lauren gasped. "I am no angel."

"How do you … a *heathen* woman … ken the words of our Holy Bible? How do ye know of our sacred stories and know the Words of God?"

"I am an educated woman, sir." She moved past him, turning her back, her mind racing to explain. "My husband and I made our home in the west. There, we have many books. I have read them all. We talk about the miracles of Jesus, and the redemption of the Holy Land over our supper. We have read the Torah and the writings of Buddha. My sons, too, are educated. Is it so hard to conceive that a woman need not be an angel to know the words of your sacred books?"

He considered her for a moment as she leaned against a tree, stretching her aching back. "Perhaps no," he conceded as he turned to face her. "But we came in search of a sign. We were told we would find an angel … and we *have*. Praise God in all His Glory!"

15

The boys had been sent to bed already, and Lauren was relieved to find them sound asleep in their furs around the fire. Rowan came in behind her, exhausted by the effort of the day's hunt. His belly was full of fresh venison and raw liquor. Lauren had returned to camp after her visit with Prince Sinclair, to find the basket she had just made, filled with corn, squash, and beans. She prepared a rugged succotash to go with their meal and the feast had been a pleasant one.

She hadn't had a chance to tell Rowan about her conversation with Sinclair, and as tired as she was, she'd already decided it could wait 'til the morning. Her back had been bothering her and her feet were swollen. All she wanted to do was rest. Still, her mind was a whirl with everything she had learned from Sinclair today.

Lauren helped Rowan out of his shirt and breeches and got him settled into their furs before she managed to get down and sit on the bedding beside him, leaning on him to ease the ache in her back as she set to untying her braid. Tsul'Kalu had given her a comb crafted from a bit of elk's horn. She set to work patiently combing out her long hair.

"When a Cherokee woman is troubled, she combs her

hair," she said, as much to herself as to Rowan. "As she combs the snakes from her hair, her troubles are loosened and allowed to escape her mind so she can sleep in peace."

Rowan's hand found its way into her hair, petting her gently. She melted into him sinking down beside him, too tired to undress. She lay her head onto his shoulder and rolled over onto her side, as he drew the furs up over her, tucking her into the circle of his arms, his hand cradling her stomach, feeling the child within her hiccupping.

"Why so troubled, my Princess ... my *Deja Thoris*?" he asked, his voice heavy. She could smell the liquor on his breath.

"I think I've been having contractions off and on all day," she said. "Probably Braxton-Hicks, but ... I'm worried that it's not."

"You said it yourself. You're not due for months ..." he said. "You just need to rest."

"We need to go home," she said. She caught his hand and pressed it to the side of her stomach, where a small foot or fist pressed against her. "Soon."

"How do we get Sinclair to restore the runes?" he asked.

"I think I may be close to answering that," she said, and told him everything.

"You don't think he's got the Holy Grail, do you?" They both knew the legends of Templars bringing the Grail to the Americas even before Columbus discovered it. He knew about the Kensington Rune Stones, and the Westford Knight.

Lauren shrugged, a foot catching her in the ribs, just above Rowan's hand. She winced and his hand moved to the spot, as if to calm the child. "I can't imagine how it feels to have a baby inside you," he sighed, sleepily.

"It's weird and wonderful, and completely exhausting," she said as her stomach tightened beneath his hand.

"Have you been drinking enough water?" he asked.

"Probably not," she said. "I've been drinking a lot of tea."

"Where'd you get tea?"

"I have no idea," she said. "It's like it just appears. I've noticed with Tsul'Kalu that things seem to appear when they're needed. Apart from the game the hunters brought to our fire, most of the meals I've had here have just always … been there."

"The mighty conjurer Tsul'Kalu is quite the chef." He yawned.

"I wish he could conjure me a cheeseburger," she mused. She hadn't had cravings with this pregnancy. She was happy with the simplest of meals. Heartburn had become her steady companion, so the blander, the better.

"When we get home, I'll take you to get one," he said.

"Home? As in Hawai'i-home, or Tahlequah-home? Or San Diego-home?"

"Wherever you want to be," he said. "We were going to take some time off when the baby came anyway, so if we need to take a break, we'll take a break."

"You may have to finish the season without me." Lauren sighed. "I feel like my belly button is a turkey timer, and it's popped already."

"Are your feet swollen?" he asked.

"No more so than with any of my previous pregnancies." She sighed.

"Just relax and get some sleep, honey." Rowan kissed her head. "Maybe tomorrow we'll see if Sinclair has the Grail. Then he can make his mark and we can go home." His voice trailed off.

She lay listening to the sound of him sawing logs, her back aching, and her muscles contracting every ten or fifteen minutes, if she had to guess. She waited until she was certain he was sound asleep, and lifted his arm off of her, sneaking out from under it. He grumbled in his sleep and rolled over, turning his back to her as she slipped out from under the furs and got up, adding wood to the fire. The fire never seemed to die.

It was like Tsul'Kalu's magic food. There was always wood, and there was always fire.

Lauren found an extra fur and pulled it over her shoulders to ward off the night's chill. She paced around the fire, stopping to stretch her back then went to the entrance of the cave and gazed out over the densely-wooded valley. She could see the wisp of smoke rising from the fire at the camp where Tsul'Kalu and the Templars were still telling stories.

"Why are you not sleeping?" The shaman's mind found her in the dark.

"My back hurts," she admitted. "I think I'm having contractions." She responded in similar fashion.

"Drink some tea," he said. "You'll feel better."

Lauren turned, finding a cup by the fire. "*Wado*." Lauren thanked him as she took the cup outside and found a rock to sit on. With the fire well-tended, the cavern was now too warm. It was humid, too. The cool night air felt nice on her hot cheeks. She sipped the tea and gazed up at a sky full of stars.

"You need to go back to your own *time-place*," Tsul'Kalu said.

"I think so, too," she said, glancing down at her stomach. "This is all happening too soon."

"It's never too soon to go home." That wasn't what she meant, but she let it go.

"Is it ever too late?" She thought sadly. She'd just found him, and she wanted to know more. She wanted to spend time with her *father*. She'd hated him for leaving her. Her whole life she'd thought he left because of her.

"Ah, little curious one." She could hear him in her head. "The problem with time is we think we have enough, but few have any command of how to make the most of the time they are given."

"So, you're not immortal?" She'd always thought of Tsul'Kalu as infinite.

"No," he said in a low tone. "This too, is not my time-place, and I must return to my own world soon. Just as you must return to yours."

"Will you ever come back to my *time-place*?" Lauren sighed, sipping her tea. She wanted him to, but she realized it wasn't so much for herself, as it was for her mother. Diana needed to know. They needed time to make amends. She needed just once, to see her mother — and father — together and happy. They deserved to be as happy as she was with Rowan.

For too long, she had not had a kind thought for her mother, and when she realized it, she felt a lightening in her heart she'd never felt before. It was true her brothers would be happy to see him but imagining the expression on Diana's face brought a tear to her eye.

"Someday. There will be a poet who says *you can't go home*," he sighed. "I do not know if he is right, but I am not sure your mother will be happy to see me. I fear too much time has passed."

"You can always come and see me," Lauren said. "I don't care how much time has passed." A deep yawn overtook her, and she felt heavy-lidded.

"Sleep now, little one," he said. "There is time enough for dreams."

"Have you learned anything from Sinclair and his men?"

"I have learned much," he said. "Tomorrow, I will tell you all about it."

"Tell me now," Lauren insisted. "And I will tell you what I have learned."

She could sense the shaman laughing. "Tomorrow will be soon enough."

~

Lauren was awake a while longer. But she lay down and snuggled next to Rowan, getting comfortable before she closed her eyes. She allowed sleep to wash through her and take her deep into the world of shadows. Dreams came in bits and pieces, with vivid images of things she couldn't remember when she woke, sometime before dawn.

The fire had faded but still crackled, and the cave was chilly. She lay listening to Rowan's breathing next to her, comfortable and drowsy. Her lids closed and she sighed, slipping back into the night.

"Momma?" A small voice brought her back before she was completely under. She lifted her head and reached into the dim light, finding Jamie's hand. "I'm cold."

Lauren lifted her covers, allowing him to climb into the circle of warmth beneath the furs. She felt at peace as he lay with his head on her arm, nestled in her hair as he patted her tummy and curled himself around it. She lay brushing his hair with her fingers, content as she remained sandwiched between her husband and her youngest son.

She hadn't expected to fall back to sleep, but she did. She slept long and hard. It was late morning when she emerged from the cave like a momma grizzly after a long cold winter. Her hair was disheveled, and she felt out of sorts when she found Rowan on the path to the river. She didn't usually wake up so bleary-eyed, especially this late in the day.

"You okay?" He caught her by the upper arms and steadied her.

"Weird dreams," she muttered, pressing past him.

He stood, frozen in his tracks. Lauren was even more irritated when he dashed down the trail to get ahead of her, and stood, blocking her path with his wide shoulders. "You don't seem yourself this morning, Lauren."

"I need coffee," she grumbled, and started to move past, but he stood fast. She glared at him with hazy eyes, and a wicked scowl. "Coffee. Now."

"I haven't seen coffee since we got here," Rowan said, watching her for signs of disorientation. "Have you?"

She didn't answer, but turned and started in the opposite direction, stumbling. He jumped forward and caught her, averting a bad fall as he yanked her back into his arms, holding her up. "Honey, this isn't like you."

John approached along the path from the camp. "Trouble?" he asked, with a bemused expression.

"I just want a damn cup of coffee!" She shouted at the top of her lungs, collapsing in tears as she turned into Rowan's arms. He collected her into him, running his hand along her disheveled hair as he wrapped an arm around her.

"Believe me, honey," Rowan said. "I'd get you a cup if I could." He patted her back, turning to John for answers, but the wise old shaman just shook his head sympathetically. "How much longer before we can go back to our own *time-place*?" Rowan asked him.

"It won't be much longer now, but I have some things to tell you, son," he said. "Perhaps Lauren should rest." Her father came over and took her arm, and she leaned on him as he led her, without protest, back to the cave. A cup of tea waited for her, and he sat her down and made sure she drank it, before he allowed Rowan to tuck her back into her bed. Without protest, she drifted back to sleep.

ROWAN LEFT HER TO REST. HE FOUND HER FATHER AT THE camp fire, banking the embers to preserve them for later. When John rose from the fire. Rowan stood behind him with his hands on his hips. "I need some answers," Rowan demanded. "What's going on with her? What's in that tea?"

John seemed nonplused. "The tea is mostly peppermint and rose," he said. "With a bit of lemon balm to help her sleep. I assure you, it's perfectly safe. Lauren is experiencing temporal displacement syndrome. It should lessen once she rests. This is the bane of those who are not bound by time and place. Those who *travel* must do so with caution. Repeated *time-shifts* can cause a wide range of illnesses. It can be as difficult on the mind as it is on the body. It is easy for *travelers* to lose their way. Fortunately, my daughter is strong." Rowan deflated, glancing back in the direction of the cave. He wanted to go to her and lay beside her. He wanted to hold her while she slept, but John motioned for him to follow. Rowan found it difficult to refuse his father-in-law.

"Our visitors from the Sunland say they came here because of a legend," Tsul'Kalu said. "They tell many stories, but not all of their words are true."

Rowan fell in beside him. "But, they *are* Templars?"

"The last of their kind," Tsul'Kalu nodded. "They have come a great distance for a legend."

"What are they searching for? The Holy Grail?" Rowan asked, in jest, but John glanced back over his shoulder at his son-in-law.

"You know their story?" Tsul'Kalu seemed surprised.

"Yeah," Rowan said. "Well, there are many versions of the legend."

"Ah." John shrugged and continued on his way down the path.

"All the legends about Sinclair's supposed trip to the *New World focus* on him coming to the east." Rowan paused. Lauren's father did as well, turning back. "But, this far west? I mean the Kensington Rune Stone, yes. The Westford Knight, sure, but Oklahoma?"

"History may need to be re-written." John shrugged.

"Won't we mess up the *time-space* continuum?"

John, surprisingly, seemed to get the joke. "But what if you correct a mistake in history?"

Rowan opened his mouth for a quick retort, but stopped, his jaw dropping slack. He paused a moment, reflecting on the question. He made as if to answer again but stopped short a second time before his hands went to his hips and he shook his head and shrugged.

"You say you know of Sinclair's story," John started.

"Which version?" Rowan continued to follow as the shaman turned to lead him down a path he had never taken. Rowan knew better than to question the wise man about where they were going. John bade him follow, so he followed.

"Which do you prefer?"

"I think it's unlikely that they were hiding the unknown bloodline of Jesus." Rowan shook his head. "That's the conspiracy theorists' version of the legend. I'm not sure about the whole Priory of Sion or the DaVinci Code version of events. Based on what I know from my studies, I do think the ancient Scots could have navigated to the North American continent and explored. Sinclair was said to have traveled to the Americas with three-hundred men on three separate ships. But there are less than ten men traveling with him now, not counting their guide. They might have even gotten back across the Atlantic, though a southerly route would make more sense for their return trip, at least based on what I know about the currents and trade winds ... which isn't much."

"Why would they come?" John asked. "Why would they leave their home to travel to an distant place, filled with known and unknown dangers?"

"Explorers don't need a reason," Rowan said. "I know that from experience ... other than being curious about the journey and what lies beyond. That's been enough to get me to pack up my bags, hop on a boat and hit the high seas more than once." He thought of his scuba diving trips with his friend Pau in

Hawai'i, or the Cousteau twins in the Mediterranean Sea. He had traveled the Nile, the Amazon and even the Mississippi River because it seemed like a good idea at the time, and he had hoped to find answers to questions he'd never imagined he would ask.

"This is true," John said. "But I have spoken with these men at length, and the one thing I discern to be true, is that their words are false ... at least when it comes to their explanation of why they are here."

Rowan's head tilted like a hound who'd just heard a sound out in the yard. "Huh?"

"I have a sense," he said. "That they have not revealed their true purpose in this land, and I think I know why."

"You think they already have the Holy Grail?" Rowan's brow shot up like a rocket.

"I didn't say that," John said.

"But you implied it," Rowan said, grinning like a Cheshire Cat.

"It is my intent to imply that they are not being truthful, and I am not sure that it is wise to trust them, especially their guide."

Rowan paused, deflated. "If you don't trust them ... neither do I."

MIDMORNING FOUND THE BOYS IN THE MIDDLE OF A STAND OF blackberry bushes, covered from elbow to fingertip in scratches and berry juice. Jamie's face and teeth were stained a dark purple. Henry and John Carter were just slightly better. They lay in the afternoon sun, with bellies full of the sweet fruit.

"Did you leave any for the bears?" Rowan chortled, glancing over the bushes, finding them barren of fruit.

A basket of dark fat berries sat on a rock nearby and

Henry grinned. "We picked some for Mom," he said. "Maybe she will make us a pie."

"Is Momma okay?" Jamie asked.

"She's resting," Rowan said.

"Well, what have we here?" Ko'i Minco wandered out of the trees. He sauntered over to the basket, and took a handful, tossing back a couple of berries. Juice ran down his chin. His teeth were instantly stained. They were already in bad shape, but the berry juice didn't help any.

Jamie rose, boldly. He ran over and snatched the basket away, holding it behind him as he backed up to his father and grandfather. "Those are for our momma to make a pie with."

Rowan put a hand on his shoulder, his eyes narrowing at the man who seemed ripe for conflict. The fact that John didn't trust him was provocative, at best. Rowan was still coming to grips with Tsul'Kalu — John — being a time-traveling Bigfoot that was a shape-shifter, who just happened to be his own father-in-law. *Where did we fall off into the Twilight Zone?* he wondered.

Sinclair appeared along the trail from camp, and approached, seemingly aware of the tension between the men. "Now, see here, fella," Rowan said, but hesitated. "You've come a long way, seemingly for nothing. We've been traveling for a while ourselves, and we'd be happy enough to see you on your way, unless there's something you'd like to tell us."

Sinclair moved closer where he could step in between them, if necessary. "Ye hae been a fine host," he said, his expression hardening as he made eye-contact with the guide. "But we hae nae been the kindest of guests. Forgive us for takin' advantage of your hospitality. We best be on our way, come morning."

"I think that would be best," Rowan said, catching John's concerned expression.

～

A pot of stew bubbled over the fire where Lauren sat. With a skilled hand, she worked a ball of dough in a wooden bowl. She stared into the fire. She did not stir when Rowan approached. He hesitated but came to sit down beside her.

"Feeling better?" he asked.

"Yes," she said. "It's been a long time since I spent the day in bed. I must have been tired."

"How's your back?"

"It's okay," she said, with an indifferent lift of her shoulder.

They sat in silence for a moment, as she sprinkled flour onto a flat piece of wood

"I have a bad feeling," he said, without preamble.

She turned and arched a questioning brow. "Oh?"

"Sinclair seems to be a genuine enough guy, but that man with him, Ko'i Minco? I don't trust him."

"What do you think we should do?" Lauren's gaze returned to the fire. She seemed numb.

"I'd send you home if I could," he said, his thumb grazing his lower lip as he thought aloud.

"If Henry and I could do it, we'd have gone home already," she said.

"I know," he said, watching as Lauren tore off hunks of the dough, and rolled them into small balls, then pressed them flat and lay them on a hot rock that sat on the coals. The dough sizzled and the perfume of baking bread wafted around her.

"Watch and wait, I guess." Rowan shrugged, no longer interested in the Templars — or their secrets. His stomach growled and his mouth watered. He was ravenous and impatient for the moment when the first tortilla came off the stone. It was golden brown with darker spots seared into it.

"More of your father's magic?" he asked. She lay it on a woven mat and passed it to him.

"This is my magic," she said. "Though the ingredients must be the work of Tsul'Kalu."

She set to work on a second ball. "There's butter in the crock over there." She nodded towards the flat stone where she'd set up the rest of the dinner's accompaniments. Rowan found a wooden paddle by the container and smeared the hot bread with the golden butter. The rustic tortilla was the most exquisite thing he had ever tasted, and when she handed him a second, he took it without reservation. He slathered it with butter, too.

He brought it back over and sat down beside her, placing a hand on her knee as he devoured his prize. "You are the most amazing thing I have ever seen in my life." He sighed as he chewed and swallowed with relish.

She seemed pleased by his response. "Do you like it?"

"I do," he said, chewing. "So good."

She handed him a third piece, and he buttered it, but handed it back. "You need to eat more than I do," he insisted. She accepted it, folding it in half, then in half again before taking a bite.

"Mmm." She licked her lips, catching a trickle of butter on her chin with her thumb, sucking it off as she patted out another tortilla. "That is good."

16

"Momma," Jamie said after dinner. "Can we go down to the meadow and get some more blackberries?" Somehow, there hadn't been enough left when it came time to make a cobbler, and the boys had been fretting over that fact all evening.

"Sure," she said, standing. She stretched out her back. "We could take a walk and stop by the meadow on our way back," she suggested, knowing her boys were as restless as she was.

"I'll go with you," Rowan started to get up. "Your mom should rest."

"No," Lauren said, knowing the evening's entertainment was about to begin. "I feel much better. A walk would be nice. You stay and keep our *guests* company."

Rowan cast her a cautious gaze. "We'll be fine," she insisted. "Don't drink too much."

Lauren got up with effort and herded her boys away from the camp.

∾

IT WAS STILL MID-EVENING, AND SHE'D OVERHEARD SINCLAIR talking with his men before dinner. He said something about turning in early because they were going to journey on in the morning. After having caught up on her sleep, and feeling human again, she wouldn't rest any time soon, and she knew the exercise would help ease her troubles.

They walked for a while, meandering through the woods on a narrow animal trail. The evening was cool and calm, and the birds were chirping a raucous cacophony in the trees. A squirrel darted across the trail, jumping up the trunk of one of the large birches pausing to turn and chitter at the boys who were making far too much noise for its liking.

"Momma." Jamie had her hand and was leading her at a faster pace than she was comfortable walking. "Did Henry tell you we found a treasure chest?"

"A what?" Lauren paused, as Henry turned and glowered over his shoulder at his little brother.

"A treasure chest," he said. "It's like a pirate lost his booty."

John Carter snorted. "You said *booty*."

"That was supposed to be our little secret, *numbskull*," Henry scolded.

"If there's a diamond necklace in it, I'm going to give it to Momma." Jamie ignored his brothers, as he picked up his feet over a fallen sapling. "Maybe there are pearls in it. Which do you like better, Momma? Diamonds or pearls?"

"I don't know that I have a preference," she said, dumbfounded by this revelation, unable to process how to ask all the questions running through her mind. "I like both." Lauren was debating how she was going to manage this situation. The boys had clearly been up to something while she was napping, and she was trying to decide if she should be mad. Then it occurred to her, they might not be joking. She stopped and turned to Jamie. "Where did you find that treasure chest?" she asked.

"It's a secret," Jamie said, his bright eyes darting to Henry.

Lauren stopped, letting go of his hand, folding her own onto her hips. "I think the cat is already out of the bag, son," she said. "Where is it?"

Jamie stopped, taking a step back, closer to John Carter. "But ..."

"Come on, Mom," Henry said. "I'll show you."

"Henry," John Carter and Jamie moaned in unison.

"The jig is up boys." Henry shrugged. "Remember what Dad says?"

"If Mama ain't happy, ain't no one happy?" Jamie asked.

"Well, he does say that, but he also says it's better to *fess up when you mess up*."

"Yeah," Lauren said. "Time to fess up." She couldn't remember hearing Rowan say that one, but she didn't put it past him. He was always inventing clever little sayings with the boys, and she had to admit, that one was rather good.

Henry led the way, deeper into the trees as the trail narrowed significantly. Branches snagged in her hair and pulled it from the plait she'd patiently woven into it earlier in the day. Something was in her shoe, and she could feel bugs — probably ticks — crawling into her boots and up her legs. As much as it grossed her out, the idea of letting Rowan check her for ticks later was somewhat tantalizing. *Stupid hormones, this was no time for such thoughts.*

The path became imperceptible as the grade increased. For at least a quarter-hour, they climbed, weaving in and out of the trees, until they came to a clear path that followed the crest of a rugged rocky hill top, lined with trees. There, in a void in the rocks, beneath a shaded overhang of stone — blocked by a large red cedar — a large wooden crate with two long poles run through braces along the side was hidden. Lauren froze, her vision blurring as she stood there gazing over the darkened wood, feeling like she was in a movie ... or a dream.

"What do you think is in it?" John Carter came up and took her hand, bringing her back to herself.

Lauren's jaw dropped and she hesitated for a moment, not sure what to say. For a moment, she thought she might pass out. She knew the legends of the Ark of the Covenant. She knew the holy canon behind it — the rules that Levites carry it and no one else. She knew that within the Holy of Holies, shielded from the eye of common men, was a piece of furniture — in two parts. The ark itself was a chest made of acacia wood, overlaid with pure gold — inside and out. It was three feet and nine inches long, two feet and three inches wide and high. The second part was the atonement cover — or mercy seat — on top. The atonement cover was the lid for the ark. It was adorned with two cherubim that faced downward toward the ark with outstretched wings. It was made from one piece of pure gold. The atonement cover was known as God's dwelling place in the tabernacle. It was His throne, flanked by angels.

Inside, God commanded Moses to place three items, including a golden pot of manna, Aaron's staff that had budded and the two stone tablets on which the ten laws of God were written. If her calculations were correct, this crate could easily hold the Ark.

"It's got to be something valuable," Henry said. "Don't you think? I mean, why would anyone bring it out here and hide it."

Lauren found a place to sit and lowered herself with effort. "Come here," she called the boys over. They sat around her as she beckoned. "Do you remember when we studied the Torah and the Old Testament?" she asked. The boys each nodded. "One of the great mysteries in the Bible is the disappearance of the Ark of the Covenant of the Lord."

"Yeah, we know that one from the Indiana Jones movies, too," Henry said.

"The Hebrew Bible says, David, united the twelve tribes

of Israelites and conquered Jerusalem, bringing the artifact back to the city. David chose Mount Moriah as the site for the future temple to house the Ark, however, God forbade him from building it because he had shed too much blood. The First Temple was built by his son."

She told them of Solomon's Temple, also known as the First Temple, which was completed in 957 BCE in Jerusalem. It stood for four centuries before it was destroyed by the Babylonian Empire under King Nebuchadnezzar II who exiled all the Judeans into the desert. "The Bible records that in the seventh month of the year, at the feast of the Tabernacles, the priests and the Levites brought the Ark of the Covenant from the City of David, placing it in the Holy of Holies of the Temple. This was the first resting place of the Ark. But when the Second Temple was blessed, there was no mention of the Ark."

"What happened to it, Momma?" Jamie asked.

"There are legends that the Knights Templar took it to Acre," she explained. "It was a Templar stronghold. Archaeologists have found fortified tunnels and storage chambers beneath the ancient city that date back to the 1100s."

"That's when the Crusaders fought against Saladin," Henry said.

"You're right." Lauren nodded, proud of her son for having paid attention during the many conversations they'd had about the Templars. "The Templars never built a tunnel or escape path with a dead end. They always had a way out. They could have gotten relics out of Acre through these hidden tunnels. They found similar tunnels in Jerusalem as well."

"So if the treasures were in Jerusalem, they could have gotten them to Acre?"

"Possibly. But, this is where history and myth have blended so completely, that no one is sure," Lauren said, shifting to get comfortable.

Henry glanced at the crate in the shadows, then turned back to his mother. Lauren continued. "In some of the stories, the Ark was taken to Ethiopia, in others, it was destroyed. But, there was no record of what became of the Ark in the Books of Kings and Chronicles. Some say the prophet Jerimiah warned the Maccabees, who spirited the Ark to safety before the Temple was destroyed. Some even say it was taken to Rennes-le-Château …" Lauren's breath caught in her throat. She winced and put a hand to her side. She struggled to get to her feet. Henry jumped up to help, his brother's following suit.

"How did you find this?" Lauren asked, her breath coming in panting gasps even as she stepped up to it and let her hand hover just inches above the rough-honed wood.

"We were playing nearby, and Jamie thought he saw a Bigfoot," John Carter goaded his brother. Lauren was amused when she realized her father had used one of his mind-tricks to make them forget having met Tsul'Kalu when they first arrived. Knowing what she knew now, she was surprised he'd even allowed them to see him in such form.

"I did see a Bigfoot!" Jamie yelled at his brother, his face turning red as he walked over and stomped on his older brother's foot with as much force as he could bear. "You're a stupid head!"

John Carter balked and hopped on one foot. His face twisted in pain. "You're the stupid head that saw a Bigfoot!" John Carter retorted, making a run for Jamie.

The littlest Pierce hid behind his mother, and she caught John Carter by the arm, keeping him from tackling his brother. "Cut it out," Lauren said, stooping down so she could get in John Carter's face. "You will not make fun of your brother. I saw a Bigfoot once and no one called me a *stupid head* for it, so cut it out. If you're lucky, someday you will be worthy enough to see one, too."

The boys all stood, slack jawed. They stared at her in disbelief. "You saw one?"

"Yes, I did." She straightened, softening. "And I consider the Bigfoot my friend."

"Even the one that hit you in the face?" Henry asked, in a tone of wonder.

"Well," she said, putting her hand to her aching back. "No. Not that one."

"But you never said anything about making *friends* with it," Jamie said.

"Well, I did. But, it isn't my place to talk about it, and it's a secret you must keep. It's a long story," Lauren said. "When we get home, I'll tell you all of it." She swallowed hard and turned her attention back to the crate. "The legends of Henry Sinclair said he … he was trying to protect a secret."

"I think it's a pirate treasure," Jamie said, as if it were self-evident.

"You think *this* is the Ark from the Bible?" Henry asked his mother, coming to stand beside her. His eyes glistened with excitement. She could practically see his mouth watering as he turned to the crate.

"This isn't big enough to hold all the animals though," Jamie puzzled, scratching his head.

"The Ark of the Covenant," Lauren said. "Not Noah's Ark."

"Oh," Jamie said.

"Do you think the Ten Commandments are inside?" Henry asked.

"You've got a pretty smart kid there, for a *half-breed*," a voice behind them startled her. She turned, slowly, and matched the wicked gaze with a stern glare. Ko'i Minco stood leaning on his rifle.

He wasn't a tall man, but he was heavy-set, though his pock-marked cheeks were sunken in. His skin was redder than hers and his nose was hawkish, which made his small deep-set eyes even more beady. Lauren hadn't liked him from the moment she first met him, though she couldn't say why.

Maybe she didn't trust him. Maybe the ancient gods had given her the ability to read people and know when they were wicked. Maybe it was just her intuition.

"Ko'i Minco," she said, curtly. "Do you want to explain this?" She addressed him in his own language with a lifted hand toward the wooden crate. A bemused expression crossed his face.

"This is no concern of a woman." He spoke the words with disdain. "Particularly one who has married herself to a white man."

"I am no different than you," she said. "You serve the white men. Do they pay you for your services?"

"Does your white man pay you?" he retorted. "Are you his whore?"

Lauren glanced nervously at her boys not sure they would know the meaning of the word, even in English. "My husband has the honor of marrying into the Long Hair Clan of *Tsalagi* he is husband to … *a powerful witch*. He is the honored son of the great *wizard* Tsul'Kalu. He is a warrior who has won battles and *counted coup* on his enemies. His own father is a great warrior. My husband is honored among his people, and mine."

The man spat at her feet, and her gaze went to the spittle that stained the dirt, just millimeters from the edge of her shoe. Then, her head lifted slowly, and her brow arched as her mouth turned down. She was insulted.

That, clearly, was the reaction he had wanted. He laughed, then bolted forward, snatching her hand, squeezing it as he dug his filthy nails into her flesh and yanked her towards him. Henry and John Carter both started to intervene, but Lauren shot a wicked gaze at them both. Jamie took a step back, sniffling. Lauren then turned her eye to the man, even though that brought her face within inches of his fetid breath. "Take your hands off me." She enunciated the words in his language succinctly.

"I don't think I will," he said, in English. "You have seen more than you should. The point of bringing this here — according to the Sinclair — was to find a magic cave where their most precious treasure could rest undisturbed for eternity."

"What magic cave?" Lauren scowled, though she already knew.

"It's an old legend among their people — one I have assured them is quite true — so that when they leave for their Sunland beyond the shining waters, I can return and take their gold."

"What makes you think there's gold inside?" Lauren asked.

"Only a white man would be so foolish to leave his home, endanger his men, and risk certain death in the first place." He sniffed. His fiendish grin made Lauren chill. "I must assume he would only do such a thing for something as precious as gold. He said his peoples' greatest treasures are contained within. White men know only greed … for gold."

Who's being the greedy one now? Lauren thought. "Why wait for them to hide it? You could have taken it at any time," Lauren said. "Why here? Why now?"

"I have visions of my own. A raven came to me in a dream and told me their treasures were of great value and would give me all the power of the heavens and the earth at my command," he said, and she winced, turning her head away. The raven was a trickster. She had a lingering fear that Enlil — or one of his minions — would take any guise to manipulate her enemies and to give them the power to defeat her. She and Michael had bound the devil with the powers of the heavens, but she feared that she had not seen the last of the Dark One. "The raven told me to wait until they hid their prize. I would then part ways with them and come back for the gold myself."

"Your deception will be your downfall," she said.

"Momma," Jamie whimpered tentatively.

"Just stay calm," Lauren said to her boys. "Everything will be fine."

Ko'i Minco leaned into her, groping her belly. "Maybe I'll just cut this little half-breed from your womb and let you watch me cut their throats while you bleed out," he sneered, glancing at the boys as he licked his lips.

"I dare you to try," she said, with equal resolve, she already had the knife she carried on her belt in her hand. She was ready to defend herself. Much to her surprise, he let go of her arm and glanced down at the blade that was dangerously close to his nether regions.

He glanced back up at her, lifting a brow as he sneered coyly and took a step back. "Any man would be a fool to challenge me and … no woman will defeat me," he said with a mocking laugh. "Let us leave this place as friends, and forget our disagreement, and all we have seen here."

"I think that would be wise," Lauren said, with a cautious tone. "When your party leaves tomorrow, it will be the last we must see of one another."

He took another step back and nodded. Lauren realized her hand was trembling, and when he turned to leave, she felt herself relax. She had been ready to castrate him and gut him like a feral hog. The thought that she could go through with it frightened her. She started to turn towards the boys, when she saw the flash of movement behind her, and the glint of a blade caught her eye. She turned and went low, driving the small blade into her target, as his wicked knife came down and buried to the hilt in her left shoulder, just between the collarbone and scapula. The force of the blow took her to her knees, but her own momentum drove her blade towards his inner thigh. It found the most tender flesh before it drove home into the niche between thigh and abdomen.

He let out a roar of pain and fury, and struck out at her, knocking her down. Henry tackled him and the two went rolling to the ground. "John Carter, Jamie! Go! Find your father! Find your grandfather," Lauren barked. Pain hadn't reached her yet, but she found her left hand useless, hanging limp at her side as she tried to get up. Blood dripped off the tips of her fingers. "Go!" she yelled again, when the two younger boys didn't move. Henry and the wicked guide were locked in combat, rolling in the needles and litter on the ground. Henry had gotten a hold of Lauren's knife, which wasn't as big as the blade that was buried in her flesh, but it was sharp. Angry, scared and committed to protect his mother, he went after Ko'i Minco.

John Carter and Jamie abruptly came to their senses, and scuttled down the hillside, following the trail back along the ridge. Lauren got to her feet and picked up a rock the size of her fist, waiting for the opportunity to get a shot in.

Henry, however, brought the knife down and around, catching the man between the ribs. He let out a yelp, and rolled out from under him, tossing Henry back into the chest. Henry landed hard. He sat stunned. It was just the chance Ko'i Minco needed. He ripped the blade out of his own flesh and tossed it aside. Hobbled, he made a break for it, headed in the opposite direction.

Lauren stumbled over to Henry. She dropped to her knees beside him. "Son? Are you okay?"

Henry sat up, shaking off the blow. "Yeah, I'm fine." He gazed at her, his eyes growing wide. "Mom!"

"It's okay." Lauren glanced down at the wound, then swallowed hard as she sat back on her heels. "Just a flesh wound."

"But … you're bleeding."

She put a hand on him, as much to steady herself as to calm the boy. "Don't worry," Lauren assured him. "Your dad can fix it."

Henry took a deep breath, taking her by the elbow. He helped her to her feet, leading her to a fallen log. He settled her there, inspecting her face, gazing into her eyes. "Are you sure? You've gone pale, Mom."

"It doesn't even hurt," Lauren assured him. She was certain nerves had been severed. Her fingers tingled. Heat washed through her body. A cold mist built on her upper lip. She took a deep breath, fighting to hold on to consciousness.

Still, she must have convinced Henry she was okay. His face reddened and he stood, turning towards the path the attacker had taken. Lauren could see that Henry was now boiling mad. He found her small knife in the grass. "I'm gonna kill that guy!" He wiped the blood off of it onto the knee of his pants, before he raced off down the trail, in pursuit of their attacker.

"Henry," she called after him. Lauren swallowed hard, now aware of the burning fire in her shoulder. Gasping to catch her breath, she struggled to keep her feet, knowing she wouldn't get back up if she went down. The pain was growing intense with each movement. She managed to stagger a few steps before she paused and leaned against the wooden crate that she couldn't bring herself to touch earlier. A comforting warmth passed through her body, and she felt her resolve strengthen. She straightened and made every effort to follow Henry. Lauren couldn't move as fast as her son. He was young and strong. She was not. Willing her feet to move, Lauren placed one foot in front of the other.

She managed to make it down the hill and back to the trail that turned and led toward the swamp. Her vision was blurring, but she caught sight of a flash of blue, the color of Henry's jacket. Lauren wanted to stop and turn to camp. She wanted to find Rowan, but she was concerned for Henry, and she knew if she stopped, she was done. Henry's life was in jeopardy. He was just a boy. He had no business trying to fight a grown man — even an injured one — much less in physical combat with just a small knife.

Tears threatened to form in her eyes, but she fought them

back, refusing to let anything come between her and her son, even her emotions. He needed her. "Henry!" She tried to shout, but the pain in her shoulder gripped her throat, and it came out as a gasp. One minute she was staggering in the quagmire, the next, she was behind Ko'i Minco, as he hid in the tall grass, ready to jump out at Henry.

A fury washed through her unlike any she had ever experienced. At that moment, she knew just how the *Incredible Hulk* felt, and she roared with an inhuman ferocity.

Ko'i Minco had terror written in his eyes. That was the last thing she remembered, as the rage overtook her, and she unleashed the bloodlust on him with a savagery she could not control.

17

"Lauren!" Rowan found her on her knees, near the still form, with Henry wrapped in her one functioning arm. They were both bloody and in shock. Henry jumped up when the men approached, wiping the tears from his eyes — smearing blood on his tear-stained face — trying not to let his father see him cry.

"Dad!" he called, as Rowan raced through the murk, struggling to keep his feet. "Mom's hurt."

Rowan rushed over and dropped down beside her. He glanced at the unmoving form of the guide, laying in the bog in front of his wife. She was white-faced, trembling, and clearly in shock as she sat on her knees, staring at her bloodied hands. Blood smeared over the front of her clothing. Crimson flowed down her arm and dripped into the bog. A deer-antler knife handle protruded from her shoulder at a wicked angle. Rowan caught her before she could go over. A blood-curdling yelp escaped her throat, and her eyes rolled back. John scooped her up as Sinclair and his men caught up, taking in the scene.

"What the hell happened?" Rowan barked at Henry who stood trembling.

"I don't ... I don't know ..." He stepped back, as John lifted his mother effortlessly.

"What do you mean you don't know?" Rowan demanded. He knew he shouldn't yell at the boy, but he needed answers. John Carter and Jamie rushed over to stand with their brother, both pale, and afraid, watching as their grandfather headed off with the limp form of their mother.

"I saw what happened, Dad." Henry swallowed hard. "But ... but I don't think I believe it."

"It's Ko'i Minco," Sir Gunn, inspecting the body, said to Sinclair, who scowled.

"He attacked our mom," Henry said. "He pushed me down and he stabbed her with his knife. He tried to kill her. He threatened to kill me and my brothers ... even the baby. He was going to kill you and your men and take that crate you hid up on the hill."

Rowan's expression changed immediately, as he turned to Sinclair.

Sinclair's face had gone red. He was as angry as Rowan was. He was almost as angry as Henry. "I should hae' kent nae tae trust that ... *bawbag*." His brogue was particularly strong.

"Somebody better start explaining," Rowan started but realized John and his wife were gone from sight. He caught Henry by the hand. "It will wait, but I want answers," he said, as they started after Lauren. "Later."

"What do we do about Ko'i Minco?" Rowan heard Armstrong ask.

"Leave him." Sinclair scowled. "Let the alligators hae' him."

ROWAN FOUND THEM BY THE FIRE AT THE CAVE. JOHN CARTER and Jamie were sitting across the fire, tearfully watching the shaman work over their mother. Tsul'Kalu had cut away the shoulder of her blouse. Her bra strap had been severed in the attack. Blood marred her exposed flesh. Kneeling beside her, Lauren's father cleansed the wound around the impaled blade. The furs beneath her were red with her blood, despite his efforts to stop the flow. He had torn strips of linen cloth and wrapped them around the blade.

Rowan dropped to the ground beside her, and inspected the injury, taking over the work of holding pressure against the dagger. Rowan could feel the force of her pulse surging beneath the bandages. He suspected the artery had been damaged.

"The blade will have to be removed," John said.

Her eyes opened, and closed just as quickly, rolling beneath the lids as she fought for consciousness, turning her head away from Rowan, wincing as she began to tremble violently. Her teeth chattered audibly.

"Not in the field," he protested. His paramedic's training kicked in. "She needs a hospital."

"There is no time, son." Her father spoke calmly, resting his hand on Rowan's upper arm. "She's in shock. Your wife is losing too much blood."

Rowan knew she would need help beyond his skill level. This was work for a surgeon, not a medic. John nodded and instructed John Carter to bring him the bundle of furs in the back corner of the cave. He boy did as his grandfather instructed, despite the terror written on his small features. He helped the shaman put them under her feet, elevating them. John Carter rushed back to his spot next to his frightened brothers, glancing up. Sinclair and some of his men stood at the entrance of the cave.

Rowan was so focused on Lauren, he paid no attention to what John — *Tsul'Kalu* — was doing until he came with a cup of tea. He lifted her head, holding the cup to her lips. Her uninjured hand came to the cup and her lashes fluttered open as she drank greedily, coughing then sputtering to catch her breath, before she collapsed to the furs, wheezing. Rowan realized she needed to sit up to avoid choking. He lifted her and moved himself to a seated position under her. Here, he could hold her upright, letting her head rest on his shoulder. She winced and groaned with each jostling motion. Her lids closed, and she went limp against him.

"Come on, honey," he whispered as he patted her cheek. She flinched, barely rousing. "Here, drink some more." He found the cup and held it up for her. "You've lost a lot of blood. You need the fluids."

"Henry?" She panted.

"He's fine," Rowan said. "What did you do to Ko'i Minco? Talk to me." He made eye contact with John — *Tsul'Kalu*— as he finished his preparation. More linen bandages sat by his knee, though Rowan had no idea where anything came from in this crazy freaking *time-place*.

Rowan turned and pressed his lips to Lauren's temple as her head rolled away from the injured shoulder. John reached for the knife and gripped it in his gnarled hand. Without so much as a nod, he removed it from its sheath.

Blood gushed from the wound, spilling down Lauren's shoulder and over the furs that covered her. A blood curdling scream echoed in the cavern ceiling. Rowan held her tightly in his arms, burying his face in her hair. His tears mixed with hers on her torn calico blouse.

"Rowan. Son." John brought him back, lifting his hand over the bandages he'd stacked on the deep wound. "Hold this. Apply pressure." Rowan did as his father-in-law instructed. Lauren was now a limp form that lay heavy against him. He could feel her pulse coursing and his hand warmed with fresh blood with each beat of her heart. He prayed the faint would be kind and he could tend her without causing her to suffer.

"How bad is it?" Rowan asked.

"The wound is deep." He produced a leather pouch from

his belt. Bidding Rowan to lift the bandages, he sprinkled dried herbs over the laceration. At his nod, Rowan placed his hand back over the linen. "It doesn't appear the ..." he paused as if seeking the words. "*Subclavian artery* is severed, but it does appear to be nicked. How are you at vascular sutures?"

"Trained, but ..." Rowan hesitated. "I've never done a procedure like that. I've seen it done by a surgeon, but ... I've never done it. I don't have the equipment for it. I need a vascular needle and sutures ..."

John nodded as he reached for another leather pouch on his belt and opened it. He took out a paper packet. There were three curved needles of assorted sizes, along with lengths of suturing thread. "Your knowledge is sufficient. Lauren needs you."

Rowan felt his brow lift and his stomach drop into the hollow of his gut. "If you've got some morphine in there, I'm sure Lauren would appreciate it." Rowan scowled.

"Just herbs," John said. "But they will serve us today."

Rowan took the bundle, inspecting it, sizing up the situation and considering what he needed to do ... and in what order. He noticed how pale Lauren had gone. Her lips were dry and cracked and were turning ashen. He shook his head and accepted what he had to do. He knew he didn't have time to wait. "Trade places with me," Rowan said, with conviction. "I need both hands free."

John took his daughter in his arms, placing his body behind her, supporting her limp form while Rowan worked on her to get the bleeding to slow enough for him to visualize the damage.

The blood made it hard to find the nick, which was larger than he'd feared. To make matters worse, her faint pulse made the tiny spaghetti-like structure quiver, so he would be aiming at a moving target. He kept reminding himself that a moving target was a good sign, it meant her heart was still beating and she hadn't bled out completely.

"She needs fluids," Rowan said. "And I need boiling water to sterilize things."

John lifted a hand towards the fire and the cavern seemed to lighten. Rowan glanced up and found a kettle of steaming liquid suspended over the licking flames.

"Henry, come help me," Rowan said, pointing to the kettle. Henry jumped to his feet, finding a vessel and a ladle. He scooped up the water, filling the container, bringing it to his father. He was careful not to spill any.

John instructed him on procedures to clean the implements, allowing Rowan to focus on cleaning up the wound.

"Any alcohol?" Rowan glanced up at his father-in-law.

"Perhaps," John nodded to the flask at Rowan's knee. Rowan shook his head wondering where it had come from, but he recognized it as the flask that had been passed around the fire by their guests.

"That'll do." Rowan used it to wash his hands. He put his hand on Lauren's chest to steady her and splashed a generous dose on the wound. She flinched, moaning, but never fully awakened, much to Rowan's relief. "Hold this." He started to hand Henry some of the linen bandaging but noticed the boy was already pale, seeing his mother's injury so close.

"Maybe Jamie would be better suited," John said, drawing Rowan's attention to the boy's distress.

"No, I can do it." Henry said. He swallowed hard and swayed as he sat on his knees.

"It's okay." Jamie came up behind his brother. "I can do it."

Henry nodded and made a hasty retreat to the furs where John Carter sat in silence. Henry managed to stay both conscious and kept his stomach from revolting on him, which made Rowan proud.

"What do you need me to do?" Jamie asked, his voice trembling, but his courage steeled.

"You are my surgical assistant," he said. "Stick out your

hands." The boy did, and Rowan poured the last of the liquor over his small hands. Jamie instinctively rubbed the amber liquid on his skin, as if washing them, then shook them dry. He recoiled at the smell of the strong booze. Rowan proceeded to instruct him on the names of each of the implements in his father-in-law's kit. "When I ask you to hand me one be careful not to touch anything else, especially not your nose and face, or the dirt floor. We have to keep the surgical field and all the equipment sterilized. Can you do that?"

"Yes, sir."

With the implements sterilized, Rowan returned his attention to the wound, and the needle with an ample length of thread upon it. He took up the needle holder and prepared himself.

Jamie sat at his dad's elbow watching carefully. Rowan found himself talking his way through the procedure. It wasn't so much as to instruct his son, as it was to calm his own racing heart and steady his trembling hand. It was a mental practice he'd learned in the military to make sure he didn't miss a step. In a way it was a lot like saying the rosary. It was the regimen that kept his head and heart as calm as possible, in turn steadying his hands.

"I'm going to go with a simple interrupted stitch," he said, as he took the bandages John had been holding and dabbed at the wound. "A continuous stitch is quicker, but I can't risk the stitch failing if I cut the suture in the wrong place. I'll finish with a surgeon's knot."

Despite his age, Jamie made an excellent surgical assistant, blotting the wound when Rowan needed him to, even without being asked. He watched with the curiosity of youth, and never flinched when Rowan started tugging on the threads as he tied the last knot in the wiggling artery. Rowan sat back and took a deep breath, putting a hand on the boy's shoulder. "Good job. That ought to take care of the artery."

John inspected the stitches, nodding. "The bleeding has stopped."

"How's she doing?"

"Pulse is faint, but steady," the shaman said. "Best hurry and close the wound before the medicine wears off."

Rowan nodded, wiped his brow on his shirt sleeve and set to work with the rest of his suturing. When he cut the last thread all the tension he'd been holding in his shoulders, neck and back, seemed to melt. He let out a deep sigh. "That ought to do it," Rowan said.

"SHE LIVES?" A VOICE FROM THE ENTRANCE OF THE CAVE found them as Rowan sat back feeling relieved. He glanced up and realized Prince Henry and his men collected in the entry way of the cave.

"She does," John answered. He rose and summoned them. "Come in. There is room for all."

"John Carter." John turned to the boys. "There are furs back in the corner. Would you please bring them to me?" John Carter rose and several of the Templars offered the boy a hand. The rest dropped to one knee and crossed themselves, taking up their rosaries to pray on Lauren's behalf.

Rowan glanced at John wondering if he should ask how anything he needed was just *there*, but the old shaman cast him a sidelong glance. Rowan thought better of it. *Why look a gift — Bigfoot — in the mouth?* He decided. Once Lauren was settled on the pile of furs, her head and shoulders elevated, Rowan used the bandages to cover the stitches and create a sling to support her limp arm while her injury healed.

"Is she going to be okay, Dad?" Jamie asked, curling up next to her, resting his head on her uninjured arm.

"Yeah, son." Rowan nodded. "She just needs to sleep and let it heal."

"It's late," John said to Jamie. "You and your brothers should get some rest."

A flash of lightning illuminated the outer edge of the cave, and the miasma of rain was immediately evident on the night air. "Your men are welcome to take shelter with us here tonight," Rowan said.

"I thank ye." Sinclair nodded. He gave instructions to Gunn to have the men gather their things and move them to the cave.

The taller dark-haired Scot, Sir Armstrong, came over and knelt at Lauren's side, his hand went to her abdomen. "She will deliver soon," he said. He bowed his head, crossing himself as he reached for an amulet beneath his armor. He clutched the charm in his hands as he folded them together to pray. "I call upon thee, Saint Anne, Mother of Mary. Glorious Saint Ann, filled with compassion, I invoke thee with love for those who suffer, heavy laden. I cast myself at thy feet that thee see safe this mother upon her bed of pain."

"Lord Armstrong's wife recently died in child bed," Sinclair informed Rowan as he watched, unmoving. "They prayed for children for years but were not so blessed until she was late in her days.

"Cease not to intercede for me and behalf of all women who suffer for want of a child and safe delivery." Armstrong held out the amulet, folding the beaded chain with the small ornate cross that appeared to be made of bone and gold. He took it and opened Lauren's hand, coiling the chain in her palm, closing her fingers around it. He crossed himself again, rested his hand on her belly a moment, then rose.

Rowan could see a glisten of tears in his eye, but he remained stoic as he came to stand behind his Prince. "Thank you," Rowan said, turning back to him. He extended his hand, and the dark Scot took it with a firm grasp.

"By the Blood," Armstrong said.

Rowan remembered the inscription on the wall over a

hearth in Rennes Le Château. "Through His Blood we are saved," Rowan replied.

Armstrong met Sinclair's gaze, their eyes communicating something Rowan read as surprise, or perhaps … shock.

Sinclair put a hand on Rowan's arm and nodded. "We thank you for your hospitality … again." The thunder outside punctuated his appreciation.

"Please," John said. "Make yourselves comfortable. I will make tea and we can rest until the storm passes."

The cavern was big enough and soon, they bedded down, except Rowan, Sinclair, and John. They kept watch over Lauren as she slept, with Jamie curled up beside her. The glint of firelight flickered on the chain that remained in her limp hand. Rowan could see the details of the cross between her fingers.

"It was a gift from my grandsire to Lady Armstrong," Sinclair said, noticing his attention on the relic. "He found it whilst heading to the Holy Land in France. *Asāsiyyūn's* raided their party and took a precious artifact that had been protected by our order. This was one of the many artifacts among them. It is the Cross of Saint Ann. It is said to be made of the arm bone of Her Holiness. It is said to ensure fertility and protect a woman in childbirth, for she is their patron saint."

"It's beautiful," Rowan said, appreciatively. "But we don't need help with fertility." A blush came to Rowan's cheeks. He could feel his ears grow hot as well. "Mercifully."

"It will carry her through her impending time and even beyond, when the bairn takes to breast."

Rowan studied his wife but settled back as the conversation waned. "So, what was this crate the boys were talking about?" Rowan thought to ask.

Sinclair gazed at him cautiously, hesitating, but answered. "I dinnae ken ye'd believe me if I told ye," he said.

"Try me," Rowan said flatly. He was too tired and too worried to mince words.

"The Cross of Saint Anne is no' the only relic we carry." Sinclair studied him a moment, then glanced at Lauren and nodded, as if making up his mind. "We bear the burden of a sacred oath," he said. "We serve the *Order of the Sacred Heart of the Rose*. Ye've heard of it?"

"I've heard of the *Order of the Rosy Cross*," Rowan said, puzzling.

"A fellowship of ours." Sinclair nodded. "Are ye a Christian man?"

Rowan nodded. "I was raised in the Presbyterian Church."

That seemed sufficient for the Prince. "Then ye kent we are holy warriors, *Soldiers of God*, aye?"

"Aye. Yes." Rowan grew impatient. "There are legends about the Templars and the Holy Grail. I've heard the tales since I was a boy."

"Aye, then." Sinclair nodded. "I'll tell ye more tales." Sinclair seemed to settle in, and Rowan got the sense this would not be a short story. "There is an ancient legend, of Our Lord. He had a love for all mankind, ye ken. But he had a special love for one woman."

"Mary Magdalene," Rowan said. "Yes, I've heard the legend. If you have the Holy Grail in that chest, I'm going to lose my mind."

Sinclair hesitated. "Nay," Sinclair explained. "Ye ken, the Grail, originally had nothing whatsoever to do with the Last Supper. The first appearance of the Grail is in the Perceval of Chrétien de Troyes. There was a golden serving dish that descended before Perceval in the castle of the Fisher King. But Chrétien does nae call it holy, nor call any special attention tae it, as opposed tae the equally sacred lance that pierced Our Lord's breast. A hundred or more years before I was born, Sir Robert de Boron told a different tale."

Rowan leaned forward, listening intently at this new spin on history. One he could never have imagined. "Joseph of Arimathea had received the Holy Chalice that caught Our Lord's blood when the sacred spear pierced His heart. He sprinted it away tae Scotland and founded a line of knights tae guard the sacred vessel. My father told this tale tae me, as his father told it tae him. I will tell it tae my sons."

"But ... the Grail ..." Rowan started.

Sinclair raised a hand. "Lost to antiquity, but as sae often occurs, the legends were merged, and a myth arose that a line of sacred knights guarded the *Chalice of Our Lord Jesus Christ*. My father understood the tale as one of courtly fiction. He kent it was no' a report of actual fact, because he kent all tae weil the true tale."

"So, no Grail." Rowan deflated.

"No," he said. "But we have many of the sacred relics. These are important, but our charge is to protect the *Sacred Heart of the Rose* above all else."

Rowan sat up, feeling his features withdraw in disbelief. "The *Sacred Heart of the Rose*? Do you have ... the heart of *Mary Magdalene*?"

He glanced at Lauren, who'd asked the same thing. "No," he proceeded to tell of the *Heart of Sarah* and how his family played into the legend. "My grandsire was among members of the Order who intended to return *the Sacred Heart* — along with that of our King, Robert — tae the Holy Land, but Saracens assassins attacked them and took the relic. Brothers of our Order came to their aid and rescued the *Sacred Heart of the Rose*, returning it to Scotland where our family has protected it. We protected other relics including the Holy of Holies that were spirited from Jerusalem when it fell."

"Holy of Holies?" Rowan's brow lifted towards his hairline. Then his eyes narrowed. "You mean ... *the Ark*?"

"The Ark, containing Aaron's rod and the sacred pot of manna," he said. "Along with a few other things."

Rowan sat gob smacked. He gazed into the fire, trying to form a rational thought and turn it into a logical question. "You said there were other relics?"

"We carry the sacred Ark of the Covenant, the Spear of Longinus, and a fragment of the True Cross of Our Lord, but we also carry Robert's *Bannatyne mazer*." Rowan knew that to be a communal feasting cup from the middle ages. It was made of turned maple wood with a silver foot. It had been given to the Bruce by Walter Stewart — the father of the first King of the Stewart line — and Rowan's own ancestor. "When Robert defeated the English at Bannockburn, Bruce was essentially excommunicated from the church. He wrote a letter to the Pope in Avignon," he said. "We bear that letter with the original seals of each of the signatories intact."

"The Declaration of Arbroath?" Rowan said, his voice just above a whisper. He quoted from the document, "...*for as long as but a hundred of us remain alive, never will we on any conditions be brought under English rule. It is in truth not for glory nor riches, nor honours that we are fighting but for freedom — for that alone, which no honest man gives up but with life itself.*"

"Ye've read it?" Sinclair's face lightened.

"One of my ..." *How should he word it?* "One of my family members signed it." Sinclair's brow lifted and his head tilted in inquiry. "Walter, High Steward of Scotland. He was just twenty-one years old when he fought with King Robert at Bannockburn. He commanded the left wing of the Scots army ... along with Lord Douglas."

"Aye, Walter was marrit tae King Robert's daughter, Marjorie and is also a friend to Clan St. Clair. My father, too, signed the *Declaration* ... which makes us ... *Brothers*," Prince Henry said, bowing before Rowan.

"Cousins at the very least." Rowan bowed back. "I am honored."

"We carry the *Heart of the Bruce* ... and ... the *Sacred Heart of the Rose* ... for our King so loved Our Lord, Jesus Christ that he promised to protect Christ's sacred secret with his very life. It was his will that his heart be interred in the Holy Land with hers but alas, it was not to be. My ancestors fought to see her heart safely delivered to Rosslyn Chapel, where we have kept it safe for many years."

"Why risk taking it back to the Holy Land?" John asked.

"Ye ken, when Our Lord returns, according to the Revelations, His Trumpets will sound. All who have gone to *glory* shall be recalled to fight for *The Lord, Our God*. In that great and terrible day of the apocalypse — the final holy battle for heaven and earth — the *Soldiers of Christ* will take Jerusalem once more and our Holy City will be restored."

Rowan was again dumbfounded and unable to draw breath, much less speak for a moment. "You mean to tell me," he began, when he could find words. "Armies of the *dead* are going to rise and fight in the Apocalypse?" He tried to remember every detail of the story Lauren had told him about the battle with Enlil. It had been a hellish conflict, to hear her tell it. Macabre and unholy beings rose to fight against the Army of God, an army she and her brother led. She'd said she wasn't convinced that was the *final* battle for good and evil. *Had she been wrong?*

"The dead restored," Sinclair said.

Rowan sat shaking his head as he tried to process it all. "Wait. I thought the heart of the Bruce went to a cathedral …" Rowan stopped, afraid to say too much.

"My forefathers were intent on taking it to the Holy Land, along with *the Sacred Heart of the Rose*," Sinclair explained. "When the assassins attacked, my great-grandsire knew it could not be risked. His brothers in arms gathered an army of a hundred knights and three hundred infantry and archers and set off to recover the *Sacred Heart of the Rose*. They placed it in Melrose Abby with the heart of our King."

"Why did you bring them here?" Rowan puzzled.

"When enemies threatened our sacred relics, my grandsire

ordered us carry it here where we would find a sacred cave where these treasures would be protected for all time. I knew it when I saw the signs while your wife and I walked last evening. This is the cave … this is where our journey ends."

John took in the news nonplused, as Rowan's gaze turned to him, then back to Sinclair. "We have awaited your arrival, Lord Sinclair," John said. "I could not say this before, not in the presence of the traitor, whom Lauren killed today. But, we have come to receive your treasures and see them safely hidden."

Rowan's head whipped back around to his father-in-law, straining a muscle as he did. "Say what?"

"That is why we are here," John said to Rowan. "My daughter and I." He turned to Sinclair.

"Our missive was to find a sacred cave where our treasures would be safe," Sinclair said. "The legend foretold that we would know this cave by the sign of the cross and the crown and an angel would be here to receive our treasures. I have seen all the signs we seek. My grandsire instructed me to leave my markings upon the stone to honor God who would protect our treasures."

John raised his hand toward the wall. The fire in the middle of the cavern rose, illuminating the wall above the reach of any man. Sparks raced through the marks as they seemed to illuminate as if lasers had engraved the stone. There, the symbols Rowan had seen in his own *time-place* now appeared deeply and clearly carved into the stone.

Rowan stood, stunned. Sinclair rose beside him, taking a step back. His men, those who were still awake rose, too. Someone set to work waking the others. When Rowan turned around they were kneeling, crossing themselves and praying under their breath.

Lauren stirred in her sleep, her eyelids fluttering open. She lay with her gaze already pointed in the direction of the inscription.

Rowan dropped to his knee, but not for the same reason. His hand went to her cheek, and he could feel the heat rising from her flesh. "You're burning up, honey." Rowan reached for one of the linen cloths and dipped it into the cool water, mopping her brow with it.

Her good hand reached up and caught his. "We can go home," she managed, barely above a whisper.

Rowan turned to John, "Is that right? Can we?"

His father-in-law nodded, dropping beside him. "But you must take the relics," he said. "Take them and keep them safe."

"What?" Rowan sat down hard, stunned by the directive. "Me?"

"Lauren has her gifts," he said. "This is your gift, and your missive. You are *The Protector*. You must keep them safe but tell no one of their true origins. Protect them with your life, and if be, with your blood."

Rowan's mind was spinning, trying to fathom what was being asked of him. John rose and turned to Sinclair. "Have your men bring the relics," he said. "My son ... your *Brother* ... will keep them safe in his own place and time. Your crusade is done. Your journey complete."

Sinclair rose and turned to his men. "Go. Bring back the chest. Do as he commands."

They didn't question their Prince, and headed out into the storm, mindless of the fury that raged.

John turned back to Rowan. "You will do it?"

"I ... I ..." he gasped. "I will."

Sinclair drew his sword from his sheath, laying it on the ground between them, and commanded Rowan to kneel before him. Rowan furrowed his brow. He did as Sinclair beckoned. As he knelt, he studied the Templar sword before him. The pommel was a circle of metal with a Templar cross — inlaid with copper — at its center. This sword was the kind that could hack through mail, plate, or chain, and was sharpened to a wicked edge that could take a man's head with a strong warrior wielding it.

"I have no armor, no spurs, nor shield to bestow upon ye, as is fitting," he began, peeling off his own white tabard with the red cross on the chest. Like the others, it had a rose embroidered in gold upon the cross. "Our order ha' taken a vow of poverty, ye ken? But I shall gie ye this holy armor," he said, draping it over Rowan's head, girding the tabard with his own belt. "White is for purity, and red is for the Blood of Our Lord and Savior, Jesus Christ. The rose for the Fruit of His Love. It is for his wife and child." Rowan studied the cross on his chest. "State thy full name."

With a quavering voice, he spoke. "Rowan Charlemagne Pierce."

"Do you, Rowan Charlemagne Pierce, vow to never traffic with traitors, never give evil counsel to a lady — whether *marrit* or no — tae always treat thy woman with great respect and defend her against all? Do ye vow to observe fasts and abstinences, and hear mass, and make an offering tae the Church?"

"Define abstinences?" Rowan puzzled.

"He means ye must lie with your wife and no other." John's voice found his way to his ear, though the wizard said nothing.

"Do you?"

"I do," Rowan said, solemnly.

The blade of Sinclair's sword came down flat on his shoulder, then over his head to the other side. Lastly, it came to rest upon his head, before the Lord Sinclair turned it, hilt up, in the form of the cross. "Press thy lips and make thy pledge," he instructed. Rowan leaned forward and kissed the cross before him. "Rise, then, and be recognized. Hence forth thou shall be known as Sir Rowan Pierce, Protector of the Holy of Holies, Bearer of the Secret, Protector of the Sacred Heart of the Rose … Knight of the Cross, and *Brother* of Prince Henry Sinclair."

Rowan rose and found the sword laid in his trembling hands. "If any harm should befall these relics, may this sword defend them, or take thy life," Sinclair said, bowing deeply before him.

"I pray to God it never comes to that." Rowan reached up and wiped his brow with his arm, almost dropping the sword, which was heavy, but razor sharp. He regained control and held the sword by one hand. He realized Sinclair's scabbard was still seated on his belt, and Rowan returned the blade to its sheath. He returned the bow and turned back to Lauren. "Honey?" She had slipped back into the darkness, the fever breaking out into a mist over her skin. Her cheeks flamed pink, even after the fire died to a gentle glow.

"Gather your sons," John said. "There isn't much time."

Rowan went and woke the boys, explaining that they were preparing to go home. The boys rose, reluctantly. "Can't we wait 'til morning?" John Carter complained.

"No," Rowan said. "You're mother has started to run a fever and we need to take her home as fast as we can."

"If I may." Sinclair held a hand out towards his sword. Rowan handed it to him.

"Young men of Clan Pierce, you have proven your nobility," Sinclair said in a strong voice that echoed around them. He turned as his men set the crate on the ground beneath the inscription. He waved his men over, taking a tabard from each who bore them, and presented them to the young men. "I command thee, kneel," he said. The knighting ceremony repeated for each of them, and he granted them similar titles to the ones he bestowed upon their father. Henry was named the Guardian of the Rose, and Protector of the True Cross. John Carter was named the Protector of the Divine Secret and Holder of the Spear. Jamie was declared Protector of the Heart of King Robert and Defender of the Faith.

"Gae now … and remember yer sacred duties. Bear this secret in your heart, as you bear my memory in yer mind. Gae with m' thanks, and … m' blessing."

"Wait," Jamie protested. "What about our mother? Doesn't she get some sort of title?"

"It is not customary to knight a woman, but … it is not unheard of." Prince Henry hesitated a moment. He lifted his gaze to Armstrong, who still wore his tabard. Without orders, he peeled out of it, and presented it to his king. Sinclair took it with a nod of thanks and knelt at Lauren's side, laying it over her, drawing out his own rosary, letting the string of wooden and glass beads slide between his calloused hands. He lay them on her chest, adjusting the cross over her heart.

"Having been tested and found worthy before man and God, Mistress Lauren Pierce, I lift thee up to the Most High. Keeper of the Sacred Relics, I name thee. Sister of the Sacred Heart of the Rose … and Mother of New Jerusalem. Keep safe our holy treasure and see it returned to the Holy Sepulcher … when the time is right."

He made the sign of the cross over her forehead, over her heart and then over his own head before he rose and turned to Rowan and the boys. He rested his hand on Jamie's head as he bowed to Rowan and to his father-in-law. "I pray we meet again on the field of battle outside Jerusalem on that beautiful Day of Glory."

Rowan bowed, as did the boys, each unbidden. John extended a hand to the King, which he accepted. With farewells made, John nodded at Rowan. Rowan returned the sword to its scabbard before he bent down and scooped Lauren up into his arms. Her head lay limp against his chest. Henry lifted his mother's arm into the cradle of what was left of her lap. Her belly had grown even bigger. Rowan hadn't carried her in some time, and he struggled to balance her weight in his arms. Once he had her settled, John went to the wall, beneath the inscription and turned to Henry. "I will need your help," he said. "Boys, all of you." He instructed Rowan to lay his wife on the crate, and the boys to lay their hands on their mother. Rowan leaned her against his body. He turned to John, glancing back at Sinclair who nodded, with a beatific expression on his face.

Sinclair raised his hand and made the sign of the cross. "Go with God," he said, and the world around them vanished.

18

Rowan turned around and realized they were alone in the cavern. Just his boys, his wife, and the wooden crate. The fire in the pit had faded to little but glowing embers, and a chill hit him square in the face, coalescing into a cloud that was his breath.

"Daddy, I'm cold," Jamie moaned, shivering.

Rowan pulled him in, and held him, rubbing his arms. "Boys, find some firewood," he said. "Let's get that fire going. We'll warm up and then I'll find help for your mother."

There was a bundle of wood in the same spot it had been in the other *time-place*. Henry took care of the fire, while Rowan collected Lauren and moved her closer to it, covering her with the furs they'd brought with them. She winced and her brow furrowed. She stirred but he settled her on the pile of furs that were still there. Rowan leaned down and pressed his lips to her fevered brow and lingered as long as he dared.

"Help me move the crate into the back of the cave," he instructed. "We will need to hide the tabards, too." He unloosened his belt and removed Sinclair's sword, laying it on top of the chest as he took off the tabard and folded it. The boys took off theirs and placed them with their fathers. It took all of them to move the crate to a hidden niche, dragging it across the slick mud floor. Rowan used his foot to scuff up the ground to hide the marks left behind, and hoped it was far enough out of sight that no one would find it before he could return for it later. They would have to leave without it and get Lauren to safety first. It was their only choice.

He turned to the boys and gathered them around, making sure each of them were wrapped in a warm fur. "Listen to me," he said. "Stay here with your mother. I am going to find help. Hopefully Jean-René and the team aren't far."

"Daddy, I don't want you to go." Jamie sniffed. "I'm scared."

"I'm scared, too, son," Rowan admitted, pulling his youngest into his arms. "But you know I have to go. Your mother needs medical attention. You understand, right?"

"I do." Jamie nodded.

"A knight has his errand," Rowan said, kissing his head. "Mine is to find help. Yours is to stay with your mother, Sir James." Jamie balled up his courage and nodded, taking a step back.

"Stay close to the fire," he said. "Henry, keep it stoked. I won't be long."

GEORGE AND THE TEAM RETURNED TO THEIR MOBILE COMMAND post. The fire chief stood eyeing the skies as they darkened. The sound of ice pellets hitting the ground reached a crescendo as the storm approached. "We're gonna have to call it." The Choctaw County EM shook his head as the returning search teams gathered under the plastic canopy. George turned his attention back to the map on the table in front of him. They had marked each section of the grid as it had been searched, and there was still a substantial portion of the map unmarked.

"Strike Team Alpha is still out in this quadrant," George said. "We'll wait 'til they finish their search and then re-evaluate."

"The National Weather Service has issued a winter storm warning," the emergency manager said. "If we don't get out soon, we could get iced in."

"We've got supplies to last us a week," George said calmly. "I'm not leaving here without my sister."

"I can't risk our teams," the EM protested. "We can come back."

"I'm not leaving." George tapped his finger on the map in an empty square. "I'm going to go search this section," he said. "Radio me when Alpha team returns. Delta team, you're with me." George pulled on his ski cap and zipped up his coat. "We won't be long."

ROWAN HAD WRAPPED HIMSELF WITH ONE OF THE FURS, HAVING thrown it over his shoulders to ward off the bitter cold. It also kept the stinging ice from hitting his neck and kept the wind out of his ears. It was treacherous, trying to scale down the narrow trail from the cave. One missed step and he could end up tumbling down the side of a jagged cliff. He took a step back, away from the edge, pressing his back to the rock face behind him, not willing to risk it.

The distant rumble of thunder made the trees shudder, and the sleet came down with a ferocity he was ill-prepared for. He stopped at the base of the trail, glancing back up to the hidden entrance of the cave, debating his chosen course of action. He thought about having to drag Lauren through this weather, carrying her on rugged terrain, with their children in tow. The dread of all the *what ifs* strengthened his resolve and convinced him, this was what was best for Lauren and the boys. What was best for him, well, that didn't matter. His family was everything.

He continued on. Finding the campsite abandoned, he wasn't surprised. He wasn't sure how long they'd been gone from this *time-place*, and Tsul'Kalu — John — had said time passed differently there. By the swell of Lauren's belly, he suspected time had moved faster there. Her pregnancy had advanced farther than he would have expected here.

Rowan stood by where the campfire had been, blinking back the freezing rain as he gazed up, studying the sky. The sun was completely obscured, and the slate gray sky was over taken by darker shades as the clouds thickened, and the rain grew more intense. *Where would the team be if they weren't here?* He thought to himself and decided to hike the path down to the trail head where they had parked.

The landscape was familiar, but with a layer of ice on everything, it wasn't exactly as he remembered. He wondered if the time-shifts had addled his brain. He paused at the fork in the path, trying to remember which led to the trailhead and which led to the meadow. He stood clutching the fur around his shoulders and decided. *Right.* It had to be.

Lauren came to her senses with a screaming headache to go with the agony in her shoulder. John Carter was sitting on one side of her. Jamie sat on the other, holding her uninjured hand, petting it. Worry was carved into his small features, and she thought how much he resembled his father. "Momma," he said. "We're home."

"Home?" Her voice was gruff. "Where's your dad?"

"He's gone to find Uncle Jean-René and get help," John Carter said.

Lauren nodded, swallowing hard. "Is there water?"

Henry got up and inspected the cave, then returned to his mother's side. "I'm sorry, Mom. I can't find any."

"It's okay." She winced. "Don't worry."

Jamie leaned in, inspecting the bandages. "Mom, your shoulder is bleeding again," he said, scowling.

"Pressure," she said, trying to see down at the stain spreading across the bandages. "Apply pressure."

Henry did as she instructed, but recoiled when his mother gasped, wincing. "Sorry, sorry!"

"It's going to hurt, it's okay." Lauren peered at him with unfocused eyes. "You have to do it. It's okay."

"I can do it," Jamie said. Henry moved aside. Jamie did as he'd seen his father do, despite his mother's response. He spoke soft words of comfort as he held the wound bravely.

His mother's brow knitted in pain. "Good job, sweet boy." Her other hand went to her stomach, as the muscles seized, and her face contorted with the pain that spread through her body.

"Are you okay, Mom?" Henry scowled.

"Yeah," she panted, through the contraction. "Yeah ... I'm okay ..."

"What's taking Dad so long?" Henry stood, pacing, much as his father did when he was trying to think.

"He's only been gone about thirty minutes," John Carter pointed out. He stood too and went to the entrance of the cave. "It's raining," he said. "Do we have anything we can catch water in? Something?"

Henry searched, finding nothing of use. A flash of inspiration hit him, and he went to the crate hidden in the back of the cave. "John Carter, help me," Henry called his brother over. "We have to get this lid off." Henry tossed the sword and tabards aside. John Carter and Henry both put their all into it and barely got the top to budge. "Try harder," Henry grunted.

"This is the hardest I have," John Carter replied. Then, as

if by an unknown force, the lid popped off. "What are you doing?"

There was a second crate inside the first, but several items lay wrapped in fine clothes. Henry rummaged through these relics finding a metal cup. It was relatively shallow, almost like the soup dishes in his Grandma Martha's China cabinet — the ones he and his brothers weren't allowed to use.

He blew the dust out of the bottom and wiped it off with the tail of his shirt. The bowl was flat with an effigy of a lion in the bottom. "Henry? I don't think that's supposed to be used for …" John Carter stopped when Henry took it outside and held it up in the rain. It took a moment to fill it, getting the boy's arm soaking wet in the process. "That's King Robert's cup! We're supposed to protect it. Not use it!"

"Mom needs water." He glared at his brother sharply as he passed.

"What if the cup has magic?" Jamie asked. "What if it could make Momma better?"

Henry scowled at his little brother. "This is King Robert the Bruce's cup. It's not the Holy Grail. You've been watching too much Indiana Jones."

"Wait," John Carter said, putting a hand on his brother's arm. "It's been in the same crate as the Ark of the Covenant. How could it not have magic?"

Henry scowled at them both, gazing down at the ancient cup. With a shrug, he dropped to his knees. "Mom." He lifted her head and held the shallow bowl to her lips. "Drink this."

Lauren managed a few swallows, draining the dish. They all sat back watching, waiting for the magic to happen. Their mom settled back and seemed to melt into sleep, but there were no sparks, no flickers of magic surrounding her as they'd expected. "*Brackium Emendo!*" Jamie said, waving one of the sticks from the fire kindling over his mother as if it were a wand.

Henry glowered at him. "Harry Potter spells? Really? That one is for mending bones."

"Well I don't know what a healing spell is," Jamie huffed, tossing the stick into the fire.

"It was worth a try." John Carter patted Jamie on the back.

"Dad better hurry," Henry said.

THE SLEET HAD TURNED TO A FREEZING RAIN, MAKING THE trail a hazardous quagmire. It was difficult to navigate. His hiking boots squished as they sunk ankle deep and the effort required to free himself became exhausting. Each mile passed slowly, and he cursed the weather, and his fate with each step.

At one point, he fell hard, wrenching his knee as his foot stuck in the mud. "Holy hell!" He shouted in agony. It felt good, so he let out another expletive-laced tirade that matched his mood. Roaring it at the top of his lungs, he balled up his fists and pounded them into the mud, splashing it into his face as he lay there and had a temper tantrum 'til he was spent.

Come on, Rowan, he chided himself, working to get his boot out of the quagmire. Pain shot through his knee, and he roared again. "Bloody hell." He winced, then thought to simply remove his foot from the shoe.

A bolt of lightning crackled overhead. Thunder crashed at almost the same moment. Then, a large hail stone bounced off his head, and he threw an arm up to protect himself, but the stones multiplied, bouncing like giant golf balls off the ground around him. They pelted him from head to toe. His arms went to his knee, protecting the injury at risk of his skull.

"Rowan!!" He heard a voice on the wind and turned to identify the source. "Lauren!!!"

"Over here!" Rowan yelled over the rumble of thunder.

"Henry!!!" The voice carried the name on the wind, but

Rowan still couldn't tell the direction from which it was coming. It wasn't Jean-René, and it wasn't Bahati, of that he was sure. "Jamie!! John Carter!?"

"Over here!" Rowan shouted again, scanning the trees around him. "*Heellppp*!!"

Rowan rolled up onto his hands and knee, unable to bear weight on the injured right knee. He was barely able to bend it. He pushed himself up, standing on one foot, testing the injured knee, finding it hurt to bear weight. He did anyway. Lightning bolts shot up the side of his leg, but he refused to stop. He managed a feeble limp. Mud squished through his sock and between his toes. He repeated the effort, but it was so bad, he could hardly bear it. Somehow, he kept himself upright, but caught a hailstone in the cheek and it almost blinded him. It stung like fire. He shook it off and managed a few more steps, seeing a movement in the woods.

He made it to the edge of the trail, leaning on one of the trees, throwing off the fur he'd kept on his shoulders, he waved it like a flag, as a form appeared in the dense cover. "Here! Help!"

"Rowan?!"

"George?" Rowan called out, a wave of relief washing over him. He realized George wasn't alone.

"Rowan." His brother-in-law scrambled through the underbrush and made it to him. "Are you okay?"

"My knee ... I think it's just a sprain," Rowan said.

"Where's Lauren? Are the boys with her?"

"Yeah," he said. "I left her in a cave not far from here. She's hurt."

"What happened?"

"I'll explain later," Rowan said. "We have to get her out."

"We thought you were dead ... search teams found a body in the swamp," George panted, hugging Rowan fiercely. "An old one."

Ko'i Minco? Rowan thought to himself. "It wasn't me."

"They said it must have been there a couple of hundred years or more," George said, letting go of his brother-in-law. "Tell me how to get to the cave," he said. "Mario can take you down and get that knee tended. You may have torn a ligament."

"No," Rowan said. "I can't tell you how to get there."

George scowled, reminding Rowan of his father, then turned to one of his firefighters. "Go alert the team. Get medics on standby. We'll need to transport as soon as we get her out. Bring up a couple of litters and triage kit. Meet me right back here." He pulled off his pack and pulled out a roll of hot pink plastic ribbon, drawing off a length of it, tying it around the tree Rowan leaned on. "Radio me when you get back here."

"Yes, sir!" Mario turned and headed back down the way he'd come.

Lauren lay staring at the fire, realizing she was awake. The boys were sitting nearby, but their gazes were distant and as unattached as hers had been. She felt horrible, and she was terribly uncomfortable. She groaned when she tried to move. Henry came over and knelt beside her. "What do you need, Mom?"

"Help me." She held up her uninjured hand. "I need to roll over. My back is killing me."

"Here." Henry got one of the furs he'd been sitting on and folded it up, tucking it under her head as he helped her get into a more comfortable position. "How's that?"

"Maybe sitting up would be better," she said, swallowing hard.

John Carter came over to help his brother, and they got her sitting upright and propped up on all the furs they found.

Jamie came over and sat by her. "Is the baby okay?"

Lauren's hand went to her stomach. "I think so."

"Dad's been gone for at least an hour," John Carter said. "I think I should go find him."

"No," Lauren said, shaking her head, wishing she hadn't. The cave spun around her.

"Momma, you don't look so hot," Jamie said, concern written on his face. "Henry, do you have more water?"

"Sure," he said. He brought back the cup and helped her drink.

Jamie moved to inspect the wound beneath the bandages. "The bleeding stopped."

Lauren made a face, wincing. "That's ... good," she panted.

"You're not going to have the baby here, are you?" Henry asked. He stood with his hands on his hips, appearing so much like his father.

She stretched her back, her face twisting in pain, as she shook her head and bit her lip. "No ..." she groaned. "No, not here."

"Are you sure?" John Carter wasn't so sure himself.

"Yes," Lauren said. She made to get up, and it took all three boys to help get her to her feet.

"Where are you going, Mom?" Henry asked.

"I can't just lay there," she said. "I just need to move. I'm hot."

"You have a fever." Henry caught her arm.

Lauren managed to straighten and made it the ten or so steps to the edge of the cave, peering out. The icy air blasted her in the face. She stepped back. It was hailing viciously. "You can't go out there," John Carter insisted.

"No." Lauren leaned on the wall. "I just needed fresh air." She doubled over, panting, as her stomach seized.

"Mom?" Jamie caught her elbow. "Are you sure you shouldn't lay down?"

"No," she said, glancing up, as the hail began to abate.

"We can't stay here." She stood erect, holding her stomach. "This could be our one chance to make a break for it before the weather gets worse."

"Dad said for us to stay here," Henry agreed with his brother. "We have to stay here. Mom! He promised us he'd be back."

"Boys," she said, calmly. "I know this is scary. I'm scared too, but if we don't get out of here now, I don't know what will happen. Henry, bring me one of those furs. You should each get one, too. Bundle up. I don't know how far we'll have to go."

The three boys hesitated, but when their mom buckled again, Henry sprang into action, gathering a fur for each of them He wrapped one around his mom's shoulders, before catching her arm. "Come on then," Henry ordered.

Lauren immediately began to question her sanity as her foot skidded on the icy slope, and she almost went down. If Henry hadn't had a strong grip on her, she might have landed hard on her butt, and that wouldn't be good for her or the baby. She glanced back, finding John Carter helping Jamie behind them. She turned her attention back to her own feet. They made it to the trail below, and Lauren felt a wave of relief wash over her as they turned towards camp, along a path they had come to know well.

"Mom?" Henry patted her cheek. "Stay with me, Mom."

Lauren felt faint but her resolve carried her as she assured him she was fine, even as her knees buckled underneath her. "Mom!" John Carter bolted up and caught her by the elbow of her injured arm and she let out a gut-wrenching yelp.

"Lauren?" Their dad's voice echoed in the distance. "Lauren?!"

"Dad!" Henry shouted. "Over here! We're over here!"

Henry had just gotten his mom to her feet when his dad hobbled up the trail, along with their Uncle George. "Lauren," George left Rowan to his sons and rushed forward to help his sister. "Lauren?"

"Uncle George!" The boys cheered. Relief was evident in their voices.

"George?" Lauren's blurred as the shadow of the giant moved closer. "What are you doing here?"

"Searching for you," he said, helping her over to a fallen tree, sitting her down so he could inspect her. "What happened?"

"I don't remember," she said, trying to focus on him, but consciousness was fleeting. He did a quick assessment. Steam rose off her body, and he put a hand to her flame-red cheek, noting her temperature was dangerously high.

"Are you still having contractions?" Rowan asked, when he got to her.

"Yeah," she panted. "Not often enough to time, but ... often enough."

"Could be Braxton-Hicks, but we can't take any chances," George said. "I've called in the extraction team. They're coming with a Stokes basket. We'll have to transport you by car. The nearest hospital is about thirty minutes away, but that's in good weather. Might take us an hour today." He paused, reaching into his pack, pulling out a bottle of water. "Drink this," he said, opening it for her and holding it to her lips. She drank greedily, draining half of it before she turned away. "A little more?"

"No," she protested, her head tipping forward as she swooned.

"Henry, John Carter, you'll have to help your dad. Jamie, can you carry my pack?"

"Yes, sir," Jamie said, nodding.

"Come on, little sister." George collected Lauren and lifted her as if she weighed nothing.

~

AN HOUR AND A HALF LATER, GEORGE'S COMMAND VEHICLE pulled into the ER bay and Lauren and Rowan were both offloaded. Lauren's contractions had eased, but her shoulder was killing her. Rowan had started an IV in the car and was running saline full out as he monitored her vitals while George drove. Her pulse was thready, and she was in a state of near-faint all the way there. He fed information to the response team as he was moved to wheel chair. Lauren was placed on a stretcher and taken into an exam room in the ER.

Rowan protested when they started to take him to another room. "I'm staying with my wife."

The nurse didn't argue. They went to work assessing Lauren's condition first. Rowan chair was parked in the corner by Lauren's head where he could watch, but not interfere.

"Her temp's 103.5," one of the nurses said.

"Let's get her on a fetal heart and uterine monitors," the doctor said. "Let's get ultrasound in here, too."

"She's dilated 2 centimeters, 80% effaced."

"When's your due date?" The doctor moved closer and raised his voice.

"February 14th," Lauren said faintly.

"That can't be right," the nurse protested.

"She's delirious," the doctor said, making a quick examination. "Are you sure about that date?"

Lauren didn't answer. The doctor glanced up at Rowan. He didn't know how to explain it, and he thought better of even trying. "It's too early," he said.

"Continue to push fluids and start her on some mag sulfate," the doctor said, patting Lauren on her leg. "We're going to run some tests and address the *preterm* labor, then we'll worry about your shoulder."

Lauren nodded and closed her eyes, and left them to it, drifting off into unconsciousness. "Lauren?" The doctor called her name, pinching her uninjured shoulder.

"BP is 89/50," the nurse announced

"Get that equipment in here."

"Lauren?" Rowan used his uninjured foot to pull the wheel chair closer. "Honey? What's going on? What's wrong?"

"Take Mr. Pierce next door," the doctor said. "We're still trying to assess your wife's condition, but she's in good hands." The doctor lowered his tone as he spoke to the nurse. "Get OB down here, now."

"Rowan Pierce?' Rowan was smoldering when a different doctor came in. He could hear them next door and knew Lauren's condition had stabilized but he was still worried.

"What brings you in today?" Rowan's swollen knee answered his question. His pant leg had been cut to expose the injury. The nurse had removed the field brace George had put on him at the command post. Now, he was sitting up on a gurney with his arms on the guard rails. "Ouch." The doctor laid the chart down. "Slip and fall on the ice?"

"Lost my boot in the mud." Rowan scowled. He wasn't happy he couldn't focus on what was going on next door. "Twisted my knee."

One of the nurses came to check in with the doctor. "Let's get an x-ray and see what we're dealing with. We'll need an MRI, too. Just hang tight Mr. Pierce. We'll patch you up and have you on your way."

"Don't worry about me. Just take care of my wife."

The doctor looked puzzled. "Mrs. Pierce is being treated next door," the nurse informed him.

"How is she?" Rowan asked.

"The contractions have slowed," she said, as she took his blood pressure. "They're running some tests. The good news is the babies are fine."

"B-b-babies? As in … more than one?" Rowan's brows shot up.

She looked at him sideways and her brows knitted. "You didn't know your wife was pregnant with twins?"

"T-t-twins?" Now Rowan felt faint. "No …" He swallowed hard. "No wonder she's as big as a house."

"Mr. Pierce," she scolded.

"Sorry." He shrugged. "But she is," he added.

"She seems to think she's not due until February."

"It's too soon, but … she's not thinking straight," Rowan lied. "That was when our first was due." He glanced up as George came in with the boys. Rowan was absolutely convinced something about the *time-shift* had accelerated her pregnancy. That wasn't something he felt like he could share, though.

"Hey, guys." Rowan's attention turned to his sons. "Everybody okay?"

"Yes, sir," they chorused.

"Is your knee broken?" Jamie asked, screwing up his face as he inspected it. "It sure looks broken."

"We're about to find out," the doctor said. "But I'm going to have to ask you guys to wait in the waiting room." He turned to Rowan. "All yours?"

"All of them except the tall one." He grinned at George. "That's their uncle."

The doctor chuckled. "Okay, guys." He put a hand on Henry's shoulder. "We're going to run some tests and see what's going on with your dad's knee. You can see him once we're done."

"What about our mom?"

"They're still checking on her," the doctor said. "We'll know more in a little bit."

"I'm hungry, Uncle George," Jamie said.

"Me, too," John Carter admitted.

"Of course you are." George chuckled. "We'll go see what

they have to eat in the cafeteria," George said, then glanced at Rowan. "I'll check back in once I get them fed."

"Hey, George," Rowan called after him. They all stopped and took a step back. "How do you feel about being an uncle to twins?"

George's brow lifted, and the boys looked surprised. "Twins?" George gulped. "I have been a brother to twins." He glanced at the boys. "You guys are in *soooo* much trouble," he chortled.

Rowan could hear the boys chittering between themselves as they passed down the hallway, until they were out of earshot. Rowan lay his head back on the pillow, and tucked his arms in, laying there trying to process the idea of twins. It never occurred to him to ask if they were boys or girls.

"Okay, Rowan." The nurse returned with an orderly pushing a wheel chair. "Let's go see what's going on with that knee."

19

Lauren sat in front of the fire, gazing into the flames, deep in thought. Tsul'Kalu sat across from her. The fire flickered in his eyes as he lifted his head to speak. "How goes it, daughter?"

She glanced up, her blank gaze evolving into an expression of joy. "It is well," she said. "And with you?"

"The crusaders have begun their journey home," he said. "The relics?"

"Safely hidden," she said, her hand going to the amulet that lay on her chest. "For now. They'll have to be moved … eventually."

"And with you?"

"The fever is abating, but … I do not think I will be able to come to you again," she said. "Not any time soon."

"I will find you, *Truth Seeker*." The kind face of her mentor morphed into that of her father. "You are in safe hands, and you will not need me much longer."

Lauren melted. "I will always need you."

The wizard's eyes sparkled through her father's face. "I am never more than a dream away," he said, and rose slowly. "I am with you always."

"You are always welcome." Lauren assured him and nodded as his image faded in the darkness. "Come home."

~

"LAUREN?" A VOICE ECHOED IN THE DISTANCE. SHE FOUND herself laying in a hospital bed. A large bouquet of flowers set on the table beside her. She lay on her side, with a pillow tucked behind her back. She made to roll over, but stopped, realizing her left arm was completely immobilized in a sling. She reached for the button to raise the head of the bed, surprised to find Bahati at her elbow. "Hey, boss," she said. "Welcome back."

Lauren grinned sheepishly. "How long have I been out of it?"

"Couple of days." Bahati pulled up the stool beside the bed and leaned on the rail. "Kind of feels like *déjà vu*, you know."

"Days?" Lauren groaned. "*Déjà vu*? I feel like I've been gone for months."

"No, not quite that long," Bahati chortled. "But while we're on the subject could you not do that again? It's starting to get old."

"Sorry about that," Lauren said.

"The doctor thinks you'll deliver early." Bahati reached over and rested a hand on Lauren's stomach.

"Early?" She seemed to perk up. "Wait, what's the date? What is today?"

"October 27th," she said.

"Are you sure?" Lauren asked, blankly. If she were right, they'd completely missed Rowan's birthday.

"Certain. Remember, *I've* been *here* the whole time," she said. "Unlike *some* people."

Lauren startled, her hand going to her stomach, as if she'd forgotten she was still pregnant. "Is … is the baby okay?"

"Yes. The *babies* are fine." Bahati moved a lock of hair off her forehead. "Both of them."

"Both?" Lauren's eyes crossed a moment, then realization washed over her face. She seemed to blanch. "Twins?"

Bahati nodded. "You seem surprised." She leaned her ear on her fist, studying her best friend's face.

"Well, that explains a lot," Lauren smirked. "But … I'm not due until February."

"You must have your dates mixed up." Bahati shrugged. "The doctor says you're right on track for going full term, if you don't domino right here and now."

Lauren shook her head and nodded, now comfortable enough to lay in silence. She knew when she'd conceived — had been 100% certain of it from the get-go. Rowan had called to Freyja, the fertility goddess — *that was it*! It all made perfect sense now that she thought about it. Of course it was twins. She was lucky it wasn't a whole litter, to hear him talk about how he had prayed. She felt her cheeks warm into a blush remembering how fervent he had been. "Where is everyone?" She diverted the conversation.

"Jean-René and the boys are at your brother's place," she said.

"What about Rowan?"

Bahati nodded to the side of the bed, and Lauren had to wrench her neck around to see him sleeping on a low trundle, with his knee elevated on a pillow, wrapped in bandages, and splinted.

"Torn ACL," Bahati informed her friend. "He's going to need surgery, but he refused to go until he knew you were all right."

"Oh, man!" Lauren said.

"The doctor said it was a complete tear and it was a miracle he could even walk on it."

"Well, I'm all right," Lauren said. "He needs to get it fixed."

"He'll be so relieved to hear that," Bahati said.

"Is everyone else okay? Nyota?"

"She's fine," Bahati said. "Chance took a tumble and is going to be out of commission for a while, but the Network flew him home to San Diego, along with all our equipment and film. They want us to come back when we can. They want us to do our post production in San Diego."

"I'm surprised we're not fired," Lauren said. "I'm sure this hasn't been the best press for us."

Bahati shrugged. "No, not really, but Jacob hopes you'll have a *good story* to dispel the bad press."

"Oh." Lauren yawned. "We have a good story all right."

But Lauren realized they had yet another truth they couldn't tell. But, the markings in the cave — they could talk about that, she decided. "Henry Sinclair was here …" she smirked to herself, deciding to play her delirium up. "We met him."

Bahati's brow shot up and she stood, leaning back, her eyes going wide as she crossed her arms and cocked her hip to one side. "Mm-hm," she scoffed. "Sure you did."

20

A little over a week later, Lauren was sitting in the rocking chair in George's living room with a baby in her arms. Her mother was sitting in the recliner beside her with his twin sister. "Lauren, she's beautiful," Diana said. "But this name? *What* were you thinking?"

"I was thinking if I didn't come up with *something*, Rowan was going to name her Leia Organa, LeeLoo Dallas ... or Dana Scully."

"But where did you come up with the name Kathryn Jane?"

"In keeping with our theme, Kathryn Janeway was the first female captain featured in her own Star Trek series," Rowan said from the kitchen. "And Kathryn is a nod to Kitty."

"Michael will like that." Diana beamed. "Kitty will, too."

"It could be worse, Mom," George piped up as he came in and sat down on the sofa. "She could be named Katniss Everdeen or Hermione Grainger."

"So, where did the name Samuel Beckett come from?" Diana asked, leaning over to inspect baby in Lauren's arm. "Murder in the Cathedral?"

"That was Thomas Becket."

"So you do remember some of your education from catholic school," Diana said.

"Sam Beckett was a character in the show *Quantum Leap*," Lauren said, deciding it was more than appropriate. Sam Beckett had been a time traveler, too. "And, the actor who played Sam went on to play a Captain on the *Enterprise* in one of the many evolutions of *Star Trek*."

"I wanted to name him Duncan McCloud," Rowan said, hobbling in on his crutches from the kitchen. "But as Lauren pointed out, that wouldn't work because he was a twin."

"Well, what does that have to do with anything?" Diana scowled. She was not a science fiction fan.

"Duncan McCloud is a character from *Highlander*, and ... as anyone who knows anything about *Highlander* knows ... *there can be only one*." He lowered his tone, trying to sound like Sean Connery.

"One what?" Diana puzzled as everyone else laughed.

"We debated naming them Freyja and Thor, seeing as how they were born on Thor's Day and Freyja's Day." Kate had been born on Thursday at 11:58 pm, and Sam had arrived shortly after midnight on Friday. It gave each of them their own separate birthdays. "But we didn't want to do that to our kids."

"Thank heavens," George smirked. A knock at the door interrupted the friendly banter. George rose. "Sit here, Rowan. Put your knee up." Rowan took him up on the offer and propped his splinted leg up on the recliner.

"How's your knee?" Lauren asked.

"Nothing that a new piece of ligament and a couple of screws couldn't fix," he grunted, getting comfortable. He'd undergone surgery two days before Lauren went into labor. He'd coached her from a stool beside the bed. "Now, I just need six to twelve weeks of physical therapy."

Lauren's attention went to George as he came in grinning

wickedly. She realized someone was behind him in the hall-way. Everyone turned to see, but George said nothing. He just stepped aside and let the man in.

Diana gasped, her hand going to her mouth. In a frantic panic, she collected baby Kate and handed her off to Rowan, as she got up from her chair and raced across the room, clipping her shin on the coffee table as she went to grab the man and pull him into her arms. She was wailing in tears. When Lauren saw who it was, she knew why.

Tsul'Kalu — John Grayson — embraced his wife for the first time in a long time. It was an appropriate welcome from a wife who'd given him up for dead. Lauren glanced at Rowan and the two shared a knowing gaze as he settled Kate on his shoulder.

Lauren resumed her rocking and waited patiently before Diana turned around, drying her tears with her hands, regaining her composure. She seemed embarrassed by the show of emotion, but managed to collect herself enough to say, "Lauren, *this* is your father."

Lauren nodded. "I know," she said. "We've met. *Osiyo*, Father."

"*Dohidjunihi*, daughter," he said, with a slight bow. He held out a brown paper bag and the perfume of fried meat and potatoes filled her nose.

"What's this?" She took it with a puzzled expression.

He leaned in to hug her. "I have conjured you a cheese-burger," he said, chortling as she sat back.

"And bless you for it," she said, sticking her face in the bag, inhaling the perfume of it.

"My son." He walked over and offered Rowan his hand in friendship. Rowan made to stand, but John waved him off.

"I didn't think we would ever see you again," Diana sobbed as she embraced John again.

"When I found our daughter, she told me of your heartbreak," he said. "I had feared I would not be welcome at your hearth. You had been so angry when I had to leave, so I stayed away. *This one* convinced me that I would be welcomed." John gave a nod of his chin toward Lauren.

Diana glared at him sharply, then turned slowly to Lauren, realizing the implication of his words. The two locked eyes on one another, and for once, the kindness that passed between them was evident. Neither was bitter, nor angry, and forgiveness seemed to abound in each of their expressions.

"Of course, you are welcome," George said, clearly oblivious to the moment going on right in front of his face. "You are family. This home is yours."

Diana's hands were trembling as she ran one of them down the collar of his shirt, straightening it out of reflex more than need. "How long can you stay?"

"As long as I can," he said. "Not as long as I would like, but … I have some business with my son-in-law."

Diana's brow shot up as high as Rowan's did. "With me?" he asked, surprised.

"You had a task that you will need help with," he said. "We will talk more of this later, but for now, I want to see my grandchildren again and meet the new ones."

"I'll go find the boys," George said, as John came over and sat beside Rowan. His son-in-law handed the small bundle to the old man. The ginger-haired baby yawned and opened her blue eyes, gazing up at her grandfather placidly.

"John, this is your granddaughter, Kate," Rowan said.

Lauren came over with the boy. Rowan took him and laid him in his father-in-law's other arm. "And this is Sam."

"They are beautiful." Lauren heard a tremble in her father's voice. His eyes glistened.

"John, did you know there would be twins?" Rowan asked.

He had that all-knowing expression that seemed so mystical and wise. Rowan had his answer.

~

"DOES ANYONE KNOW OF *THE CRATE*?" JOHN ASKED AS ROWAN poured a cup of coffee and handed it to him. It was two a.m., and Rowan had been on late night diaper duty so Lauren could get some sleep. Kate had been fussy, and John rocked her back to sleep, then tucked her into the bassinet that sat nearby. At five days old, they still hadn't gotten the twins onto a schedule that had allowed Lauren much rest, but she insisted on nursing them both. She slept whenever she could.

"No," Rowan said. "No one has been into the cave, and Lauren spun a wild tale about having been attacked by a hunter. The sheriff bought it, even though it seemed like a lame story to me."

"You might call it … a *Jedi Mind Trick*," John smirked. "I have mastered the *magic* of the Ancient gods." Rowan's brow went up. "That is how you do not remember me from Mt. St. Helens. As you have learned, *her* powers come from the gods as well. She will someday be as great a *jedi* as her father."

"As long as you're not *Darth Vader*, I guess we're okay," Rowan said, amused at the thought.

"I use *the Force* for good, son. Always."

Henry appeared at his dad's elbow, rubbing his eyes. "Hey, buddy." Rowan reached out a hand and pulled his son into him. "What are you doing up?"

"I smelled coffee," he said. "I thought it was breakfast time."

"You are a couple of hours early, son," John said. "But you are not hungry."

"I'm not hungry," Henry said.

Rowan cast a suspicious gaze at his father-in-law. His brow twitched. Clearly he was impressed with the trick. "Henry, we haven't had a chance to talk since your mom and I got home. Why don't you have a seat?"

Henry sat down, peering up with a sheepish expression, as if he were in trouble for something. "What?"

"Back in the swamp in the *other* time-place, you told me you saw what happened with your mother and Ko'i Minco, but you didn't believe it. What did you mean by that?"

Rowan noticed John's knowing gaze but focused his attention on Henry.

"Dad, I don't think you'd believe me if I told you." Henry shrugged. "Heck, I don't believe it."

Rowan felt the bemused expression wash over his face. "Try me, son. After seeing some of the stuff your mom can do, little surprises me anymore."

Henry glanced over at his grandfather who gave him an encouraging nod. "Okay." Henry folded his hands on the table in front of him, appearing mature beyond his years, and terribly serious. He took a deep breath and continued. "When that guy attacked Mom, I was sure I was going to have to kill him," he began, his voice shaking as he spoke. He swallowed hard and continued, steadying himself. "I followed him into the swamp. I had Mom's knife, and I was ready to stab his eyes out if I had to. I don't know how she did it, as hurt as she was, but Mom followed us. I didn't see Ko'i Minco at first, I just saw Mom. She was hurt … hurt bad … but I don't know what happened … one minute it was Mom, but then … it wasn't Mom …" he hesitated, his eyes darting between the two men, nervously.

"What do you mean?"

"Tell your father, son." John already seemed to know.

"It wasn't mom that attacked Ko'i Minco … it was … a … a *Bigfoot*."

Rowan's whole face dropped, and he sank back in his chair, his grip on his coffee cup going slack. "Your … mom? But *not* your mom."

"A Bigfoot, Dad," Henry repeated.

"Your mom … turned into … a *Bigfoot*?"

"Uh, huh," Henry said, nodding.

"Your mother was ... a Bigfoot." It was a statement, not a question.

"I told you that you wouldn't believe me," Henry said.

Rowan shifted in his chair to peer at John. "Did you know about this?"

"I knew her *powers* were growing," John admitted easily. "*Wizards* like me ... like her ... have many disguises we must use. Like any mother, she will use everything within her power to protect her children."

Rowan sat contemplating this idea for a moment. He thought back to Mexico, when he'd been injured. She said she pushed Santiago Mateo into a cenote, but ... he'd seen a jaguar go flying into the air as Mateo went over. Had she used the form of the jaguar to save him from the killer, too?

"Grandpa," Henry said to his grandfather. "Mom said if I were lucky, someday I would get to see a Bigfoot. She said the Bigfoots were her friends."

"*The People* — that is what the Bigfoot tribes call themselves — they are the friends of the *Tsalagi*."

"Have you ever seen a Bigfoot, Grandpa?"

John chuckled. "Your mother is my child. She is blood of my blood and bone of my bone," he said. "The powers that flow through her, flow through me as well." John gazed at him intently, and Rowan suspected he was using those *Jedi Mind Tricks* on him. "And ... through you, too."

"Cool," Henry chirped, then yawned. "I'm gonna go back to bed now. Wake me up when breakfast is ready?"

"Sure, son," Rowan said and hugged the boy before he wandered back to bed.

John grinned at Rowan when they were alone again. "Your sons are good boys." He nodded. "That one though ..."

"I realize now why he's been such a challenge," Rowan said. "Never is where he is supposed to be, always late for dinner. He's not a bad kid. He's been testing his *powers*."

"He will grow to have as much magic as his mother," John said. "They all have their gifts. A wise father will find a way to manage them. You, Rowan, are a wise father."

Rowan pursed his lips. "Thank you, John."

"Now, we need to do something about the chest."

EPILOGUE

"So where do we hide it?" Rowan asked, thinking aloud. John had extracted the crate from the cave. Rowan still wasn't sure just how he had done it, but the crate now sat in a U-Haul truck at the edge of the forest.

"One of the practices of The People, is to hide in plain sight," John said, firing up the engine. "We are often confused for tree trunks, or shadows in the mist."

Rowan furrowed his brow as John put the truck in gear and revved the engine into motion. That gave Rowan an idea. "It seems sacrilegious," he said. "These treasures should be in a museum … or a church."

"Perhaps in time," John said. "But you have been given your divine missive, and your wisdom will serve you well."

They drove the truck to the UPS drop-off in Tahlequah and Rowan arranged to have the crate shipped back to *The Veritas Codex* headquarters, under the guise of being part of the equipment used for the television show. Rowan paid extra to ensure the shipment received care, and was properly insured, though no amount of money was enough to protect such sacred objects. Still, Rowan had no other choice.

"Thank you for bringing your father home," Diana said as she rocked Kate. Sam had been fed, changed and was asleep in his car seat carrier to await his father's return and their journey back to San Diego.

Lauren had a minute to rest before Kate would demand similar attention. "I wish I had known," Lauren said, curled up on the sofa.

"Known what?" Diana asked.

"The truth." She yawned.

"About your father?" Diana asked. "You would have thought I was crazy."

Lauren lifted her head, raising up onto her elbow to meet her mother's eye. "I thought he left … because of *me*. Because he didn't want another kid. I thought *you* hated *me* for that."

"Sweetheart …" Diana shook her head, leaning forward. "I found out I was pregnant with you two months after your father left for good. You were a product of our last night together. I loved him just as much as you love Rowan. He was my everything. Our souls are connected with a force stronger than any in the universe," Diana said. "I knew what he was when we married. I thought … if we tried hard enough, we could make it work. For years, we tried. But as time passed, he grew weak. His magic grew weak. We both knew he needed to go back to his own place, or he would die. We found ways to buy us time. But people talk. So I told them he'd gone to war. The longer he stayed, the longer it took for him to regain his strength. It affected his mind, too. He would forget about me, for a time. When he remembered, he would come home. He couldn't stay indefinitely, and soon he had to leave more often."

Lauren swallowed hard. She felt sick thinking about how she would have reacted if it had been Rowan who had to leave her. She couldn't bear it.

Diana continued. Her expression spoke of melancholy. "He gave me seven beautiful children, and I was thankful for that … but … when he left that last time and didn't come home … it gutted me. I thought I was strong enough to endure anything, but a life without John? I just couldn't do it. I did what so many do. Over the years, I started drinking. I lost myself in my grief, and a bottle. I wasn't the mother I wanted to be, but … I couldn't bring myself out of it. Once the house was empty, and all my children were gone, I thought it was over. I was ready to surrender …"

"How did you …?" Lauren couldn't even finish the sentence. She had created a vivid image of how she would feel if it were Rowan who left and couldn't come back. That was one of her biggest insecurities. The thought terrified her.

"He came home one last time," Diana said. "It was while you were in college in California. He told me that he'd found you in another *time-place*, and he promised me we'd have this moment. He didn't give me any details, but he gave me advice on many things, so I could prepare for trouble, or make sure the family was taken care of. John even left a pouch containing uncut diamonds once."

"Diamonds?"

"I knew they were from him," she said. "Even though he didn't leave a note or anything. He'd do that kind of thing when he could. I cashed in some of them and used them to pay for the trip to come to your wedding. I'm saving some to help with your children's college tuitions, if they decide they want a PhD … or two."

Lauren's heart chilled. She'd been so rude to her mother. It crushed her to think of the angry stare she'd given to the woman after their wedding ceremony.

"Don't blame yourself, Lauren." Diana squeezed her hand again. "We all managed in our own ways. Once I knew we'd be okay — you and me — then I trusted your father."

"But he never came to see you," Lauren said. Her brow narrowed.

"I knew he couldn't," Diana said. "I also came to realize that as long as he was out there, I would be okay. As long as he was safe, I could endure anything."

"Thank you for not giving up on me," Lauren said. "I always thought it was my fault … that you hated me for him leaving."

"I hated myself."

Lauren's brows knitted and a lump formed in her throat. She shook her head, turning away as her mother squeezed her hand. "I was so … wrong," she squeaked, her voice cracking as she pushed the tears off her face with her free hand.

"I was wrong, too," Diana said. "But … the past is the past. We have our whole future to grow close again."

"I'd like that," Lauren said.

Diana nodded. "Then let us move forward as friends."

"Done." Lauren rose and reached over the baby to hug her mother.

"Besides," Diana said, pushing tears off her face. "You are going to need me."

"I am?" Lauren asked, sitting back down, snatching a tissue from the box by the chair. She handed one to her mother before she took another for herself.

"You will want to go back to work soon," Diana said. "You will need someone to care for the children while you travel."

"You'd do that?"

"I have done it for all my boys … I am available whenever you need me. You need only to ask."

∽

By the time John and Rowan returned to George's house, Lauren had the children packed and ready to head to the airport. The babies had been changed and fed. Both slept in their car-seat carriers.

"Everything okay?" Lauren kissed Rowan as he came in, surrounded by the cold he brought with him.

"Yeah," he said. "How's your shoulder today?"

"Still sore, but not bad," she said. "What took you so long? I was starting to worry."

"Took a little bit to get the truck loaded," John said.

Rowan inspected her line of suitcases and duffle bags as the boys came bounding down the stairs, so loud he thought it might wake the twins. "Is everyone ready to go?"

"Everyone's been fed, and everything is packed," she said. "I think Kate and Sam will sleep at least until we get to the airport in Tulsa."

"Here." George followed the boys down. "Let me help." He took Lauren's bag, and the diaper bag. "I'll take these to the SUV."

"Thank you," Lauren said. "Come on guys, get your stuff and take it out to the car."

"What did you tell Jean-René?" Rowan asked.

"I sent him on to the airport with Bahati and Nyota. I told him you had to file a police report with the Sheriff," Lauren said. "They're on the same flight, so, it's not like they'll leave Tulsa without us."

"They didn't have a problem with that?"

"No. I don't think they wanted to be crammed in an SUV with George, three rowdy boys, two crying babies, a dude with his knee in a splint, and a woman with her arm in a sling."

"Valid point." He leaned on his crutches and gave a nod.

"They said they'd meet us at the airport and help us with all our stuff," she said. "Let's not keep them waiting. I don't want to miss our flight."

∾

Monday morning, they arrived at the studio in San Diego, and it was a joyful homecoming. They hadn't been back to the *mothership* in some time, and it was good to be there. The staff was happy to see them. From Amy at the front desk, to Zack, the security guard, they were greeted with well-wishes and congratulations. The Exploration Channel staff gushed over the babies and raved about how big the boys — and Nyota — had gotten.

Jacob greeted Lauren with a big, albeit gentle, hug. Rowan got a handshake, and he invited them into his office. Jacob greeted each of the boys and asked them questions about their travels and their harrowing ordeal. Lauren had coached each one of them, and they understood the magnitude of their secret and their sacred duty to protect it. They had their cover stories well practiced. Each of the boys delivered their stories with impeccable timing and no variation from the set story.

Bahati set Kate's baby carrier next to Lauren's chair, while Jean-René carried in Sam. Jacob inspected each of their sleeping faces, nodding with approval as he pushed his glasses up his nose. "They are beautiful, Lauren," he said, as he sat on the edge of his desk, casually. He eyed Rowan with his knee in a brace, and Lauren with her arm in a sling much more critically.

"I'm hungry, Mom," John Carter said.

"Of course you are," she said, rolling her eyes.

"Come on," Jean-René said. "Let's go find a bagel." The boys followed Jean-René and Bahati to see if there was anything to eat in the employee break room.

"I'll take a coffee," Rowan called after them, setting his crutches aside as he sat down.

"How's the leg?"

"It still hurts," he admitted. "But the swelling is coming down."

"Well, that's good," Jacob said. "Probably best to stay off it a while longer."

"That's what the doctor said."

"And what about you, Lauren?"

"I'll have to do some physical therapy before I get my range of motion back. But it's not as bad as when I broke my arm in Washington State."

"I'm sure it's hard juggling twins with a lame flipper," he smirked at his own humor.

"You could say that," she said politely.

"So," Jacob said. "We've been reviewing the video you sent back, and I must say, there's some pretty provocative evidence."

Lauren glanced at Rowan, puzzling. "What part?"

"What part? What do you mean, *what part?*" Jacob gesticulated wildly. "You have video of a skunk ape, and you act like it's no big deal? The pictures of the mark on Lauren's face? Are you kidding me?"

"Oh," Rowan said, ducking sheepish. "Well... yeah, but …" He managed a shrug.

"You got video of a skunk ape?" Lauren's brow knitted.

"Sorry. I didn't get a chance to tell you about it." He shrugged. "Since that video was taken, my wife and sons were kidnapped and attacked, I got lost in the woods and blew out my knee, and my wife gave birth to twins. We weren't expecting twins, so cut me some slack, will ya?" There was a hint of jest in his voice.

"Forgiven," Lauren said with a nod. "I can't wait to see it."

"Oh, by the way," Rowan said to Jacob. "I'm expecting a crate to be delivered here in the next day or two."

"Oh?"

"Yeah, I bought some old movie props off the internet," he said. "It was a whim, but I got a heck of a deal."

Lauren scowled at him and shook her head. "Two new babies and he's blowing our money on movie props."

"Would you expect anything different?" Jacob mused. "Well, while we're on that topic, I have a feeling when the studio sees the post production on this episode, they're going to want to renew for another season or two. I'm giving you a boost in your budget and we're moving you to the Sunday night 7/9 pm slot."

"Would that include a raise?" Lauren asked. "To help me cover his movie memorabilia habit?"

"As a matter of fact, it does," he nodded. "Fifteen percent sound fair?"

"Twenty-five percent sounds better," Rowan said.

"I'll make it twenty percent and include a generous housing allowance to help you find a place here in San Diego."

"San Diego?" Lauren and Rowan asked in unison.

"I know you're probably anxious to go home to Hawai'i, and if you plan to take some time off with the babies, of course, that would be fine, but ... the studio wants to do the post-production here. I know you both used to like living here."

"We only moved to Hawai'i because we couldn't find a place we could afford." Lauren nodded.

"That won't be a problem with this housing stipend," he said. "Want a place on the beach? I'll make sure it happens."

"Are you serious?" Lauren's brow lifted.

"As serious as a shark attack," he said, borrowing one of Rowan's favorite quips.

Rowan arched a brow and tilted his head. "That's pretty serious."

"Just let me know how soon I can expect you back, and I'll get a realtor to work finding you a place to live."

"We'll need a room for my mother," Lauren said. "She's going to come stay with us to help with the babies."

"Your mother?" Rowan's brow lifted. "Are you sure?"

Lauren nodded. "We'll need her here, so she can watch the kids while we travel."

"What about Bahati and Jean-René?" Rowan turned back to Jacob.

"Yup," he said. "We'll take care of them, too."

"Well, I guess I better get to work researching some new mysteries to solve." Rowan grinned, glancing at Lauren. "Work for you?"

"Well, I was thinking about taking some time off to author a book ... I'm thinking of calling it *The Ultimate Guide to Crypto-zoology*."

"That has a nice ring to it," Rowan said.

"So, write a book," Jacob said. "We'll get it to a publisher for you. Does that work?"

"I think that will be perfect," she said. "We've suddenly outgrown the house in Hawai'i anyway."

Jacob sat back, appearing placid. "So, how long do you need? Six weeks? Six months?"

"Twelve weeks more or less, if Rowan's knee heals well enough, and I get use of my arm by then. Of course, I won't want to travel while I'm nursing the twins, but we'll figure something out."

"I'll check back in with you in twelve weeks," he said. "I'll get crews started building out a studio office to film your post-show recap for future episodes."

"Oh, can we recreate my office in Hilo?" Rowan asked.

"Sure," Jacob said. "Send me all the details."

"I'll bring all my mementos to decorate it," he said.

"I don't know what movie props you found, but if they'd be great for background effect, you could expense your purchase ... get you out of the doghouse with Lauren," he suggested. Rowan's eyebrow shot up, thinking of John Grayson's advice about hiding things in plain sight.

"Expense it, huh?" Rowan thought aloud. "Shipping, too?"

"Fine," Jacob said, rolling his eyes. "Shipping, too."

"You know what? That just might work." Rowan grinned.

"Props from the set of *Indiana Jones*," he said, thinking quickly.

"Oh, really?"

"Yeah." He lifted a shoulder, shaking his head. "Just some stuff from some of the Indiana Jones movies. You know, a couple of crusaders tabards and a few other things."

"You can use those as props in your office," Jacob said. "I can't think of anything else that represents Rowan Pierce and his adventures better."

Lauren scowled clearing her throat overtly. "What am I? Chopped liver?"

"You want a studio office, too?" Jacob blushed, realizing he'd slighted her.

"No," Lauren said. "Maybe not a separate one … but you could put a desk in there for me, too. May I remind you, this *was my* show before Rowan stepped in and usurped me."

"You have a point, of course," Jacob said. "I can't think of a better way to show you are both partners in these adventures. You need more voice overs and screen time in the intro and wrap up. Heck, Lauren, we can set you up with an office where you can direct the field research until you can travel."

Lauren nodded. "That sounds fair."

"So we have a deal?"

"We have a deal," Rowan said, glancing at Lauren for confirmation. "We have a deal?"

"Yes," she said. "We have a deal."

SIX MONTHS LATER, THEY RETURNED TO SAN DIEGO. ALL their possessions had been shipped back to the mainland to their new beach-front home. A studio office was waiting for them at the Network's headquarters. Rowan and Lauren each had a desk, and there was a sofa with a coffee table, and even a play area for the kids that could be used on air, or not.

The set designers had free reign to decorate Lauren's portion of the office. Her desk was a rustic slab from a single fallen tree cut at an angle on the bias. The smoothed-off bark surrounded most of the exterior. The rings were stained into alternating ovals of light and dark, polished to a sheen. Pictures of her children lined the floating book case, and she had a lamp that one might find more suited to a bedside table than an office, but it worked. The artwork in her space included paintings by a Cherokee artist the Network had commissioned. There was a hand-painted statue of a warrior spinning in the Eagle Dance, and a similar statue of a Pretty Woman in her blue fringed shawl, and ribbon skirt. The details were delicate and so amazingly intricate.

Lauren admired them in wonder, as she sat in the chair behind the desk, before turning back to Rowan in the desk behind her. Jean-René had informed her that they were arranged that way, so that when they filmed, the camera could focus on her, then shift to focus on him as it panned passed her. He promised her it would be a cool effect and would ensure they were both in the frame for a portion of the segments they would film together.

Rowan's desk from Hawai'i had been shipped back state-side, and photos had been used to ensure every trinket and item had been placed in the exact same spot it had been back home. The studio had done an amazing job to ensure the feel of his home office, including the window behind him, which was a projection screen so they could simulate different back-grounds. "We can make it rain, or make it appear to be night, even when we're filming in the middle of the day," Jean-René explained. "I can control shadows that might interfere with getting the shot."

"It's brilliant." Rowan grinned from ear to ear.

And there, behind Rowan's desk — in place of the credenza he had in the office beneath the window in Hawai'i — sat the crate that secretly contained the Ark of the

Covenant. His favorite treasures sat on the corner book case, along with his favorite well-worn copies of *A Princess of Mars, Stranger in A Strange Land, Ready Player One, Outlander*, and a few of his other favorite books. The cast of the first Bigfoot print he'd taken in Washington State was framed and hung on the wall above a shadowbox containing his Star Wars action figures. His model replicas of the Millennium Falcon and the Starship Enterprise each had their own shelf.

And there, on the top shelf, in a prime location, and place of honor, sat the unassuming cup of King Robert the Bruce. The small chest holding the *Sacred Heart of the Rose* sat discreetly in the corner, a soft incandescent light gave it an ethereal glow. The scabbard with the sword Sinclair had given him hung from a hook on the wall above it.

"So, what do you think?" Jacob asked, as Lauren and Rowan stood, their arms linked, admiring the set up.

"I think it's wonderful," Lauren said, leaning on Rowan's shoulder.

Rowan pushed his glasses up on his nose, his teeth shining white against his tanned skin. "This is amazing, just ... amazing."

"I do have just one favor to ask," Jacob said.

Rowan's expression faded and a curious lift came to his brow. "What's that?"

He leaned in, lowering his tone so Lauren wouldn't overhear the conversation as she went to inspect her desk. "I got the invoice for the movie props," he started, but hesitated, and Rowan felt his heart quicken. He'd been dreading this conversation. "Next time you feel the need to decorate your office, try not to spend an arm and a leg?"

AFTERWORD

Thank you for reading **The Lost Templar**. If you've made it this far, I can assume you were with me the entire time and you bought into the myth I have attempted to weave here. The story of Prince Henry Sinclair — and the Knights Templar — are the source of much debate. While I never want to create controversy, I simply weave my tale as a further adaptation of the Templar legends, with a nod to one of my favorite authors, Mr. Dan Brown. This story is not meant to offend and is not offered as dogma, but rather a tasty bit of fiction that I hope you enjoyed.

For many of you *Templar buffs*, there are sure to be a few times when you found yourself thinking *Well, that's not right*, and yes, you are correct. I took some historical liberties on the gamble that you would trust me. *Thank you for that, by the way.*

For those who didn't know, I'm sorry to have to tell you, but there is no evidence of the Knights Templar ever having a treasure — one of the oaths of the Templar Order required a man to give up all his land and worldly possessions — nor of a fleet of Templar ships sneaking out of Europe to Scotland. Yet, the Sinclair family in England and Scotland did quite well for themselves, holding both land and positions of power. The evidence of them having come to the Americas is still up for debate, but I cling to Lauren's words, "absence of evidence, is not evidence of absence."

Like Rowan, I am a descendant of Robert the Bruce, with some ties to the Sinclair family, though I'm still working to document those. I have done extensive research for this book, so I would know when I was blurring the lines. (Like bigfoot, I blurred a lot in this book.)

If you care to learn more about the real Knights Templar, and maybe get a glimpse into my mind, I'd like to share with you a few books about the Knights Templar (among other things) from my reading list:

1 Jerusalem: A Biography by Simon Sebag Montefiore. The audiobook was 25 hours and 22 minutes long and it took me nearly a month to finish it. I enjoyed it so thoroughly that I also bought the paperback version.

2 The Greatest Knight: The Remarkable Life of William Marshal, the Power Behind Five English Thrones by Thomas Asbridge. Another great, albeit long audiobook, this book provided insight into the life of a working knight in the medieval era.

3 **The Templars, The Secret History Revealed** by Barbara Frale

4 The Sword and the Grail by Andrew Sinclair

And last but not at all least, I would be remiss without a nod to Diana Gabaldon, author of the ***Outlander*** series. I found her through the book ***Dragonfly in Amber***, which was the 2nd book in the Outlander Series that I picked up in a bookstore back in 1992. I happened to mention the book to my mother and said to her I felt like I was missing something as I was halfway through it and finding reference to happenings that were alluded to but hadn't happened in the book. My mom reached into her book bag and pulled out ***Outlander***, pointing out that I had missed the first book, and she had just finished it. We swapped books, and I was hooked from the get-go.

Diana wrote **Outlander** "for practice" which was exactly what I did with **The Veritas Codex**, and the series that followed. While Diana takes years to write a book (usually writing more than one at a time, along with everything else on her plate), I have a much more expedited process. Book 4 — **The Monk's Grimoire**, was originally drafted in 23 days. When you write that fast, the edits take a bit longer. I am efficient, but not always accurate.

I still enjoy having a day job, so balancing my writing with my occupation isn't always easy, but I know there will come a time when I can retire —again — and spend my days happily lost in the heads of my characters. In the meantime, I hope my readers will find delight in knowing that I have already completed first drafts of eleven books, with a twelfth currently in progress. It is my sincere hope to see the sixth book of **The Veritas Codex Series — The Pirate's Curse** in 2023.

The new research vessel was a wonder of modern engineering. The craft, freshly launched from dry dock, still had that *new-ship-smell*, accented with the tang of salt and the sea. In the months to come, the heady aroma of fish-guts would meld into a nauseating miasma that would surely send more than one member of the crew heaving over the side to bid goodbye to their previous meal. But today, was not that day.

Today, the ship would take her maiden voyage. Her hull was a bright and unblemished white. Crisp blue lettering across the back, named her THE EXPLORER OF THE DEEP. The Oceanic Channel had invested $1.2 million to ensure she was fitted with all that was needed for long voyages in the search for the answers to the mysteries of the briny depths. An American flag billowed in a gentle breeze from the pole at the pinnacle of the craft.

The day was bright. A light breeze rustled through the palm trees along the nearby boardwalk. The song of gulls pierced the sky as their shadows cut across the sun and cast shadows on the deck. Eric Sherwood peered out over his sunglasses towards the horizon, studying a towering stratocumulus cloud that reached for the stratosphere in the distance.

The prospect of sailing the ocean had always had a certain appeal to this stalwart adventurer and scientist. There was so much left to be learned about the Seven Seas and the waves called to him like a siren's song. To Eric, there was nothing better than standing on the deck, watching as each wave barreled over one another. What lay hidden beneath the dark waters? To plumb its depths was to discover a world filled with creatures and lost relics. Sleeping on a gently lulling craft in the middle of a calm sea was one of the most relaxing things he could think of. Sunrises were only slightly more inspirational than sunsets over the expanse of water.

When the sea could calm itself, Eric could still his own racing thoughts, and when the sea grew wild, his own thoughts were focused on the peril at hand and his troubles could be held at bay — at least for a time.

Yes, today was the day. It had to be. It was time to take this girl out and see what she could do. Everything was ready. It was time to go.

Eric ordered the ship's kitchen to be stocked with only the best ingredients for the meals and cocktails he would make for his guest on this voyage. Expensive tins of beluga caviar were stacked on the shelves in the ships pantry, along with fresh produce, French cheeses, Kobe beef and the finest champagne. The local bakery also dropped off a dozen loaves of sourdough bread, some of the unbaked loaves had gone to the freezer for later use, but already thoughts of a pâte and Swiss cheese sandwich made Eric's mouth water.

As he made his way up to the helm, his hand ran along the smooth mahogany handrail and his leather-soled dress shoes clapped against the metal stairs. The sound of them echoed up the stairwell. As he entered the bridge he was in awe of the large console of readouts, buttons, knobs and other input and output devices. He had radar, sonar and even satellite global positioning equipment with large high definition readouts.

Pressing the main power switch, Eric stood back, listening to the ship come to life, feeling the hum of it through the soles of his shoes. Tucking his sunglasses into his shirt pocket, he gazed out over the bow of the ship. His eye went to the horizon as thoughts of home escaped him and he dreamed only of the sea.

Amanda's perfume preceded her as she found Eric at the helm. She came up behind him, snaking a hand around his waist. "Everything ready?" She asked.

"No." He turned, scowling down at her.

"No?"

"You didn't ask for permission to come aboard," he growled. "You never board a ship without permission."

"Is that like having to invite a vampire inside?"

"It's a custom that dates back to ancient times. In the age of pirates, it could get you keel hauled," he stated.

She reached up and caught him, pulling his lips to hers, kissing him full on the mouth. She tasted of cherry cola and her lips were as soft as a prayer. "Permission to come aboard?" she whispered once she'd greeted him properly.

He eyed her a moment, a broad grin lighting his tanned features. "Permission granted."

She giggled and loped towards the door. "I thought you might say that," she said. "How long 'til we set sail?"

His eye went to the clock, then to the read out on the board. "I just alerted the port authority of our intentions to cast off in the next half hour." He climbed into the captain's seat, surprised to find it conformed to the curve of his backside. The soft leather was supple against his bare legs. "I'll need your help on the deck in twenty minutes."

"I'll go change and meet you at the port rail," she said with a half-hearted salute.

Eric turned back to the view from his command post and

sighed. Yes, he was a man of the sea. This was his home and his sanctuary. It was his escape from the burdens of the world. At sea, he was the master of his own destiny — the captain of the world.

"I hope we get lost," Eric said as he popped open a bottle of champagne. He added it to the flute that already contained orange juice. "Have you ever seen anything more beautiful?"

Amanda rolled over on her towel and held her hand up to shield her eyes, taking the glass from him as he leaned down to kiss her. The sun had broken over the horizon less than an hour before, and the water around the yacht was the most beautiful shade of turquoise. The sky seemed almost magical, radiating shades of gold from the sun streaking through varying levels of pink into purple hues. "I hope you're talking about my tan." She grinned up at him, giggling.

"Well, that is one way to make sure you don't get any tan lines," he said, gazing at her devilishly. Her bikini top had been untied and she clutched the minimal cloth to her chest as she sat up on her elbows.

"Well, we are a hundred of miles from any land, right?" She shrugged, knowing the effect she was having on him.

"More or less," he said, appreciating the view as she rolled onto her back and stretched out her long slim body, tossing the bikini top aside.

"So, who's going to see me naked?" She lifted her glass toward the empty horizon. "Besides you of course, and you certainly don't seem to mind."

"But it would be a shame for you to get a terrible sunburn."

"So? Care to rub some sunscreen on for me?" She reached over and picked up the bottle beside her, holding it up for him.

A breath of wind rose to a gust, followed by a gale that seemed to come out of nowhere. The ship was cast up by a hearty swell and nearly born aloft. Amanda's mimosa went everywhere as the ship dropped out beneath them. He caught one of the ropes at the last second and saved himself from being cast over the rail. Amanda jumped to her feet, catching his arm, the champagne flute shattered as it fell to the deck. "What was that?" She shouted, as the wind picked up, and the sea grew more unsettled.

"There's a storm coming." He turned into the wind. "Holy …" His voice trailed off. Amanda grabbed her towel, wrapping it around her body as the temperature suddenly dropped. Behind them, a giant egg-shaped cloud hovered high above. The skies behind it grew dark as more towering thunderheads boiled up quickly to the west. A crackle of lightning broke the sky and spread out through the lenticular cloud, illuminating it. A silver craft shot from the middle of the cloud, as if the lightning had launched it high into the atmosphere.

Eric's gaze followed it as the triangular shaped object tumbled end over end, as gravity took over and the craft began its free-fall. The sea lifted and fell beneath him as the aerial craft's engines fired and it swooped up just meters from the roiling sea's surface. It shot through one of the large waves and appeared on the other side as the now brackish sea churned with foam.

Rain began buffeting them as the vessel lurched again, the bow twisting against the pull of the waves. The silvery craft was now lost in the maelstrom. "Get inside!" Eric shouted. Amanda wasted no time following instructions, heading below deck to find clothing while Eric headed up to the bridge.

The technology aboard the craft was state of the art. Eric pulled up the radar and got his first look at the storm that had appeared almost out of nowhere. The nautical forecast from the National Weather Service had called for five days of mild weather, calm seas, and no predictions of potential storms, least of all a hurricane. Hurricanes didn't just pop up out of nowhere.

"Eric!" Amanda cried as she was tossed about on the

stairs. "There's water coming in below!" She staggered in, with her hand to her head. Eric turned and noticed blood seeping beneath her fingers.

"Are you hurt?"

"I hit my head," she said. Eric inspected it, as the ship lurched, nearly upending both of them again. He caught her and kept her upright. "Is there a breech in the hull?"

"I didn't see a hole…" she said. "I think the water is coming over the deck…"

"There's a first aid kit under that bench. I'll go make sure all the doors are shut and latched!" Eric had to raise his voice. "We've got a huge squall building right on top of us!"

"Is it a hurricane?" She caught his arm.

"It looks like it, but there's no way…"

"You said it was supposed to be smooth sailing!" she snapped angrily having to raise her voice over the roaring storm that was raging outside now.

"It was!" he shouted back.

"I'll get the doors," she said. "Have you called for help?"

Stupid! How could he not have done that first? "I'm on it!" Eric picked up the receiver on the radio and held down the button, all the while trying to set a course back towards Miami. He switched the radio over to channel 16 and triggered the distress signal. "Mayday. Mayday. Mayday," he said as calmly as he could, yet still conveying the urgency of the situation. "This is the *Explorer of the Deep* … *Explorer of the Deep* … *Explorer of the Deep* – FL1727." He proceeded to give them their coordinates. "We are caught in a storm that came on without warning! We are taking on water. Repeat we are taking on water. *Explorer of the Deep* is a blue Stampede class expedition yacht with two souls aboard. One is a twenty-six-year-old female with a minor head injury with no LOC. We need rescue. Over."

There was a long pause. Eric lifted the mic to his mouth to repeat the message when the radio squelched. "*Explorer of the*

Deep, this is *Rubber Duckie*," a female voice responded, she had a thick Caribbean accent. "Repeat location and nature of the emergency."

Eric did as instructed. "We're encountering twenty to thirty foot swells ..."

"*Explorer of the Deep*, the *Rubber Duckie* is less than five nautical miles west of that location. Sun is shining and no signs of storms in your direction."

"*Rubber Duckie*, notify Coast Guard ... we're going over ... MAYDAY! MAYDAY! MAYD..."

Jacob took his favorite putter from his golf bag and laughed at Curt as he tapped his putt in for a double bogie. "You know the loser buys the first round of drinks in the clubhouse, right?"

"If you sink that putt on the first attempt, I'll buy you the biggest steak they have," Curt ribbed. Jacob hadn't sunk an easy putt all day. If it hadn't been for the lucky birdie on the 3rd hole, the score wouldn't have been so close.

"Don't worry, Curt, he'll choke," Everett prodded back. The Oceanic Network's CEO was in last place, so he wasn't one to talk, but he wasn't about to let the rest of the bosses give Jacob a hard time without getting in on the fun. Jacob was always a target for good-hearted teasing, at least on the golf course. In the boardroom, he was the top dog of all the Networks in the Exploration Channel Family of Networks.

"Step back." Jacob put a hand out, pushing his sunglasses up his nose as he stepped on the green, his ball less than three feet from the hole. He consulted with the caddy and studied the landscape for any hidden slopes or divots. "Let me show you boys how it's done." He could be a cocky bastard and he knew it. This was an easy putt. He couldn't possibly miss.

Lining up his shot and preparing to draw back the putter, his cell phone suddenly blared in his pocket, and he flinched. Without meaning to, he tapped the ball, sending it awry of the hole, and over to the sand trap. He stood, watching it roll down the edge and come to stop in the sand. He threw down his putter and dug in his pocket, profanities spilling from his lips as his buddies laughed and slapped their knees behind him.

"You know the rules, Jacob!" Curt ribbed. "No cell phones on the course!"

Jacob turned and glared at the men as he pressed the phone to his ear. The look on his face must have conveyed the seriousness of the call. "Hannah?" He hesitated, his face dropping. "Dear God! Hannah … what happened?" he asked, putting his hand on his hip as he turned his back on the crowd. "Oh dear Lord, Hannah. I'm so sorry to hear that. No, of course. If there's anything I can do." His brow lifted and he sucked in a breath. "Actually, I think there is something I can do. Send me all the details. I've got some connections. Let me start yanking some strings. We'll see what we can find."

"What is it?" Everett asked when Jacob hung up the phone.

"The *Explorer of the Deep* has gone missing," he said.

The next morning, Jacob called all the Network executives, including the Legal Department together in the boardroom at the main office in San Diego. "Good morning, Ladies and Gentlemen. I do hate to be the bearer of bad news, but I got a call from Eric Sherwood's wife, Hannah. He was taking out the *Explorer of the Deep*, the Oceanic Channel's newest research vessel for a test run from Miami to Bermuda. Yesterday morning, a sailboat called the *Rubber Duckie* received a distress call from the *Explorer*. The captain reported the craft was experiencing severe weather, including large swells, and indicated they were taking on water and needed help."

"Is Eric okay?" Everett asked.

The look on Jacobs face said more than he ever could.

"The Coast Guard is still searching for the *Explorer,* and Eric." Jacob pursed his lips. "The really crazy thing is, the *Rubber Duckie* reported the seas were calm and the sun was shining in the area. After notifying the Coast Guard, the *Duckie* made efforts to render aid, but when they reached the coordinates Eric reported, there was nothing there. Calm sea. Blue skies … but no sign of the *Explorer.*"

"But …" The executive from the Oceanic Channel shook his head. "The *Explorer* is brand new, state of the art. It has some of the most high-tech navigation and weather-detection systems on the Seven Seas. We had Jean-Pierre and Nina Cousteau's team work with us on designing everything."

"Did you say …" Curt started. "Did you say he was sailing from Miami to Bermuda?"

Jacob turned to the Escape Channel's boss. "I did," he said. "And I know what you're thinking. That is part of the Devil's Triangle. In fact, several other vessels have gone missing in this general region over the past five years."

"Jesus," Everett rolled his eyes. "You don't believe any of that superstitious nonsense? Really? I thought we were a network of scientists."

"We are," Jacob said. "And I have a couple of scientists in mind to go help us find Eric and our ship."

ABOUT THE AUTHOR

Betsey Kulakowski has thirty years of experience as an occupational safety professional and recently completed her degree in Emergency Management. Betsey and her husband live in Oklahoma and have two grown children. She has been writing since she could, and created her first book at the age of six cardboard cover, string binding and all.

The Veritas Codex (Book 1 of The Veritas Codex Series)

The Jaguar Queen (Book 2 of The Veritas Codex Series)

The Alien Accord (Book 3 of The Veritas Codex Series)

The Monk's Grimoire (Book 4 of The Veritas Codex Series)

The Lost Templar (Book 5 of The Veritas Codex Series)